Ashes
Edited by David Edgar Grinnell

Curious Corvid
PUBLISHING

To my Family, Friends,
& Those Dearest to Us Deceased.

Foreword

I will never forget my first meeting with David. After launching my publishing house, I waited for authors whom I honestly did not believe would come. I was new to the scene, underexperienced, and a little bit odd. But strange and unusual folk have a tendency to gravitate toward one another and one day whilst refreshing my inbox, David's email popped up, promising a gothic novel of mysterious intrigue.

Ashes was strange, it was curious, and it delicately cradled the tragic tale of an all-consuming loss and the grief that follows. *Ashes* was special. It reached into the heart of family trauma and pulled out an experience that beats in many of us. Whether we have lost a parent or parents, been alienated from our family, missed universal childhood milestones, or had to grow up too fast because of circumstance, *Ashes* touches a bit on all of that. It is painful while also healing. It acknowledges those deep wounds, validates our experiences, and then encourages us to continue on, down through the tunnel and out the other side.

A book is nothing without its author which brings me back to David. Our first meeting was over zoom where we talked on gothic literature, inspirations, expectations, rejections, and the future. I saw an author with potential and passion, someone who genuinely loved their creation and had breathed their own life into the pages. David was exactly the person I wanted to work with. He was odd, a bit socially awkward, entertained by darkness, and absolutely, unquestionably on fire for words. I also saw a grief, a responsibility, a person who wanted to write while also making the world better, brighter, and more inclusive.

Besides the resplendent tale of grief and healing, David also chose to introduce a queer love story. While I've found many queer love tales written by men to be diminutive and infantilized, David approached the subject with respect and reverence. The romance between Viviana and Alice is soft and gentle. It is two souls enraptured in each other, finding comfort and companionship. It's not sensationalized or sexualized—it's sacred. Just as it should be. Inclusion is so, so important and the more I learned about *Ashes* and its gothic creator I knew that the heavens had surely aligned.

On November 12th, 2021, *Ashes* debuted for the first time. It was a very exciting moment for both David and me. It was David's first published novel, and it was my first time publishing one. It was not without its stressful moments but from the beginning, David and I had decided that we were a team. I will always be grateful for his understanding, his grace, and his unwavering belief in our vision, all of which still continue to this day.

Three books and several projects later, David has become much more than *'just'* an author. We have a very lovely friendship and it's been a joy to watch him grow and blossom, find love, and begin a new kind of living that comes after life changing loss and grief.

Sometimes sorrows must be felt, pain must be expressed, and we all must learn how to walk alongside grief. Though it may overshadow us, it needn't bury us. We are all, in the end, ashes to ashes, so we may as well learn how to dance in the breeze and flutter in the sunlight for all of our days.

—Ravven White

Prologue

It has been two years since my father died.

"Paul Reaper was a good, honest man!"

Or, "Mr. Reaper always put others before himself," were common phrases they had said about him.

"You'll be ok Alice, your father is at peace."

Almost everyone had told me this, but what about me? My hometown had admired my father, but I had no one. My mother died giving birth to me and my father had been consumed by his work as a groundskeeper and a funeral director. No one had ever been there for me. My best friends left for different colleges, and one would think with social media, it would make communication better or easier but, in fact, it hasn't. It has only made me cold, isolated, alone, and afraid. Everyone seems so happy…

They post pictures online with their boyfriends, girlfriends, and pets. I don't have any of that. Why? I left my hometown with what inheritance was left after my father's death. Now, I'm a simple girl working at a coffee shop part-time while attending Cleveland State University. I still feel bitterness and dismay at the happiness of my friends on social media, though authors like Edgar Allan Poe, Nathaniel Hawthorne, and Emily Dickinson always keep me in good company.

The last gift my father gave to me before he passed was a complete collection of Edgar Allan Poe's short stories and poems. It's most precious to me. Sometimes, on my days off, I go to the coffee shop and sit there to read. I love the coffee shop. It's in the small town of Bedford, Ohio and the townsquare sits across from it. The winters are long and cold, and some are not as bad as others. The town is usually quiet until the night falls. The trains echo in the far distance and sing a lullaby.

I don't sleep well. Nightmares filter my mind with my father. I have one specific dream involving him that starts out beautifully. I stand inside the old antique house where we had lived in Boydton, Virginia. It's a grand Victorian; blue and white. It has elegant see-through windows and a dark gray roof with spires. A large porch wraps the entire front of the house and through the front door is the foyer with its grand stairway. I'm in a strapless black dress with my hair tied up in a ponytail. I go up a set of wooden stairs that lead up to the attic. In the attic, I see my father dressed in a fine, fancy suit. He smiles warmly, his dimples showing, and his light blue eyes aglow. He bows before me and offers out his hand.

In the gentlest voice he asks, "Take this dance?"

I smile, touch, and hold his warm hand. Around me I begin to feel others watching me.

"Do not look at them," my father says.

I see a few of my family relatives, such as my Uncle Vincent and Aunt Ophelia who are from Oregon.

"Alice, please don't look!" persists my father.

I look over to my other side and spot a woman whom I've never seen before. She's beautiful, with long, dark raven hair, green eyes, and pale skin. She wears a dark purple dress and as her eyes lock with mine I call out to her.

"Mama?" I cry. I know she has to be my mother even though I have never seen her. I just know. I look back to my father and right before my eyes he disintegrates into ashes as everyone else around me withers to dust. I scream as my father's ashes seep out through my fingers and my dream ends.

Ashes • David Edgar Grinnell

Chapter 1

"Those who dream by day are cognizant of many things which escape those who dream only by night."
~ Edgar Allan Poe, Eleonora

Whenever I'm not at school or in the coffee shop, I love to be with nature. It's when I'm most at peace and find solace to read my books. It's a habit I picked up as a little girl when my father cared for the grounds of the cemetery near our home. I'd sit by my mother's grave and read to her. As I would read, I kept a close eye on my father as he worked, cutting the grass, placing flowers on the graves, and caring for the gravestones. Eventually, I'd read myself to sleep, hearing the soft winds whisper, the birds singing, the blades of grass touching my feet, and I would imagine that it was my mother holding me to sleep. Some time later, I'd wake up in my room or in the house knowing my father had carried me inside. Now, here I am at the Bedford Cemetery reading to strangers I do not know.

There's a comfort about cemeteries. My eyes strain from reading and I decide to lay upon the grass. I stare up at the sky, shut my eyes, and listen. The birds chirp, the sun warms my face, and all is peaceful. Nature's rhythms soothe my worries of loneliness, of my past, and time flees from my subconscious.

During my slumber, I see a fire lit in a blaze. The flames roar high, and burn, crackle, and snap. The night is black and a nibbling sound echoes nearby. A little girl sits across from me and a black bird nibbles upon her face.

She stares, looking just like me, and finally speaks, "Can you hear it breathing? I can…"

I scream and flail my arms about until I look around and realize I had fallen asleep. I pant haggardly as flashes of the little girl come into my mind. It triggers memories of the past, and all is silent until I hear a car with flashing lights roll by. I panic, not because of the flashlight coming towards me, but because of the fire, ashes, and shards. My hands shake. I stare at them, as I can't get the horrid images out.

Fire. Ashes. Shards.

"Ma'am, what are you doing here? It's after hours, and you are trespassing."

I don't answer, my breathing unnerved, and the flash of the red and blue lights remind me of that day. "You look pale. Have you been drinking?"

Fire. Ashes. Shards. Say something.

"No, I-I-fell asleep. Nightmares," I answer. The cop studies me and purses his lips.

"Well, I hope I don't catch you here after dusk again. I don't feel comfortable leaving you here especially at this time of night. Where do you live?"

"Up the road. Glen Valley Apartments." There's a pause.

"Very well, I'll let you go with a warning. Don't stay here after dark."

I stutter, "Th-thank you officer…"

I snatch my book and hastily leave the cemetery. The flashing lights of the cop car make me think of the moment when everything changed. I don't want to remember… I don't want to remember.

I cling to my book, press it tightly against my chest, and tears stream down from my cheeks. My footsteps echo as my mind consumes my vision. *The memories.* It forces me to remember how it all started.

In my early teens, my father bought me a dog, a hound named Viktor. He had the cutest brown eyes, floppy ears, and a dark nose with a white stripe on the top of its bridge. He brought me so much comfort and so much joy. I believe my father knew of my loneliness, so he gave me Viktor for companionship.

Our Victorian home in Virginia was also the funeral home of the city. Viktor and I stayed in my room and he laid with me and watched out of my bedroom window. I'd sit there next to him reading a book. It wasn't just any book, but Mary Shelley's

Frankenstein. It was a leather laced softcover with ruby red edged pages. It was slightly worn as it once belonged to my mother. As I'd read to myself, my father worked around the first floor. It wasn't until a few years later that I was able to work with him.

My father did the embalming process. Step by step, he showed me the surgical portion where bodily fluids are removed and are replaced with formaldehyde-based chemical solutions. Sometimes I would cut hair, style it, add makeup, and set the facial features to make the corpses presentable for those who held funerals at the house.

My father was a heavy smoker. Every time before and after preparing a body he would smoke cigarettes. He would always say, "Helps calm the nerves…"

I don't know if he was always a smoker or if it was something he picked up after my mother died. He never talked about when he started smoking, but from his coughing and hacking, I imagine it was years. I hate the smell of smoke, especially now more than ever.

The thick fumes haunt my dreams. The nightmare about my father in the attic is only one of several dreams. Sometimes they repeat and at other times they change. It's always the same though: *fire, ashes, shards.*

I have another nightmare as I go to bed after coming back from Bedford Cemetery. In the darkness I hear a whimper, a whimper of some kind of dog in pain. Viktor. I reach into my pocket, grab my phone, and turn on the flashlight.

My mind races, and I quicken my pace to follow the sound. I have to save Viktor; he is still crying out to me. Further into the woods I cut through branches, trees, and bushes. The whimpering sound becomes less faint and for I know, I'm closer. In the distance I glance ahead of me to a steep hill from where the whimpering had come from. I place my phone back into my pocket, and begin to climb, pulling myself up with anything I can grab onto, including rocks and trees. The further I climb up, the steeper the hill becomes. My feet slide and my hands clench into the ground. My fingernails collect dirt as I continue to crawl my way up.

"Hold on, I'm coming!" I cry aloud, hoping that Viktor can hear me. I stop climbing to catch my breath. "Must keep going…"

I grip onto a tree branch nearby and hoist myself up. Finally, I'm at the top and that's when the whimpering stops. All is silent as I slowly trudge across the top. With each step I take, the leaves crackle and the twigs snap. I stop.

"Viktor?"

His long ears and droopy face stare at me.

"It's ok boy…" I say calmingly. He scurries away. "Hey, wait!" I call.

I chase after him and in moments I come to a sudden halt. I gasp, my mouth ajar, an ill feeling taking over. My stomach knots and twists inside as I see Viktor about to cross the street.

"No!" I shout.

As my arms reach out, a loud horn wails, and the sound of flesh and machine crackle. I scream, tears line my cheeks, and fire surrounds me within my old home. My father stands across from me—*fire, ashes, shards.*

Chapter 2

It's always the same after my nightmares. I bolt up, drenched in sweat and my skin hot. I cry. Life goes on. College keeps me distracted.

The city of Cleveland with its discombobulating paradise keeps me busy. It's different from what I'm used to, but I enjoy the lights and the tall buildings. Today though, the weather is quite nasty with gray clouds, mist and fog shrouding the university grounds. It's very Poe though, and comforts my soul. I look up to Rhodes' Tower and the fog seems to veil the top. As I walk promptly across the courtyard, my backpack the burden of academia, my shoulders weigh down, and I clutch my Edgar Allan Poe book close to my chest. It shall keep me company as I wait for class. Berkman Hall, or what other students call the Main Classroom, feels spacious. It's my first time as a student here, but not my first time as a student since I had attended Longwood University. I can't get over how many stairs there are in this building. A person my age shouldn't be huffing so much...

Ugh. I have no idea where to go—ah, finally, my classroom. I sigh as I glare at my phone for the time.

I mumble to myself, *"It's not even close."* I look around the fourth floor to find a place to sit, but the darkness of the night shrouds the windows in pitch black. There's one section on the fourth floor with a view of an Episcopal church. I would love to sit in view of it, but to no avail.

"I'll just sit outside the hall of my classroom…" I plummet down in the hall, shove my backpack next to me, and stretch out my legs, adjusting my skirt. I open my book to where I had left off, reading Poe's *"The Fall of the House of Usher."*

Suddenly, someone across from me sits and sets their bag down. It's a man and he's looking right at me…

"I'm just going to focus on read—

"Once upon a midnight dreary, while I pondered, weak and weary," says his voice.

My eyes peer over my book. His accent is not from here. I wonder if he knows the third line.

"Over many a quaint and curious volume of forgotten lore," I reply.

He interjects, "While I nodded, nearly napping, suddenly there came a tapping." He chuckles. "It doesn't sound like you're from here," he adds.

"You aren't either."

His dimples show from his smile, "How very perceptive of you. What is your deduction, Dupin?"

I study him. His hair is medium-length, brown with light blonde highlights, his eyes brown, his face clean-shaven, and he wears a green flannel shirt with a checkered design. I think about his accent.

"Polish?"

There's a pause as he nods his head. "Yes, only half though."

I squint my eyes. "Russian."

He shakes his head.

I bite my lip. "German!"

He laughs, "No, Romanian."

My eyebrows rise and I slightly nod and state, "Huh, interesting combination. However, your accent is not as thick as I'd imagine."

He smiles again, "Right you are. I was born in Romania, but my parents are first generation immigrants to the U.S. Your accent sounds strong. I know you're not from Ohio."

I close my book and set it next to me. "Indeed, I came here two years ago from a small town called Boydton, Virginia."

He stretches his back from sitting, "Awesome, explains the Southern accent. I'm Ionel Dragomir."

"Alice Reaper."

Ionel's eyes are wide. "What kind of a last name is that?"

I find myself smiling and I chuckle "A special one…" I haven't smiled or laughed like that since… I don't know when.

"Dark and mysterious. How do you like Cleveland?"

I take a moment to think. What are my thoughts about Cleveland? "Eh, honestly, I haven't seen much of Cleveland."

Ionel's jaw drops. "What? You've been here for two years and haven't explored Cleveland? What rock do you live under?" he says jokingly.

His joke deflates my feelings. Silence.

"I apologize. I feel from the silence that I perturbed your feelings."

I flash a smile. "It's okay…"

Another awkward pause.

Ionel clears his voice. "Perhaps, you'd like to see Tremont or Coventry?"

I open my mouth, but Ionel interjects, "There is a bookstore called Mac's Backs-Books!"

I close my mouth to think. When was the last time I was in an actual bookstore? Oh, my…I don't remember when—any books I have read were always from my mother's book collection—wait, I think I remember.

"Sure, I haven't been to a bookstore in a long time!"

A student goes into our classroom. Ionel starts to get up to stretch. He grabs his bag and says, "You should go check it out sometime. I would go with you, but unfortunately, I have a TA assistantship that consumes my time during school." He goes into the classroom with a smile.

I look at my phone. Fifteen more minutes. I groan "Ugh, this is going to be a long class…"

All throughout class, my mind is distracted by the last time I went to a bookstore. It was with my best friend, Camila. She had been my childhood friend for as long as I could remember. We had been inseparable, until she…developed unique spiritual views.

One of the things that bothered her when we were together was my 'energy'.

"I can feel your energy. It's dark and full of despair. Honestly, it's hard to be around it."

When I tried to reach out to her, she kept saying, "I can't help you." But I didn't want her help, just her support in talking about my grief. She finally told me that I wasn't allowed to talk to her about anything negative, which I didn't like. Camila was even uncomfortable in my Virginia home because she felt the despair from my father.

I remember when we went to the bookstore in town. I called out her name, and she said, "Alice, you need to stop it! I can't help you and you're being needlessly negative. You need to work on yourself."

The last words I said to her still ring inside my head, "I am working on myself Camila! You're being so difficult. You tell me I can't talk about negative stuff because of something I don't even believe in!" She left me there in a rage.

Vulnerability is difficult. Tears silently stream down my cheeks. I miss her. I glance at the clock as the professor announces a five-minute break. I quickly get up, exit, and leave the school.

Chapter 3

I'm tormented by the thought of sleep.

Fire. Ashes. Shards.

Nausea rots my stomach in knots. The thought of sleep is something I desire, but dread. Darkness swallows my room. The streetlights illuminate behind the blinds. Tightness fills my chest and my heart races as I think about sleep, the nightmares, my father, and Viktor. My sheets are drenched in sweat, chills run through me, and my breathing is wild.

Tears fall. "Mama… Camila…"

I want them here. I cling to my phone as the time passes. Two-a.m., three…It's not possible to entirely avoid sleep. Four a.m.….Almost—alarm rings. Time to prepare for work.

Some days when I don't sleep, coffee becomes my closest friend. It's not just any coffee that will suffice my sleep deprivation, but Death Wish Coffee. Its black bag, skull, and crossed bones call to me. It keeps me awake, keeps me safe from closing my eyes, and is a safeguard against the nightmarish visions inside my head. Yet, I know this coffee can literally kill me. The activities at work keep my mind active until things get a bit… strange.

I'm standing at the cashier, when I notice some movement from the corner of my eye. I turn but see nothing. My eyes are heavy, and I blink. Shadows. I look closer at the shadows and they seem to churn, almost like smoke. I know they aren't real; they can't be. I ignore it to help a customer order. A few moments later, however, I notice more movement from the corner of my eye; only this time, I don't turn immediately.

Instead, I focus on completing the order. I don't look at them directly but can feel their presence. I catch glimpses of them. It's a group of five human shaped forms made of three-dimensional shadows, that rise up from the floor, and begin walking towards me, arms extended in my direction. I swivel my head to look at these beings, and I'm able to see them for a brief moment before they dissipate back into the shadows. My body shakes, but I can't distinguish whether it's from the caffeine jitters, lack of sleep, or the shadows. I try ignoring them. Terror fills my heart, and after what seems like ten minutes of looking at them, I close my eyes. Fire, ashes, and shards consume the shadows of my eyelids.

When I open my eyes, they're gone. The coffee beans grind in the machine as it reverberates. The ground coffee seeps out of the machine and into the bag and the reverberating sound reminds me of that day.

Fire. Ashes. Shards.

I breathe sharply while specks of dark coffee residue land on my hands. I give the customer their ground coffee, flash a quick smile, then flee to the back of the room. I cry. My head, hot and achy, pounds.

"Ashes-ashes-ashes; get off!" I cry brushing my hands.

"Alice?" calls my boss. "Alice, it's just ground coffee residue…"

My hands are frantic, "Must get them off!" Tears flood from my cheeks. Shards of the urn, ashes, and fire flash simultaneously.

"Alice, go home!" My boss's voice breaks my trance.

Silence.

"Come back in a few days. You need rest."

There's no rest for the wicked.

I don't go home. The autumn brisk composes a dreamy air. Across from me I see the trees in Bedford Square and all of the orange, yellow, and red leaves that shroud the grounds and monument stones. I don't want to go to my apartment alone. There's no solace there. The only solace I have are the cool winds that flow into my lungs and the sway of my dark hair against my face. I want to escape.

It's still early in the day so I decide to go to Coventry, the place Ionel told me about. From my phone, I look up the route to Coventry and take a bus there. In about an hour, I arrive. I'm in awe of the atmosphere. There's a mixture of artistic, musical, bohemian, and hippie communities. Coventry Village boasts a thriving music scene, restaurants, coffee shops, and of course bookstores. Some places that catch my attention while strolling Coventry Road are Phoenix Coffee, Tommy's, and of course... Mac's Back. I stand at the front of the door. A neon light illuminates with the word "Books" in the window glowing softly on the paperbacks and hardcovers sitting delicately on display.

Books are real. I open the door and a bell rings. I soak in the smell and the touch of ink-stained pages. Books are the souls of the people who wrote them and the hearts of the people who read them. Books are also like people as they too come in different sizes, hardcovers and paperbacks and even eBooks. Which book to choose? Which one is the one? Like many people, books are fragile and have history.

Which book—ah, my eyes, I think, deceive me... My hands tremble around a phantom of my past *Frankenstein*; a copy almost like the one I once had.

"That is a special book you have there." That voice.

"Ionel?" I shift my head to face him as he studies me.

His eyes and face squint in puzzlement, "You look pale. Is everything alright?"

"Yeah, I'm fine." Hah, the lies I spew.

"Hmm… Well, I came to pick this up." It's a hardcover with a red jacket cover of a black and white photo.

"*This Side of Paradise*," I say holding the book.

"Yeah, it's a book I am thinking of using for my thesis. I can't decide if I am going to focus on this novel, *The Great Gatsby*, or perhaps both…"

I hand the book back with a smirk of encouragement. "It's still early in the semester, so I'm sure you will have time to look over both novels."

Ionel flashes a smile and my heart melts, but I ignore the feelings. I grip and squeeze the *Frankenstein* book in my hands.

"Indeed. Um, this is spontaneous, but would you like to go to Bd's Mongolian Grill with me?"

I put *Frankenstein* back in its place as he says this to me. My ears turn beet red and are warm.

"Eh, um…" I'm tongue tied.

"Oh, I mean as friends. No pressure." His words stutter, but I can't tell if his true intentions are that he wants to be *'just friends'*.

"Uh, sure…" I flash a smile as we make our way out of Mac's Back.

As we stroll over to the restaurant, the wind tickles my legs and ruffles my hair. We are silent as Ionel and I walk side by side. His scent is mixed with various incense, and I become curious and ask, "Do you use incense or smoke?"

He opens his mouth slightly with a little smile, "Neither, but my sister Viviana uses incense in her room." He looks down at me and sees me squint my eyes in perplexity. "Oh, she's into tarot card readings and every now and then 'cleanses' the cards with mugwort."

I shake my head in disbelief, "She burns what?"

"Mugwort… She believes the smoke clears and cleanses her cards of past energies."

I roll my eyes as Ionel's words 'past energies' makes me remember Camila.

"What? You don't believe in spiritualism?"

I sigh dimly, "I'm not sure…It just reminds me of someone I once knew who shunned my presence because I seemed too negative or didn't appreciate her views. All because she wouldn't allow me to open up…It's complicated." It becomes quiet again as we approach the restaurant.

"The restaurant is in this building" says Ionel while opening the door.

I walk through. "Wow, it's downstairs?"

"Yeah, you'll like it!" We are seated at a random table as the mixture of smells, spices, and food fills the atmosphere. The sound of voices and food sizzling consume my ears. It's warm and cozy.

"Hmm… I'm not a fan of spicy food," I say to Ionel. He's looking at the menu.

"It's all good. There are more options than spicy food."

I look down at the menu and notice the options for the cocktails. I turn over the menu as Ionel speaks, "You know, I was thinking…perhaps you should come over Friday night. My sister is holding her annual autumn bonfire and insight from her readings might help you."

I glare up, my lips sinking. "How can she help me when I don't believe in spiritualism?"

Ionel chuckles, "No, no… It's not about believing or not. Tarot cards are about guidance and interpretation, kind of like when you study literature. Instead of analyzing the language and breaking it apart for meaning, the tarot cards are a vessel for a physical representation. It's to help you understand your question or concerns and based on what my sister gathers intuitively from the cards, you interpret them as you would in studying literature."

The hamster wheel in my head spins around Ionel's explanation of the tarot cards. On one end, I think a reading may help address my nightmares and my torments about my family and Camila. I've never thought about flimsy cards in such a way of interpretation, as I find comfort from the interpretation of books. Perhaps this is what I need? My mind becomes restless. How will I take the reading? Will it all be hogwash from her words of interpretation? I dislike being vulnerable, but it is also necessary in order to find peace. To make it all go away: the fire, the ashes, and the shards.

"Alright, I'll come." I finally answer.

"Great, it starts at seven! If you stay on Coventry and go past the gas station, there are rows of houses. My house is on the left side, it's dark gray with red shutters." A waitress comes by and asks us what our names are. After we say our names, she writes them down on a slip of paper. She hands me one and Ionel as well.

"Thanks" says Ionel as he signals me to get up. We get in line to order our food. I learn more about Ionel during our time at lunch. He's a musician. Ionel plays piano, some guitar, and cello but what he enjoys most is singing. Before graduate studies in English, he shares that he once strived for an undergraduate degree in music for performance at the University of Rochester in New York, but he dropped it due to financial difficulties. We finish our meal.

"So, why are you doing a master's degree in English?"

"Eh, well. I'm thinking the degree will help in the long run because I can apply it to several different fields. I feel it will give me better financial security than music."

I bite my lip and stare at him. "Well, I would like to hear you sing or play sometime."

He chuckles, "Yeah, I'll play something at the bonfire tomorrow." We both rise from our seats and begin to leave after splitting the bill. We make it outside as we say our goodbyes and exchange numbers. I go back home, tired, drained, and weary.

Chapter 4

As soon as I slam my body against my bed, I can't move. My body becomes stiff and aches from not sleeping. My eyes close heavily...

My old Virginia home flashes before me and once again I'm in a black strapless dress. I creep up the grand staircase and every creak and board wails. An uneasy feeling takes over as my chest tightens. I hear a scraping of some kind, like chalk rubbing against a surface. I follow the sound to my room as a flash of lightning illuminates my room. I catch a small figure on the floor of my room as I open the door. Engraved on the floor by my bed is a pink pentagram with a circle drawn around it. The figure stops, holds the chalk, and turns its head to me. Another flash of lightning reveals the figure is a little girl. It's the same little girl whose face is deformed from the bird nibbling on her. She looks a lot like me, but there's madness in her eyes and my attention is completely fixated upon them.

Without understanding or making sense, I find myself lying upon the pink pentagram. Something keeps me from moving and getting up. The floorboards start to shake like a mild earthquake, and hands, countless hands extend from the surface and shroud my eyes. I suffocate, feeling the touch of dirt and the smell of blood mixing together. It feels as if I'm being burned alive, the smell of rotting and burning flesh. The ceiling above me decays, the wood rots beneath me, and my body falls through the floor.

Everything around me fades. I know I'm awake, but half asleep. My eyes open wide, but my body is paralyzed. In the far corner of my apartment room, a streetlight illuminates the corner and I see a human shadow standing there. It terrifies me as I know this figure is not meant to be here. I'm on the verge of tears, and I repeatedly cry out, "What's that? What's that? Leave-leave-leave…"

I can't look—I don't want to look and so I shut my eyes. Memories flash in the darkness.

Fire. Ashes. Shards.

It's my fault. I dropped Viktor's urn. His ashes scatter in a house of fire. The shards. My hands try to gather the ashes as I listen to my father's screams, and smell his burning flesh. The thick fumes of the fire suffocate my lungs, and my body tingles as I shake and violently thrash my legs, desperate to fully wake up. I scream, open my eyes, and the figure in the corner is gone.

I bolt up in bed and sob while listening to the rain hitting against the roof and windowpane. All is quiet as I breathe restlessly and clutch my body close to me. My hair falls upon my face, frail and sweaty. The image of the figure in the corner flashes through my mind as a delicate spark of lightning illuminates my room, the rumble of thunder following.

I let out deep sighs trying to catch my breath while focusing on the melody of the rain outside. In a few moments, the rain picks up and the storm outside becomes more violent. The wind howls and rattles my windows. An ill feeling takes over me; I don't want any of this anymore.

I rise from my bed and the sweat-drenched sheets stick to my bare thighs falling once I stagger out of my room. My body aches. I'm hot, then cold, and chills run down my spine. My teeth clatter and my breathing unnerves my body to shiver. A small night light illuminates my bathroom, and I switch on the main light. I see myself in the mirror, pale, sickly, red rimmed eyes framed in dark circles.

I open the medicine cabinet behind the mirror to take ibuprofen. Anything to stop the aches, the pains, and the feverish chills. I shove the ibuprofen in my mouth, bend my head towards the faucet, and gulp the tap water. I glance back into the mirror seeing the water trickle down from the corners of my mouth. I swallow. My grim appearance makes me remember Viktor's cremation and how grieved I was to lose him.

My father had worked on Viktor's body in the preparation room of our old home. Viktor's body wasn't embalmed, but my father cleaned him to the best of his abilities to represent our loving companion. I wasn't there when he did this because he didn't want me to see Viktor in that state. After he was done, I heard my father's footsteps as the sound of metal tags clinked. I was in the parlor when my father approached me.

"Do you wish to keep Viktor's tags?" he had asked. My father presented Viktor's blue-worn collar with his tags still attached. I stared at them. My father's wheezing agitated my ears from the brief silence that filled the room. I took the collar into my hands, and looked at Viktor's tags engraved with his name, the veterinary hospital he went to, and his identification numbers. I took his tags off, clutching them in my hand as I gave the collar back to my father. He took the collar as I opened my hand and kissed the tags.

"I do wish to keep them."

My father nodded his head with a breathless cough and plodded back into the preparation room to finish his work. As I waited for my father to finish and place Viktor in a vessel that was combustible and strong enough to hold his weight, I remember staring into the parlor room's mirror above the mantel. My skin was pale and my eyes were red rimmed with dark circles from crying and not sleeping.

I didn't know how long I stared into the parlor mirror, but my father's approaching footsteps and tireless breathing disrupted my trance.

"It's time Alice. Time to put our dear Viktor to rest." He signaled me with his hand to follow him into the preparation room.

Inside the room was a separate space for the pet cremation chamber. Fire-resistant bricks lined the chamber. My father had taught me the cremation process and that the bricks could withstand temperatures up to two-thousand degrees. The furnace hummed as it preheated, and I saw the result of the hard labors of my father as he showed me the craftsmanship of the special vessel for Viktor.

Viktor was already prepared and ready for cremation, housed in a 'green' casket, one made from renewable sources and easily biodegradable in the earth.

"I used willow to build Viktor's casket. It's simpler, greener, and more unique for a clean cremation," said my father, stroking my shoulder. It was a beautiful woven casket, natural and beige, just like Viktor. I smiled with tears streaming down my cheeks as the casket before me reminded me of when Viktor and I would go on walks together and into the nature of the countryside. It was perfect.

My father walked to Viktor's casket and signaled me to assist him saying, "Give me a hand."

I went to the bottom side of the casket as my father was on the left side.

"One, two, three."

Together, we pushed the casket into the furnace. Flames spewed out from the top like a flamethrower and the top of Viktor's casket caught fire. I rushed to the side of the furnace and pressed the button to shut the furnace's door. I plodded to the front of the furnace and stared into the black abyss of the chamber door. I glanced over to my father, watching him count the minutes go by from his watch. Time passed as I thought about memories of Viktor and I growing up together—playing with his first rope chew toy, him dragging me across the hardwood floors; my echoing laughter and my father making a joke that the hardwood floors didn't need dusting due to all the dragging Viktor did to me. The times when we laid and snuggled on my bed, and I teased him by making bunny-ears behind his head. His ears would perk up seeing my two fingers playfully dancing up and down in the mirror in my room. Viktor hogging the bed, snoring like a double stereo system with the deep and yet contented sigh. His howling and chasing in his puppy dreams. Me scratching his favorite spot that made his leg thump against his skin. As I thought of these memories, my father called to me.

"Alice…"

The memories stopped, and father signaled me to open the furnace door. I pushed the button as the flames roared high. Father took a specialized tool, stoking the fire. At the same time, he broke down Viktor's remains and tapped against the furnace. I knew the heat dried Viktor's body, burned his skin and hair, contracted and charred the muscles. It vaporized the soft tissues and calcified the bones until they crumbled. There wasn't really a smell because the emissions were processed to destroy the smoke and vaporize the gases. The gases themselves were released and discharged through our exhaust system.

Finally, after a few hours of cooling, Viktor was reduced to skeletal remains and bone fragments. My father brushed the remains into a pan below the cremator. He bent downward and opened the hatch to grab the pan, taking it over to the main room where we did the preparation. In one of the corners of the room was the animal cremulator machine, a green shaped blender that stood on four legs. He placed the pan close by and unscrewed the top of the cremulator, lifting the top and moving it to the side. Carefully, he emptied the remains into the machine's chamber and closed the lid. He screwed it tightly and set the timer for the remains. The rotating blades reverberated like a coffee grinder Viktor's remains were pulverized, and the ashes poured into his urn.

Chapter 5

Thinking about Viktor's cremation makes me reflect on what happened at work. How the coffee grind machine is similar to a cremulator. Perhaps I should tell my boss why the ground coffee and the grind machine made me freak…Or maybe he will fire me because of my behavior? I don't know. I just know I can't live like this…I need help but I don't know how to ask for it.

A flash of lightning disrupts my thoughts. I look at myself in the bathroom mirror dreading sleep. Dark thoughts consume my mind. I no longer wish to suffer but that isn't the answer. I shuffle to my room, look for my phone in the darkness, and find it plugged into the wall by my bed. The light from it automatically illuminates. It's a quarter after four. I decide to brew coffee for myself and ponder what to work on for my master's thesis. In my parlor is a bookshelf with three shelves. Some books are from past courses I've had since my two years being here. I miss going through my mother's book collection in the library of my old home.

My father told me on several occasions that I reminded him of my mother who always had a book in her hands. She would drink tea, spend time in the library, and read a diverse range of literature. My father avoided the library after her death as he said that he could still smell her scent among some of the books on the shelves. Nor could he bring himself to view the pictures of her and him together upon the tables in the room. My bookshelf looks despondent or sad compared to my mother's collection.

I shut my eyes to recall some of the books she had that perhaps I can find online or at Mac's Backs. *The Count of Monte Cristo, The Strange Case of Dr Jekyll and Mr. Hyde, Dracula,* all of Ann Radcliffe's novels, Jane Austen novels, *Frankenstein…*ah perhaps *Carmilla.* I glance at the top of my bookcase. Maybe Edgar Allan Poe…I go through my phone to order some of the books I don't have in my collection. With my coffee, I shamble to my kitchen table, open my laptop, and start to research the academics on some of these works of literature. Academia is good for me; it keeps me busy and focuses my attention away from my past and the baggage that comes with it.

Sometimes, though, there are times when even academics are not enough to numb it. It comes in waves, the depression. Even though I haven't been officially diagnosed with it, enough web searches have matched me with the symptoms. I haven't sought help. I'm too afraid of what the end result may be. If it's antidepressants, the thought of that makes me paranoid of how they will affect me.

When I was at Longwood, I attempted to seek help by using their counseling center years after Viktor passed. I didn't tell my father about it, but I went to one session. The therapist wasn't very helpful. I understood he was there for an evaluation, but the most annoying question he repeated often was, "How does that make you feel?" I felt he wasn't listening to what I was trying to open up about with the guilt of my mother passing away.

She died because of me. I killed her because she birthed me. And because of her death, my father threw himself into his work. Perhaps, that was his way of coping, but it isolated me. A drafty, cold Victorian house in the middle of the countryside was nothing but solitude—peaceful but secluded, a place which hid and fueled the darkness in my mind. I had no one after Viktor's passing. My best friend Camila had already left me, acquaintances at school were consumed by their lives, responsibilities, and their own problems. My father's health was declining. From a distance I heard his violent coughing, hacking, and spitting in the sink. It made me cringe, but his presence was all I had.

Sitting at the kitchen table in my apartment triggers another memory as I think about my father's health. In the library of the old house, he knocked upon the archway entrance of the library. I peered over from the study desk as I was typing my final paper for my undergraduate senior seminar. He was short of breath and slightly wheezing.

"Alice, I would come in, but you know how I feel about the library. Could you please come here for a moment?" The tone of his voice was stern and melancholy. Whatever it was, I knew it wasn't good, and that's when he told me.

He had received news from the doctor in town about his unhealthy coughing and hacking fits. He was coughing up bright red blood, and the x-rays lit up to reveal what the doctor called 'Squamous Cell Carcinoma of the lung.' Lung cancer. Stage three. The disease had spread from his lungs to the lymph nodes of his throat. The doctor estimated my father to live at least five more years even with the treatment of chemotherapy. I didn't know how to react to the news. I stood like a corpse; my stomach knotted. I didn't want him to die, to be taken from me. He was all that I had. As we stood between the doorway of the library, he hugged me, yet I could smell his unfiltered cigarettes on his suit jacket. Emotions overtook me inside; I was angry, hurt, sad, distraught. I shut down. I hate the smell of smoke, and I smelled it on him.

Getting him to quit smoking was draining. One moment he had stopped smoking for a few weeks, but then he would oddly disappear into his room or some part of the cemetery nearby. Deep down I knew it was to smoke, but I dared not interfere or accuse him, even when his appearance said otherwise.

He had pale, light nodes of yellow skin. Underneath his red eyes were dark circles. He was not sleeping well and continued to seclude himself into his work. He had to keep working in order to keep the health insurance to pay for his chemotherapy. That was it for me.

The birds chirping outside my apartment break my thoughts as the screen on my computer shows six in the morning. A part of me is happy that it's Friday and the other part is afraid. I think about my upcoming tarot card reading and hope it will give me comfort. To kill the time, I decide to explore the Bedford Metro Park.

Hiking and wandering through the woods, I discover an abandoned campsite. Usually, exploring the metro parks helps clear my mind when books aren't enough. When I come to this campsite, I'm unnerved. Surrounding the fire pit are stone thrones with a variety of symbols. Some of these symbols engraved are the peace sign and the Nazi sigma. One chair has the words, *"Jesus was here"* in bold and capitalized letters. Broken bottles, punctured beer cans, and cigarette buds scatter and surround the pit. What unnerves me most are the stone thrones. How did they get here in the middle of these woods and why are they excellently crafted? My feet are sore from all the exploring and hiking that I decide to sit in one of the chairs. I lean back, shut my eyes, and listen. The birds' chirping lulls me, the rising sun warms my face, and for once I'm at peace.

Darkness consumes my vision and yet I don't know how long I've blacked out from the tiredness. My feet scrape against a dirt road. The night is black, but I can still see what is ahead of me. The gates to the Boydton Cemetery lie before me, opened, and in the far distance by my mother's grave I see a human shadow. I'm in the black strapless dress again as I feel the crisp breeze hit against my bare legs. My flat heels scrape against the dirt as I tread through the gates. As I approach, the shadow turns away from me at a slow pace. I follow it and as I listen, the apparition hazes and steams like smoke taking its form. I gasp, my mouth opens awestruck, and an ill feeling takes over me. My stomach knots and twists inside as I observe the form take the shape of my father. This form—my father— goes inside an old house. Not just any old house, but one that looks just like my old home. How can it be, though? The house is decayed, molded, and the paint withered and weathered so much I can't quite tell. It's a grand Victorian house just like my old home, but the windows are nailed shut with rotted boards, and the porch floorboards are filthy and worn, the steps to the porch caved in.

A terrible feeling overcomes me as my father goes inside. I still have no idea if it's actually my father, but I'm curious. I plod onto the porch and with every step I take, the floorboards squeal. I call for my father as I go inside to search for him.

"Dad!"

I don't know how long I search for him. Minutes, hours, and all through the house. Every room, hall, and space…Molded, torn, worn, and dusty rooms; sheets, beds, couches, and chairs. As filthy as it is there are no spiders, insects, or flies. Strange…but I can't find him. Moments I think he's there, but it ends up being a sheet covering an old piece of molded furniture. I race up and down all the halls and pathways of the house, but nothing. It's like he isn't here—*how is it possible-he's here- I've seen him- clear as day. I feel a presence-I can!*

I saw him come into this dreaded place when I first entered. He has to be here! I feel something tap lightly against the top of my head. I glance up to see ashes. They gracefully fall and flutter like white tufts of snow. I look ahead of me down a narrow hallway and see my father clear as day in his fine, fancy suit. He stares at me as the ashes flutter like feathers around him. He reaches out his hand to me and the dream abruptly ends.

A vibration quakes in my lap. I feel warmed from the sun and cooled from the breeze. I reach into my pocket realizing my phone is vibrating. It's Ionel's number.

"Hello?"

"Ah, sorry. Were you asleep?"

I pause, but then speak, "Yeah, but it's fine. What's up?"

Ionel clears his throat and croaks, "I was wondering if you were still good to come to the bonfire tonight."

I remove the phone from my ear and look at the time. It's three o'clock. "Yeah, all is good, but would you be willing to pick me up?"

"Uhm…" Dead silence and static echo, "We can go together, but can you come to CSU? I have a few papers to grade from English 101 and 102."

I think about the time it will take and answer, "Yeah, I can meet you at the CSU library."

Ionel sighs with relief. "Good, that makes things easier. I'll see you then!"

We disconnect. I sit in the stone chair for a few more seconds, still drained, tired, and at unrest. My body clearly needs sleep as getting up is an endeavoring exercise. I traverse the woods, without any clear conception of where I am, but I make it back to my apartment somehow…

I grab my bag, searching my phone to plan my route to CSU by noting that the RTA bus departs in about forty-five minutes from the Maple Heights central transit stop number three. I can make the ninety-F to Cleveland if I pace myself quick enough. My heart palpitates in the sickness of my lack of sleep and I hurry on with irregular steps, not daring to submit to my tiring carcass.

Continuing onward, I come at length opposite from the buildings across from the bus stop at which various vehicles and cars are usually parked. Here I pause, though I'm unsure why, and I remain some minutes away with my eyes fixed on the approaching bus that comes towards me from the end of the street. As the bus draws nearer, I observe that it's the ninety-F-Lakeside. The bus stops where I'm standing and, on the door being opened, my vision blurs. I shut and rub my eyes. *Flashes of a burning house.* Strangers bump into me, breaking the sequence of the memory. I perceive other strangers exiting the bus.

The driver shouts out, "Are you getting on or not?"

"Yeah…"

I push my body, but it falters awkwardly forward. I grip onto the small railing inside and my Jell-O like legs ache. My arms are sore, but I manage to reach into my bag to display my student id. The driver nods and I sit down next to a window. My heart races and pounds, and my breath comes heavy and fast. I rest my head against the cold window as its coolness sweats against my forehead. A migraine ravages inside my skull as its pain triggers my eyes shut. The touch of my hand plunges against the strain.

I recall the burning house. My father's torching screams curdle my blood. He was stuck inside. I couldn't get him out. Too close to the fire, I fled to the mantle and snatched Viktor's urn. Debris showered in front of me from above. I fell, and the shards scattered. I laid beside my loving companion's ashes and pulled them close as everything went up in smoke. The flames were getting bigger as a shadowy figure within the smoke broke through the debris in front of me.

A random stranger disrupts the memory by sitting next to me on the bus. The stranger has earbuds in that play the heavy song "Made of Stone" by Evanescence. Amy Lee is my favorite singer, and I haven't thought of her since Camila. I turn to the window looking upon my reflection. I see tears stream from my eyes and stain my cheeks. I appear sickly, unwell, and as pale as one of the many corpses I've worked on with my father.

My stop coming up, I stand and pull the rope above me to depart. The bus stops, and I swing my bag upon my shoulder, and exit. The clouds are gray. It's wet and damp. The moisture in the air smells heavy and is eerily gloomy. Mist upon CSU's grounds rises and flutters like a burning flame.

Students all around the world commute and go to and from classes. I know the middle of the fall semester is approaching fast as the conflict of the cold and the barren trees collide. It's the time when students do or die in academia. Such is the position of many students like me.

My thoughts remind me of a demanding first draft paper due in my seminar course. In the courtyard, I push open the revolving door and enter the lobby of the library. I pull open the glass door that leads inside and hastily make my way to the strain of grueling research. I have at least an hour before Ionel, and I will meet. I text him, letting him know of my arrival. I wake up the computer, toss my bag to the floor next to the desk, and plummet onto the chair. It sinks… I sigh and roll my eyes. I'm like a toddler in this chair. This is an 'angry chair' if I'm ever in one.

I slouch, drop my head against the edge of the desk, and mutter under my breath. "Ugh… Must. Write."

The time flies by, an energy drink here, there, everywhere. Suddenly, I find books and papers scattered around my area like a violent hurricane. Empty canned energy drinks lay around me as I plump my elbows upon the desk. My forehead rests upon my palms; the screen is blank. Unconsciously, my ears listen to a slam of a book. My mind becomes rapid and alert. My most precious book! The pages slap together and apart as I pick it up to a random passage. I glance over it, but my eyes blur, the words on the page jumble, and my ears start ringing. I slam my book shut. My vision waves into focus, the ringing in my ears subsides, and all is silent. Not even a pin can be heard if it's dropped. I'm breathless, terrified of myself and my condition.

I think myself mad. My hands quiver but I can't make any sense of what I'm doing. I want to distract myself and so I stare at my book for comfort. The book stays within my hands, and I think I see the designs on the cover come to life. They slither like a snake. The raven feels cold, yet the touch of the picture on my bare skin musters a burning sensation. Pain crawls farther upon my shoulders, the inside of my throat twinges, and my vision blurs again. I feel my head pulsating behind my ears as if vines and thorns are crawling into them. My eyes roll into the back of my head, and my body compulsively squirms. Darkness shrouds my eyes and then—nothing. I'm still conscious, horrified, and the ringing inside my head is loud and piercing. I lurch my body away from the desk, tripping over my feet. I regain my balance as my eyes slowly blur in and out of focus. I make it to the bathroom, set my book down onto the floor and splash first cold then hot water against my eyes. I splash my eyes frantically, again, again, over and over until I feel somewhat more awake. The ringing stops. As the water falls from my face, the first thing I see is the suicide awareness sheet protected by a plastic casing. It's mounted upon the wall behind me as I glare into the mirror. I see the dark purple face and eyes of the person on the sheet as it lists the signs of someone suffering from the warnings. I look at myself. If I were dead, who would miss me then?

I snatch up my book, hug it tightly against my chest, and exit the room. A water fountain is across from me as I go up to it and slurp some into my throat. The water is cool and eases my nerves.

"Alice." A familiar voice calls to me.

It's Ionel, and he smiles at me. There's a comfort in his eyes; they're different from looking into mine. His are full of life as mine are infested with death. I can't help but smile as I see him.

"Hey."

He studies me as he hears my voice and utters, "Hmm… You seem very grim. Are you sure you don't want to talk about what's going on?" His voice is sincere, convincing.

I want to but as if in a trance I answer, "I'm just… tired."

He nods his head, "I hear you. There is no rest for the wicked, especially for academia."

I chuckle, "Ha, right you are."

We depart the library and we're on the intersection between 22nd and Chester. As we cross the street, I glance at the coffee shop 'Joe Max'. Perhaps, a coffee? Naw, probably not the best. I feel a displeasure for coffee I've never known... I can't understand it. It's something I once enjoyed but at this moment find no joy in drinking.

Nearby on 22nd street is Ionel's car. It's a dark gray Mercedes-two door sedan. The top of its roof had bubbled.

"Nice paint job," I say with sarcasm.

"Ha-ha, well, I tried re-painting it." Ionel opens the car door, sits, and starts the engine. The engine roars and the fumes of gas are strong. It makes me nauseous and dizzy. I gulp as I sit in the low passenger seat, and my hand covers my mouth. I let out a sickly sigh as Ionel sees my condition.

"Eh, sorry . This car has seen better days."

The window slides down on my side for air to breathe. "Thanks, let's just get there," I reply shortly. I glance to the side mirror and see my image is that of a crypt keeper. I loathe my appearance. I blink as the image of my father's ill face flashes within my brain. When my eyes reopen, I think I see a shroud of smoke behind me in the backseat. It churns as if it's alive! I swivel my neck and fix my attention on the radio equipment.

There's a cassette inside the slot with a cord attached to it. Ionel goes left onto Payne Avenue. "Did you want to listen to some music? What do you like?" He hands me the cord attached to the cassette as it's an aux cord. I take it while looking through my music collection on my phone. We turn briefly onto 21st and stop at the red light. My eyes quickly catch a glimpse of the see-through windows of the CSU library. Ionel's turn signal clicks repeatedly.

"Have you ever heard of The Civil Wars?" I inquire seeing their name in my collection.

Ionel pauses and purses his lips for a moment, "Eh, I don't recall."

I select their name, having to choose between their Barton Hollow album or their self-titled one. The light changes, and we go left onto Chester.

"I think you'll like them. I haven't heard them in a long while."

"Cool, inspire me my friend!"

I chuckle while choosing their first album. Their song '20 Years' plays.

The Civil Wars was the duo I had always listened to in my final year of high school. The year 2011 seems so long ago, but it has only been eight years. Camila showed them to me. She had an admiration for Joy Williams. Before she found spiritualism, she had told me once that if she were to die, it would be Joy Williams' voice that she desired to lull her asleep. Our conversation echoes inside my head.

"And what about Amy Lee?"

Camila laughed knowing she was my favorite singer whom I admired. "I think she's overrated…"

I gasped at her words but with a smile. She giggled at my facial expression and stared into my soul.

A feeling at that moment overtook me. My heart swelled but I turned my focus on the road. The drive was silent, but the atmosphere was tense. I couldn't help but slide my hand and lay it upon where the cup holders were. I had desired her touch. The delicate warmth of her hand shot an intense but gentle feeling. I felt her stroking her thumb against the palm of my hand. We held hands the entire trip. It was night when I dropped her off, raining, and she and I stood facing each other at her front door. We stared into each other's eyes and embraced. Our embrace tugged at my heart strings and an electric shock planted inside my heart. Her cat Zeus interrupted our moment by brushing against our ankles. I felt something special that day and I knew she did too.

52

Chapter 7

*"Nature is a haunted house – but Art – is a house
that tries to be haunted."
– Emily Dickinson*

Ionel's house is on Coventry Road. We pull into a dark and uneven driveway. The house is dark gray with red shutters and a porch with a swing. A diverse range of red, yellow, and brown dried-up leaves cover the front yard and driveway. The sun shines a dying red and orange as it sets. The air is cool and still.

As we walk down the drive, I hear voices in conversation. We go through a wooden gate where the backyard is completely fenced in. Tiki torches are lit in a blaze among chairs that are set up in a circle. In the center of this circle is a fire pit. The set up reminds me of the abandoned campsite I had found earlier, but this is more welcoming.

There are three other people in the chairs by the fire as it crackles and snaps. They're laughing and having a good time as they all stop to greet Ionel and me. One of the girls springs from her chair and a smile stretches from cheek to cheek. She is vibrant.

"Hello, there!" She says to me. I can't believe the excitement she has to meet me as I show her a warm smile. Her accent when she greets me is similar to Ionel's accent as I remember her name.

"Hi, there! Viviana?"

She gasps and exclaims, "Yes, I'm happy Ionel has mentioned me to you. He's told me about you." I don't know how to greet her as I take out my hand. "Oh, no need for that! You get a hug." She embraces me as I jolt, feeling the warm reception. The other people chuckle as they see my eyes wide with shock and contentment.

Ionel walks forward, near everyone. "Everyone, this is my friend Alice."

An Asian man with short black hair, honey-brown eyes, thick glasses, a gray long shirt, dark blue-jeans and drinking a clear bottle of Corona waves his hand high.

Ionel points to him. "That there is Cai!" There's a pause as I look over to the girl sitting next to him in the circle. Ionel proceeds, "And that there is his lovely fiancé, Tessa." Tessa's hair is black, she has dark-brown eyes, white-smooth skin, and wears a long-sleeved green insulated turtleneck with black jeans. She doesn't say anything but bites her lip at me as if she's staring into my soul and is plotting something against me. She nods her head in acknowledging me.

Viviana grasps my hands as she tugs me towards the bonfire and chairs. She dances as my arms do a left to right swaying motion. "Please sit by the fire and tell us of a Reaper's tale!" My breath is shot as I catch the inside context of her using my last name. I laugh short.

"Um, I suppose…?" I say next to an empty chair.

"Perhaps, get her a drink?" suggests Cai.

"No, not until she's had her tarot reading. She needs a clear mind!" Viviana looks back to me after she says this to Cai and smiles warmly. She bounces away to the chair across from me in the circle. As she walks away, I observe her appearance.

She has short blonde-hair which has a flair to it in the front. Her eyebrows are a light dark and she has hints of light purple makeup upon her eyelids. Her eyelashes are thick, tipped outward, and her eyes are blue. She wears black lipstick. In fact, her whole attire is black. She wears a leather jacket with a bushy collar of fur and has an obsidian stone pendant around her neck. A bronze antique design of roses wraps around the stone which connects to a silver chain. Her jacket is slightly open and exposes her breasts, shrouded in black fishnets. She definitely has a spooky vibe.

She sits in her chair as I sit in mine. The flames from my view almost seem to engulf her. I see Ionel to my right with a hard guitar case setting up.

"What kind of tale do you want to hear?" I ask.

Everyone is silent and Viviana leans back in her chair. "How about your favorite Edgar Allan Poe poem?" she suggests.

I have to think. There are so many.

"Ionel told me you always carry the complete poems and stories of his work."

I smile as a warm feeling takes over my heart. I didn't know Ionel spoke to others about my interests. It's quiet again as the flames hiss and dance.

"I bet you have memorized a few," chimes Ionel.

"Yes, I have; give me a second to think." I can't decide which poem as there are at least three…Which of these three poems speak the most to me? If I have to recite one of his poems to define me, which one should it be? I find it. I sit upright in my chair as all look upon me:

"From childhood's hour I have not been

As others were-I have not seen

As others saw- I could not bring

My passions from a common spring-

From the same source I have not taken

My sorrow—I could not awaken

My heart to joy at the same tone—

And all I lov'd—I lov'd alone—

Then—in my childhood—in the dawn

Of a most stormy life—was drawn

From ev'ry depth of good and ill

The mystery which binds me still—

From the torrent, or the fountain—

From the red cliff of the mountain—

From the sun that 'round me roll'd

In its autumn tint of gold—

From the lightning in the sky

As it pass'd me flying by—

From the thunder, and the storm—

And the cloud that took the form

When the rest of Heaven was blue

Of a demon in my view."

All are silent. Everyone seems as spectators to me as they reflect upon the poem I chose. Cai takes a sip from his beer as Tessa breaks the silence.

"I don't think I have heard that poem before from him…"

Viviana chimes in, "I think it's a lovely poem as the way you said it was… Beautiful."

I sink in my chair reflecting on the poem's words. It's a poem I haven't read in a while but remember clearly. I glance over to Ionel; there's a despondence from his eyes. They're sad. It's as if he knows that the poem is me. A young adult consumed by her troubled childhood which torments me. I've been different from others since my childhood, and I was not brought up in a typical family setting. I've spent most of my time alone and I've never been given the chance to share my thoughts, feelings, and experiences with others. Until now. I bet my perception toward life and nature differs from others who have enjoyed childhood. While others look up at the sky expecting to see a serene view, I only see darkness.

Everyone's voices around me fade as they change the topic of the conversation. I don't know what, but Poe's poem throws me into past remembrance. My eyes are fixated upon the fire which roars, dances, and hisses. I become lost in its trance and hypnotized by it as I recall one of my darkest memories.

A few months after the news of my father's illness, I attempted suicide. I sat in the preparation room, in a lachrymose wooden chair, I mulled and contemplated death. Across from me was the cremator furnace. I gazed into its black abyss chamber, my death bed. I wanted to catch fire and burn the pain and misery out of my body. The pet cremation chamber could be operated by computer and automated. That would give me time to lie inside it and the flames to spew. I configured the chamber settings and gave it a timer of five minutes. The furnace started to hum as I climbed inside, and the chamber felt cold lying on my back. It would start the preheating process soon. I shut my eyes, still contemplating, unsure about taking my own life. Something had told me not to do it. A voice inside my head, but I couldn't make out who or what it was, told me not to. I cried, rushed out of the chamber, and fell to the floor. When I hit the concrete floor, the furnace preheated, flames spewed from the top inside the chamber. I gazed into the fire, felt the heat upon my skin, and out of reaction I pressed the button to close the furnace door. I shut down the retort and sobbed.

When I reflect upon this memory, I feel the heat and warmth of the bonfire as its smoke wavers to me. Silent tears weep from my eyes. How can something so warm and comforting be my tormentor? I lost everything in the fire. The shadowy figure in the flames should've let me die with Viktor's ashes as they shrouded over me. The firefighter should've let me burn up in smoke with the fire, ashes, and shards.

"Alice, are you ok?" Ionel's voice halts my thoughts as he plays his guitar. He stops playing, and I realize I didn't even hear it when he first started playing.

"Yeah, I'm fine… It's just the smoke in my eyes getting to me." I say with a chuckle.

Cai laughs "They say the smoke follows the prettiest!" A loud hand-slap echoes. "Ah, that was a joke!" Tessa's perturbed emotions are radiating from where I'm sitting. I wonder secretly if Cai really thinks I'm the prettiest girl here.

Viviana bolts up from her chair and paces quickly towards me. She reaches out her hand. "Come, I think you'll love what I have to show you inside!" She seizes my hand and escorts me to the house.

Viviana and I enter the house from the side door. There's a door to my left, but it's shut. To my right, there are wooden steps leading into the basement. In front of the closed door is a doormat which reads, "A witch & her familiar live here." Next to the words is a picture of a black cat sitting upright.

"Make sure the door is closed all the way," says Viviana walking onto the doormat.

The door is shut tight as I nod, "All good!"

Viviana opens the door, "Good, one rule in this room is to make sure the doors behind you stay closed. I don't want the cats to get out."

I follow her into the kitchen. Dark green wallpaper shrouds the kitchen walls, and all the cabinets are white. The counters are a dark gray granite and a dreamcatcher dangles by the small window facing the kitchen sink. The floors are a tile gray which match the granite and there's a kitchen table against the wall by another archway nearby. The table is covered by a black cloth and a gothic-style candelabra is at its center. There are five black candles inside the holders which are shaded with red. Tiny red crystals dangle underneath each holder.

"Bathroom is over there," Viviana points out. "Wash up, take a moment, and I'll show you around."

My heart warms from her hospitality. As I enter the bathroom from the direction she points from, I close the door behind me. There are neat knickknacks scattered within. There's a skeleton decoration upon one of the shelves. It's a miniature skeleton sitting upon a toilet reading a newspaper. The shower curtain has bats scattered upon it. A picture of a human skeleton inside a tub taking a bath is mounted behind me as I stand in front of the mirror. Bubbles flutter around the skeleton scrubbing itself with a brush. I wash my hands and splash my face with the water. The cold water soothes me from my warm face being close to the fire. My clothes reek of smoke. It makes me think of the time my face was shrouded with the ashes of Viktor, my palms cut from the broken shards of his urn. I tried to scoop them up. I tried to save them. I couldn't save him. *They're gone.*

A scratching sound disrupts my thoughts. It startles me and makes me jolt. I open the door to a white fluffy cat as it meows at me and brushes against my legs. I bend down and scratch its back by the tail. The cat cozies up as it purrs from my touch. As it circles around, I see its right eye shut, and it nuzzles its head against my leg. I begin to hear voices of a conversation in the other room. It's Viviana's voice with someone else in the house. A man. I don't know whether they're speaking Polish or Romanian.

"Tato, czy Alice może zostać na noc?" The man's voice is much thicker with an accent. *"O tak; tak. Może zostać, ale chciałbym ją najpierw poznać."*

I can't make out what they're saying. All I hear is my name. I wander about into the living room where Viviana is. The room is plain but not decorated like the kitchen or bathroom.

The room has dark brown hardwood floors and light-gray walls. Tall cabinets are in the corners of the room and another door to the far right is shut. A light looms underneath the crack of the door.

"Papa, this is Alice!"

My eyes observe the form of a frail middle-aged man. His wrinkled skin speaks of a thousand lifetimes. He's hunched, hair thin and white, his eyebrows bushy, but his eyes and smile are warm and welcoming. He takes out his hand and I shake it. His hand is rough but his grip delicate.

"Welcome to our home, Alice. I am Wojciech."

Wojcie-what? I flash a warm smile to pretend I understand his name.

Mr. Dragomir purses his lips, "Ionel has mentioned you and by my daughter's excitement, I hope you too are enjoying your time?"

I forcibly shut my eyes to wear out the tiredness from them and reopen them. "Yes, I am."

"Good, I am glad. Please make yourself at home. Also, please refrain from entering that door." The old man crookedly points his finger to the door with the light looming underneath the crack. "My wife's health has not been in the best state. She is ill and is not in a condition to entertain guests I am afraid." As he says this, a large lamp in the corner catches my attention to a black and white portrait photo.

I point to it, "Is that a picture of her?"

Mr. Dragomir's eyes jolt into a downcast pain. He glances over to the photo and his voice is despondent.

"Yes, a time when she was younger and close to the time I had met her in Romania."

"I'm sorry for her health. I hope she recovers soon and gets well."

Mr. Dragomir flashes a warm smile, "I am thankful for your kindness. Please join me and my son at the bonfire for some live music."

I fumble at words. "Umm."

Viviana interjects, "She will, I promise after her reading."

The old man's eyes light up, and his worn dimples flash, "Very good. My daughter is very talented." As Mr. Dragomir says this, he limps over to an accordion in a black hard case. As he grips onto it by the handle, the case creaks as if it hasn't been picked up for centuries. "My son and I shall warm up before your arrival then." Every floorboard wails with Mr. Dragomir's heavy footsteps. Every step echoes a heavy burden as if an omen weighs in his shadow.

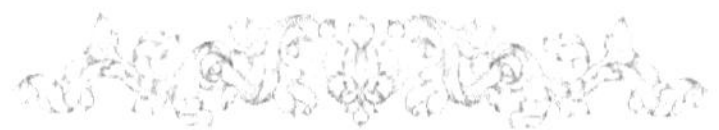

I'm in complete awe. The portrait size black and white photo of Mrs. Dragomir is well preserved behind a glass case. Her skin appears smooth and delicate to the touch as she wears a vintage-style fedora hat. Her eyes are lined in eyeliner, her eyelashes thick, healthy, and flirtatious. Her eyes radiate with a lure of seduction and of beauty. Her slim neck is extended in confidence from her narrow shoulders, as if she knows she's it.

"Beautiful, isn't she?" Viviana's voice breaks my trance.

"Yes, but what's with the fedora hat?"

Viviana chuckles. "My mother was a stage actress and opera singer. She adapted well between opera and theatre. This photo was taken when she was in her twenties during a production of *Fedora*. At the time of this photo, she played Princess Fedora Romazov. She once did the role in the theatre at Playhouse Square and then did the opera rendition on Broadway in New York."

I become puzzled. "Wait, your mom came here first?"

"Yes, before she met my father. News of my grandfather's untimely death brought her back to Romania. Then she eventually married my father and had my brother while they lived in Romania. However, my mother wanted to come back to Cleveland to continue her passions. My father gave up everything he had in his previous life for my mother to thrive and they emigrated here. She managed to get back into theatre at Playhouse, but then she became pregnant with me and could never follow up on her passion."

I become fascinated by this story as I'm about to ask Viviana about the memories with her mom. I bite my lips as I face her, my mouth opens, but she interjects.

"Anyway, I think we should do your reading now before it becomes too late to hear live music. Come." My breath deflates and I keep my mouth shut. She's right, but I still desire to know more about her mom and what it was like because that bond is something I never had. The only passions I've known about my own mother was her literature and that she attempted her undergraduate at the University of Virginia. Father rarely, if at all, spoke of her after she passed. That heavy weight of sorrow my father had carried of her death, is almost the same sorrow reflected in Mr. Dragomir.

The staircase to the second floor is narrow, uneven, and treacherous. The steps aren't completely carpeted and there's no railing to grab onto. The closer we reach to its end, the ceiling appears as if it will cave in on us.

"Mind your head. I've hit my noggin several times on this." She bends down her head and turns to the left once she reaches the top. Once I reach the top and wander over to the left, there's a brief narrow hall. Darkness shrouds the way as lighted dots cave in my vision.

"Just give me a moment. The light switch is at the end of the hall. The other one at our end does not work…" Viviana's phone light flashes, and she flicks the switch. A small bathroom is to my left in the middle of the hall, but her room is straight ahead at the end of it. I gasp in complete excitement as she switches on the main light in her room. A glass dome shrouds the light bulb on the ceiling. A rug with a pentagram shrouds her room's floor and her bed is spacious and has a quilt blanket decorated in a circle with a ginormous barren tree on it. To my far right, is a table—an altar? I become puzzled by the objects which are upon it. On the left top corner of the altar is a candle in its holder, next to a statue figure of Odin with two ravens upon his shoulders, and incense in a burner that is not lit. A dagger? And a wand…I pick up the dagger.

Viviana chuckles under her breath seeing terror start to fill my eyes. "You should see the look on your face. Don't worry, the athame is not usually supposed to harm or draw blood. I use it to cut herbs or cords. The pointy end is dull." I hear her mince behind me as I press the tip of my finger against the blade's tip.

"Oh, that it is…"

Viviana studies me and I observe from the corner of my eye. She bites her lips. "You aren't nervous being here, are you?"

I place the dagger back in its original place and study the other objects on the table. "No, I'm not. I'm just curious about all of this and I don't know what to say."

The other half of the table has a silver chalice, a medium-sized empty bowl with a smaller one beside it. There's another candle in a holder, and next to the candle is a silver statue of Freya, caressing a helmet underneath her right arm, her other arm behind her head and within her long, wavy hair. She has a sword hoisted around her waist, a shield against her left leg as a cat sits next to her right.

"This is actually quite the setup you've got here." I turn to face Viviana, "So, what made you…" I stop, not knowing how to phrase my question clearly.

Viviana laughs with a smile, "How did I come to be a Wiccan?" I nod my head like a curious child zoning in on a story. Viviana's eyes home in on me, as if she's going to tell an epic tale, but then her eyes break the suspense by a somber solace. "It wasn't much more than a feeling and seeing shadows in the corner of my eyes at nighttime. I was house-sitting for Tessa and her mom while they went to Disneyland and so I was alone. While doing laundry, there was this feeling of something following and watching me. But it wasn't ominous. Instead, I had a sense of warmth and that things were going to be okay." She stops for a moment. Her eyes lift to the ceiling as she bites her lips to think. "Almost like a grandma would give if that makes sense?" Viviana reflects upon her words. Her eyes wander back to me and never lose focus. "I was creeped out, yet I knew I wasn't in danger. The cat would follow me all around the house and stare intently at random walls and chirp. He would always pace at the guest bedroom door at night which I found comforting."

My skin churns pale. She too also saw shadows, but they weren't sullen like my experiences at work and in my apartment. Viviana stops talking. The sudden halt from her voice breaks my reflection.

"Alice?"

"Hm..." Viviana crosses her arms as if I'm a specimen for study.

"I feel like my words struck something."

"Shadows."

"You've seen them too?"

She and I stare at each other as our eyes show the answers. Through Viviana's eyes there's a warmth, sweetness, and deep sympathy. She wants to help; I know she can read the somber condition of my nature. She doesn't want to turn me away or shut me out like Camila.

Finally, Viviana speaks with sincerity, "I don't know your full story and I don't have to, but I see now what my brother spoke of when he first told me about you. There is a shadow—a heavy weight upon you. I think now is the time for a reading." Viviana pads over to her bed and bends down to reach underneath it for a few items she had stored. She places three items on her bed and moves to the side. "Go ahead. Pick out a tarot card deck. Choose one that speaks the most to you."

Three tarot card boxes lie before me as I study all of them. The first one is a box called *The Tarot of Vampyres* by Ian Daniels. The box image is a countess vampire, dressed in 19th century fashion. She has long black hair, dark eyeliner, red lips, various necklaces, and a green-black dress. Her facial expression is of a deep comfort, a warming feeling, but one that speaks of truth. The image is mesmerizing, as vampires are supposed to be.

The second tarot deck is called *Anima Mundi* by Megan Wyrewde, decorated with golden and engraved letters. It has hints of stars and the moon, with the moon half-shadowed on the top and bottom.

"What's *Anima Mundi* mean?" I ask.

"Ah, the nature deck. *Anima Mundi* is a Latin phrase to several systems of thought, an intrinsic connection between all living things on the planet, which relates to the world in much the same way as the soul is connected to the human body. It means 'the world soul'.'' As soon as Viviana says this, the last tarot card deck grabs my attention. I pick it up.

"Edgar Allan Poe Tarot…"

Viviana chuckles under her breath, "I knew that one would attract you the most."

The Poe box depicts the image of Poe himself sitting at a writing desk composing a written work. An old-fashioned pen is in his hand, with a lit candle next to him. The red curtains behind him are wide open, insinuating a flutter, and two ram heads are mounted upon the two headposts on his chair. I open the box, and find a book entitled *Edgar Allan Poe Companion*. The front cover has a raven flying in front of a parlor with a blazing fireplace. There's a table in front of the fireplace which contains a goblet, two flame candles, two coins, a book open in the center, a sword leaning against the table, and a black cauldron on the floor.

"It seems you have chosen the deck for the reading. The artwork is beautifully illustrated by Eugene Smith and the book itself is well-composed by Rose Wright."

I give her the box as Viviana takes the book out, sets it upon her bed, and loosens the black ribbon around the cards. "Come sit with me on the floor," she says pointing at her rug. We sit on top of the pentagram rug in her room. We sit cross-legged facing each other. She hands me the deck of cards.

"Now, calm your mind. Clear your thoughts. You will shuffle these cards as you think of a question in your head. It can be any question you desire for guidance. Shuffle the cards until you feel it is right to stop. Sometimes, while doing this, you may repeat the question you have. Meditate upon the cards as you shuffle. Relax your body."

As Viviana directs me, I begin to shuffle the cards, close my eyes, and calm my breathing to think of a question. My mind is daunted, and I don't know what to ask. As my eyes shut, memories and nightmares flash simultaneously. My past life from my old Virginia home, the house itself, my father, Viktor, images of photographs of my mother, the cemetery when I was a child, her gravestone, Camila, and my feelings for her. Her smile, laughter, and touch engulf the sensations of my body. Our first kiss, our bond, and our last argument. The smell of the old books from the bookstore, the bell echoing as she had abandoned me; alone. My eyes are glued shut. I don't want to open them because I need to focus—*focus* on my question. My hands impulsively shuffle the cards, over, and over, as if in a trance.

My mind is feverish with nightmares. My family disintegrates to fire and ashes, my father across from me. Viktor's urn— shattered—and then only his ashes and shards. The sound of my hands scraping them up echoes in my head and clicks in time with the cards I'm shuffling. The shadows. The figures. The firefighter

71

who saved me. My screams of pain and sorrow ring in my head as he carries me out. The flashing lights of red and blue. The water dousing the flames, sitting on the edge of the ambulance, the view of all I knew burning into ashes.

They all trigger the last dying memory of my father. After the last of the flames died, I had darted into what was left of the charred ruins of my home. The emergency crew shouted out to me, but I didn't listen. They chased after me. I went into the house; all was black ash. The room where my father had been burned alive was now out in the open. The morning dawn had penetrated through the crumbling ceiling. Specks of ashes from the house fluttered inside the light. The morning birds chirped, and there in the rubble were the bones and fragments of my father's remains. I dived into them, scraping my bare knees, wallowing and screaming in a sorrow I had never felt nor could comprehend. I sobbed uncontrollably; my soul fragmented with every scream I wailed…

Chapter 8

"Love, whether newly born or aroused from a deathlike slumber, must always create sunshine, filling the heart so full of radiance, that it overflows upon the outward world."
— Nathaniel Hawthorne, The Scarlett Letter

I breathe in a broken and deep sigh and consciously stop shuffling. My eyes open to Viviana as her hand reaches out to me; it reminds me of my father in my dreams, him reaching out to me. That brief image of my father flashes before me; the dream I had of him inside the house with the ashes. Viviana takes the deck from me and draws three cards from the deck. The top of the cards are pretty as they have a design of two ravens, one facing the top and the other the bottom with an eyeball hanging from their beak. Viviana studies the three cards without flipping them over.

"This will be an interesting reading…"

"Why?"

"It feels like two of the cards are reversed."

She flips the farthest card and begins the reading.

"The Lovers reversed. You've had a relationship that was unequal or imbalanced."

The card facing me is of Poe standing next to a woman with black-raven hair. They're upon a shore, their feet in the water as a bright full moon, and a raven, linger high above them.

"Is the woman across from Poe his wife Virginia?" I inquire.

Viviana chuckles, "No, these cards reference Poe's work. So, if you look closely at where these lovers are, it's by the sea." The reference clicks.

"Ah, 'Annabel Lee,'" I think and recite the fifth stanza from memory:

"And neither the angels in Heaven above

Nor the demons down under the sea

Can ever dissever my soul from the soul

Of the beautiful Annabel Lee."

Viviana mutters a breathy chuckle of a smile.

"True love indeed. However, this card is in reverse. So, this is telling us something about your past in regard to relationship issues, broken promises, frustration, and difficult choices. There was a close relationship you had whether it is with yourself, or another. This is about authenticity and truth to who you are no matter how difficult your situation."

I glance up to Viviana's eyes and she shifts them over to the card facedown to the middle. I can tell she is in deep thought by how she bites her lip and drums her fingers against the floor.

"Let's have a look at the present to get a possible better picture." She flips the middle card.

"The moon. It's in an upright position. You need to reflect on your needs and pay close attention to the messages, especially in your dreams."

There's a bright moon in the picture with two identical men in a courtyard facing each other. They each wear a cloak and mask to conceal themselves as they both hold swords upright. I hear Viviana's last words echo in my head. My hands shake.

"My dreams?" My voice shudders, reflecting on my nightmares. The fire, the ashes, and the shards.

"Yes, the moon reflects our innermost thoughts and dreams. It reflects our feelings, both negative and positive. This is simply advice on which you will need to meditate. Perhaps you could write down your experience from your dreams and pay attention to what they are telling you. Presently, there are subconscious fears that are haunting you. You must face them in order to cut through what is deception and illusion. Get to the heart of the matter in whatever it is that seems unclear."

There's a silence that swallows the room. My heart aches to know how accurate this experience is. I don't want to face it. My eyes fixate on the middle card. The moon. The card makes me recall Poe's short story "William Wilson." The doppelgänger exposes Wilson's mischief, causing him to flee for years. The doppelgänger is Wilson's conscience. The image reminds me of the moment in the story when Wilson looks into the mirror and says, *'Mine own image, but with features all pale and dabbled in blood'*. Rethinking this passage, I think about my own self and the restless night when I had stared upon myself in the bathroom. Or the time when Viktor had passed, and I stared into the parlor mirror for hours. How grim and pale I looked. The blood and dirt of those hands in my nightmare. The shadowy figure in the corner of my room. Is it an image to illuminate my subconscious? Nothing is what it seems in the moon's shadows.

"Alice?"

"Huh?"

My eyes refocus on Viviana. Her eyes are delicate, soft, and full of solace.

"Did you want to continue? Your eyes seem so far away in reflection like Alice falling down the rabbit hole." I laugh at the reference of my name, and it encourages me to want to continue. "Yes, I would like to see the end." I let out a deep sigh, my hands antsy. My body tingles as Viviana bites her lips, and her fingers grasp for the last card.

"Oh, the six of swords… Interesting."

"What is it?" My eyes shift between Viviana and the image of the card in angst.

"I know this card well. The image is from Poe's only novel, *The Narrative of Arthur Gordon Pym of Nantucket*. The image presents Pym, Peters, and a dog sailing towards calmer waters after a storm. A penguin floats in the water, indicating a peaceful sea. A seagull soars above to symbolize freedom. The storms are fading, and happier times are ahead."

"Isn't that a good thing?" I ask.

"Hmm… Usually, but this card is reversed." I observe her eyes studying all three cards; her mind almost seems feverish in concentration. Her eyebrows squint in perplexity as if she's gathering all the evidence to solve the mystery. She sways her body in a light-rocking motion.

"You have baggage, unfinished issues, and you're resisting change especially when these cards are present. You may feel scared to move on because of what happened in your past. You've lost yourself, and you are having trouble deciding what to take with you and what to leave behind. It could be anything from relationships, beliefs, habits, or material goods. Your personal growth depends on this change based upon the present upright card of the moon. Presently, this is your chance to reinvent yourself, reset your life, and rebuild a strong foundation from the ashes."

I'm discombobulated. I'm mesmerized by the ability of Viviana's intuition to weave my story together. She has no clue of my past as I've told her nothing of it. I'm cold, ill, just like a desolate statue. I stare at Viviana, but my eyes lose focus from spacing out. I clutch my hand into a fist, confusion fills my heart, a pain, and an emotion I haven't known surfaces. It's as if it's unconsciously suppressed. Viviana's voice speaks to me in the gentlest manner as if she sees the dismay upon my face.

"Alice, you do not have to take this reading literally. The future that it presented is never set in stone which is why readings are meant for guidance. Knowing that you have free will is imperative when understanding a tarot reading. No matter what the cards reveal, you have influence over your future. Sure, they give the advantage of gleaning into the future, but just because things are this way right now, doesn't mean that is what they will always be. Alice, you have the power of choice throughout the course of your life. The purpose of tarot cards is as a divinatory tool and to clue you in on what lies ahead if people, events, and energies remain the same."

As Viviana collects the cards from the reading, a wave of emotional drain saps my strength. I try all I can to hide my sorrow, my brokenness, and the will to keep myself together. I groan by letting out a breath of air. I run my fingers through my hair, the palms of my hands caressing my forehead. The Poe box shuts, and Viviana's floorboards creak. I can't move. My body weighs me down just like in my dream when contained upon the pink pentagram. The grace of Viviana's warm hand touches upon mine. The memory of Camila and the touch of her hand in my car flashes inside my head. The flash of Camila's green eyes to Viviana's blue are different. My emotions swallow me as if I'm on the verge of discovering something new, sincere, and real. She smiles at me.

"My mother, before she became very ill and bedridden, once told me: 'Don't be afraid of the darkness…It is where we find solitude and peace. It also gives us the opportunity to reflect on days past. You have the choice between turning the page and closing the book.'"

I grip onto her hands tightly after she tells me of her mother's words.

"Don't be afraid of the shadows," I utter.

Viviana nods her head, "Yes. As one of my favorite spiritual authors has said, *'There isn't shame in having shadows—we all have them to varying degrees. It's simply a part of being human.'"*

"But how is that?"

Viviana embraces me and answers, "I don't know the answers to that for it's something you will have to discover on your own."

I laugh, feeling her warm embrace. The scent of various herbs, incense, and smoke clings to her clothes. They remind me of my past, but a new thought comes to me. Can these memories and dreams which haunt me contain my own hidden secrets?

We stare into each other's eyes. My wounded heart bleeds with radiance. Emotions of all kinds overflow, so much so that it takes what strength I have left to conceal them. She warmly smiles; her cheeks glow and I desire to caress them. Before I do anything, Viviana speaks and breaks my trance of her, "In the famous words of my mother, I think this might help reflect everything." She scoots away from me to her bookcase. She parts a few books in a row and presents something she picks out for me.

"Here, this is for you."

Before me is a beautiful hand painted tree on a leather brown cover. It's the same design which I saw on her bed cover.

"A journal?"

"Yes, but there is more to it. It's the Tree of Life."

"Like in Norse Mythology?"

Viviana chuckles as she raises her head up to think.

"Eh, sort of…I look at it differently as a symbol of the balance it brings or of seeking to restore balance in life. So, if you are feeling out of sorts and unbalanced, look to the symbol of the Tree of Life to help find balance and equilibrium."

"Huh, makes sense that the Tree of Life is inscribed on this journal as every page is from a tree. So, it's like my thoughts or emotions, whether positive or negative, they reside in a collection of trees. The writing within these trees serves as a reminder to not dip so far in any direction that will imbalance myself. Just like the pages of every book, they are the souls of the people who wrote them and the hearts of the people who read them."

Viviana's eyes perk up. She gives me the journal as she nods her head. "That's a unique way of thinking. I really think writing in it will help. In fact, take a few moments before joining everyone outside. I know Ionel told me that you once had a friend in your past that is complicated. I don't need to know the details because it's not my place, but if you could write to your friend, what would you say?"

My stomach knots as my breath deflates. I can't believe Ionel listened to me about Camila during our time in Coventry. "You know about that?"

"I'm sorry. I'm only trying to help. Ionel told me about your time in Coventry together. He's very fond of you."

I nervously rub my hands against my thighs as I speak. "Oh, he's fond of me?" Viviana bites her lip and sighs.

"I hope I didn't upset you."

Her eyes are downcast and it numbs my heart seeing her state.

"No, I'm not upset with you. I just don't know how to react to the context of 'fondness' with how your brother views me."

"I get it. I don't even know myself where he stands with you, but I feel you should be wary of entering a new relationship at this time."

There's an awkward silence. I don't know how to react to Viviana's words or what she means. Bitterness brews, but at the same time, I think that maybe my emotions are misinterpreting what she is saying.

"What do you mean?" I finally say.

"Oh, my apologies. I just meant in general and not specifically my brother." She bites her lips again in hesitation as she wants to say something more to clarify. I give her the opportunity.

"Ok, you've read *The Fall of the House of Usher*, yes?"

I nod at her question.

"Ok, remember when the narrator flees the estate? He looks back to see the moon shining through a large fissure in the house. The crack widens and it splits in two, causing it to collapse and sink into the adjacent lake. Well, elements of this story are at play. For instance, I feel you are going through so much; I feel this darkness from you. An energy—but it is something beautiful. You have suffered from illnesses and deaths to sudden storms just like the collapse of the mansion associated with Poe's story. I don't want any relationship, regardless of who it is with, to have anything that's built on a weak foundation. Transformation is a difficult but necessary and beautiful aspect of life. You might not recognize the person you're becoming, but in time, you'll look back and marvel at how much you've grown and at all you've endured. You will be a phoenix rising from the ashes as it will portend an overhaul of your life."

"Vulnerability is difficult," I answer.

"Yes, it is, and I admire that about you." Viviana's breath deflates as she sighs, and her eyes meet mine.

"It's difficult to explain. You're vulnerable even though you try to conceal it. You stay true to yourself despite what haunts you. I may not specifically know what haunts you but there is a beauty in you. You're real; sincere. Yes, you have dark energy. But what defines a person with goodness is not a spotless life constant of temperance, but a willingness to see themselves in their deepest and innermost selves. Their complete authentic self. You are authentic as I see that in you, but look at yourself. Is that something *you* see within yourself?" She hugs me. "I'll be outside." Viviana's footsteps echo down the narrow hall. I glance down at the journal, open it, and write to reflect:

Dear Camila,

In the year 2009 I went through a very dark depression because of how things went. My father was still isolating himself and was still grieving from my mother's death. During the recession, Viktor had passed away, and I was alone. I didn't want to confide in my father because of what he had on his plate. I faced a darkness I had never known at that time. I had missed school a lot, my grades were falling, and our relationship was slowly crumbling over time. More years go by, 2016, and my father's health deteriorates; cancer, and you're not there. I thought I could escape everything by attempting suicide. 2019, I am still fighting this darkness again…Nightmares and my memories fuel them. Such memories include you dear Camila. Memories pour as I think of you. The playground where we met, the first time you held my hand, and our embrace at your front door. My heart from then knew that we were a rare set. In your room I won't forget the talks, the first kiss, our bond. Us, in palm, held and tugged. We made love and more as our emotions were pure and true. I have no regret with our time spent because as the memories flash, they will also disband.

Farewell,

Alice Reaper

I read the words I have written in the journal. A few tears stream down my cheeks onto the letter I have written for her. I know it will take time to heal from my past breakup, but this is a good start. I rip the letter out of my journal and fold it.

Chapter 9

In the distance, I hear an accordion playing lead as Ionel's guitar is playing rhythm. The music is cheerful, bouncy, and energetic. Polka music is something I never had the pleasure of listening to. As I make my way outside, I find a black kitten with green eyes. It meows but then chirps randomly at the door with the light shining underneath it. It's Mrs. Dragomir's room. The cat sits upright, stares at the white door, and meows again. Its tail flicks and swishes back and forth, almost as if it's concerned or can sense something. I think about Viviana's story about the cat. She had some sort of comfort, but the experience is different for me. I don't feel I'm in danger, but something is off—like something is about to happen but I can't quite describe it. The kitten raises its right paw only to bring it back down again, continuing to chirp. I don't know what to make of it as I exit the house.

The backyard still has the tiki torches lit in the circle. My seat is unoccupied and waits for me to join the circle.

Cai is loud, a bit too happy, definitely tipsy, and has another beer in his hand. I can't make out what he's drinking because of the darkness and the small illumination from the fire. He laughs with Viviana while they talk. Tessa is silent, sitting next to Cai like a cold-hearted wolverine ready to rip anyone to shreds. She has her arms wrapped around and underneath Cai's arm.

As Cai and Viviana are laughing, Ionel and Mr. Dragomir engage with their music. They're comfortable, content, and read off of each other in the language of music. How their bodies sway to the music gives instincts to each other on what to play. It gives me comfort seeing them interact with each other but makes me sad because that's something my father and I didn't share. As I got older, the more solitary my father had become. Maybe it was that I reminded him of my mother. She too had long dark-raven hair like me, green eyes, and pale skin. She was beautiful as I recall one of the pictures of her in the library. She had a white pretty smile, her belly swollen because of me, and my father was the happiest I'd ever seen him. He had a smile too, which was something I had never seen in my lifetime. They were happy together and I took that happiness away. My father, I secretly think, loathed me and shunned my presence. His mannerisms and his focus of all his energy on his work spoke more to me than any word he would say to me.

"Hey Alice!" The call of my name breaks my thoughts. The music stops as I glance over to Ionel.

I smile at him, "Hey, there! You two play great together." I add, crossing my legs. I readjust my chair a bit by shuffling in it. The heat from the fire is warm, but it's slowly dying out.

"Thank you. You are very kind," replies Mr. Dragomir. His dimples stretch from his cheeks. "How was your reading?" he asks.

I stand up, set the journal on the ground, and toss the letter I wrote to Camila into the fire. I know my worth to her expired as I stare into the fire and watch the paper burn. With ease I sink back into the chair. The paper burns into ash as I speak, "It was helpful. I'm glad I did it."

"Very good."

After Mr. Dragomir replies, my attention shifts to Viviana. I call to her.

"Viviana, on my way out, I saw a black kitten by your mom's room. It was acting very strangely by staring at the door, meowing and chirping…"

Viviana becomes disturbed. Her fingers drum against her thigh nervously as she tries to play it off. "Oh, really? That would be Revenant. He is quite sensitive and picks up things that sometimes aren't apparent."

My interest in her cat is piqued by curiosity. "Oh, really?"

She doesn't answer me as she pushes forward out of her chair and paces quickly to the house.

Suddenly, Tessa breaks the silence. "I think we are going to get going. It's getting late."

Cai gasps: his eyes are wide, and his mouth unlatches, "No, Alice just rejoined us. Can't we stay longer to get to know her? It's rude."

Tessa pulls Cai's arm to stand up. "I'm sorry but you have work tomorrow morning and we have obligations to attend." Her voice is short, snappy, and straightforward. I have the feeling that Tessa doesn't like my presence by the way she is treating her man.

"I'm sorry Alice. I hope we get to see you again," Cai says, almost dragging his feet. I study the abandoned beer in his chair. It's not even finished when they both disappear into the darkness. The crickets sing their song in the silence, but the distinct sounds of Cai and Tessa's voices are still heard. They're loud from arguing.

"I don't care!" cries Tessa. The car door slams and the engine roars. The wheels squeal as I look over to Ionel and his father. Ionel exhales a heavy sigh, his breath light and airy. He smacks his lips, "Well, shrewdest as ever…"

"Is she always like that or is it just me?"

"Tessa is well…I'd say snobby, self-absorbed, and a spoiled brat. She's upper middle class and her fiancé is rich because of his father. I don't know how Cai can stand her. I wouldn't even poke her with a six-foot pole."

I snort under my breath with a laugh as my hand shrouds my mouth.

"It seems that way." I mutter to myself.

Ionel's father pats his son's shoulder and grips on to it.

"Well, Ionel. It has been a good night playing music with you as always. I will check on your mother and go to bed."

"*Dobranoc ojcze*," Ionel says, embracing his father.

"*Dobranoc. Kocham Cię*," Mr. Dragomir kisses his son's cheek and with a warm smile he turns to me.

"Alice, thank you for your company. You may spend the night if you wish."

"Thank you."

Mr. Dragomir collects his accordion and lumbers away to the house.

"*Też cię kocham*," Ionel calls out.

He packs his guitar back into the case as my eyes switch between him putting the guitar away and the dying fire before me. The lit embers pulsate like a heartbeat with its last seconds. The paper I cast is nothing but blended ash into the pit. Ionel sits in the chair next to me, and he stares into what is left of the fire.

"What's your most cherished childhood memory?" He asks me.

"Oh, I…" I freeze because of how random that question is out of nowhere.

"Sorry if I asked…" adds Ionel.

"No, it's fine… Let me think." I can't find one as I ponder the many times I used to read to my mother's grave as a child. "Tell me yours first and I'll give you mine once I figure it out."

Ionel chuckles and crosses his arms to think. "Very well." A few moments later, he uncrosses his arms and shuffles his body to the edge of his chair. "It was when I was seven years old. My father, mother, and I were living here. My mom was pregnant with my sister, and she was due any day. It was the end of spring, and my mother took me on a picnic. It was at some park, I do not recall which one it was, but I clearly remember a giant pine tree. We sat underneath it, laid out a blanket, and ate food together. It is a small memory but a most cherished one as a child."

"It doesn't matter how small a memory is."

Ionel's eyes light up. "Indeed."

His face becomes despondent soon after; his lips are pressing together, and I know something is on his mind.

"What's wrong? Is it about your mom?"

Ionel nods his head. "Yes, I am afraid of her passing. Her health has not been great, and I can't imagine losing either of my parents. I keep screaming in my head saying, '*Don't you dare… Don't you dare leave me yet.*' I'm scared of getting older as I see my parents getting older. It's not death itself that frightens me, but it is the moment of losing them. Them not being here and not being able to spend time or talk with them. They have been with me my entire existence. Living without them is scary. I recall something Emily Dickinson once wrote, *'Hold dear to your parents for it is a scary and confusing world without them'*. That rings true to me."

I warmly smile at him reciting an Emily Dickinson quote.

"Classic. Emily Dickinson is one of my favorites. I can relate to your fear. I felt that way towards my father. I was afraid of losing him, but he and I were confined in our solitude. I didn't get to have the kind of relationship or memories like you did with your mom or dad. When I was a child, I was blinded and unaware of my father's torments. My mother died shortly after giving birth to me. I do remember a cherished memory with my father. Nearby the cemetery, close by our house, there was a windmill a few yards down. It was always a part of the property, but we never used it for anything except as a place for storage. It was usually used to store my father's cemetery equipment and utensils to care for the grounds…"

"Woah, wait! What, your father was a caretaker for a graveyard?"

I laugh at Ionel's interjection. His eyes are wide with interest and a smile forms around his face. "Yeah, we had a family funeral business." I'm silent as I want to get on with sharing my memory. Ionel observes my expression, "I imagine that is another discussion for sure. So, go on about your memory." I squirm in my chair and lean back to think, and I begin my childhood memory.

It was the summer of 1998. I was six years old and was to begin first grade in a few months. My father was outside in the cemetery installing a new grave marker in the graveyard. I had trouble learning and writing my middle name, so my father had me learn my middle name, Lillian, by tracing my mother's first name upon her gravestone. As I was doing this, I caught glimpses of my father installing the marker. He used a tape measure to measure out the size of the grave marker on the grave space where it was to be set. The shovel went to work to dig out the outline, excavating the dirt and setting it to the side. My father dug as deep as the marker was in its thickness. He took charge of the post hole digger and dug two piers in the width on the outer ends of the pad. He reinforced it with steel bars in each hole and used a hammer to set them down far enough so that only a few inches of the bar rose above the surface. He then placed steel mesh at the bottom and tied it to the bars with metal twist ties.

My father proceeded to mix the concrete in the wheelbarrow. He poured the mixed concrete into the ground leaving enough space for the grave marker to set flush approximately from the top. Finally, using a small board, he smoothed the surface of the wet concrete, so the marker was set flat when installed. When he had finished, he focused upon his work to ensure the concrete was level.

He wiped his brow of sweat, "Eh, a job done… Alice!" He called.

I ran up to him and remembered how soft his blue eyes were. "I'll change clothes and let's go fishing out by the pond."

I cheered and jumped up and down excitedly knowing I'd spend time with my father. I waited for him to change inside the house, wandering aimlessly around the library. My father's certificates were displayed in a row of glass cases. There was a white marble fireplace nearby with various china plates. One of them was a plate with a woman in a bonnet with dark hair smiling to admire all the men she had around her in different suits. Inside the plate was a purple bat I had randomly placed there when my father was cleaning the plates. For some reason, he kept the bat inside the plate. Old wick glass oil canisters were spaced out along the mantel. They were old-fashioned and had belonged to my mother. Through the glass I could see the green oil inside them.

The energetic footsteps of my father reverberated down upon the grand staircase within the foyer. I rushed to meet him, anxious to go fishing. He had beige shorts, black and white sneakers, and a green short-sleeve polo.

"Ha-ha, come here sweetheart!" He scooped me up in his arms. "Out to the windmill!"

I held him tightly as we made our way to the windmill. His skin reeked of the smell of cigarettes, but I don't recall if I had heard wheezing. I was too absorbed in the excitement of going fishing with him. Inside the windmill, my father collected his worn out, green-gray tackle box.

"You'll need this before we go out," he handed me a pink inflated lifejacket. He bent down, eye-level to me, and strapped the lifejacket around my body. "There's my girl. Now she's ready!"

He kissed the top of my forehead, and I giggled. I grabbed his hand as we strolled out to the pond. Nearby was a small boat ready to be pushed into the vast pond. The rods were already inside the boat as he had planned this ahead of time.

Once inside, we rowed out to the pond's center. The sound of insects echoed and sang while a few of them were attracted to us. My father slapped his neck. "Nasty devil," he muttered. My father explained gently how to set up the line on the rod, but I can't recall the exact details of what he said. I was too busy admiring him and how he glowed. He handed me the rod, saying, "Here. Take it."

As I gripped the rod, he sat closer to me; I felt his body lightly against my side and felt the touch of his rough but warm hands. He whispered in my ear as his breath tickled my ears. "Alright, Alice… Hold it gently now. You're going to cast the line out. So, take it back." His hands gripped on the rod in the same position as mine.

We swayed back the rod as he spoke again, "Now, just as you're about to cast forward in that direction, press and hold this center button on the rod. It will release the line as you cast." The rod swayed back to face him and me. "On three we'll cast together." I followed his hand motions of swaying the rod back and forth.

"One, two, three!" The line zipped and lunged forward into the pond. "Reel it in a bit." The rod clicked in my hands as I was all set.

I don't know how long we were in that boat. Eventually, I grew antsy, shifting myself. "Alice, try not to move too much in the boat. You don't want us to fall in." Sitting at the other end, he had his rod's line already cast in.

"Daddy, the fish ain't biting…" I pouted and my face soured as if drinking spoiled milk left out too long.

"No worries. Patience is the key to this. Focus on what's around you. Listen to the crickets, the frogs, and the dragonflies. The soft wind whistles and the birds chirp. Just close your eyes."

I had done this, and I found the patience to carry on. It was peaceful, enjoyable, just being out there with my father. There's solace in the feelings of human nature. Suddenly, there was a violent tug on my line. It startled me and caught me off guard.

"Daddy, daddy quick!" My voice was fevered with excitement. The patience had paid off, and my body wriggled. The boat rocked back and forth. My father was caught off guard by the excitement and the sudden struggle with my rod. He bolted up on his way over to help me, but his weight tipped him over. He and I yelped, and he splashed into the cool muddy water. I held on for dear life as the boat would not stop rocking. Everything happened so quickly that I didn't notice he was gone.

"Daddy?" I shut my eyes and reopened them. He wasn't there. I looked around and jolted from a sudden scare.

"It is I the monster! Rawr!" He made a loud-low tone and a squealing roar, his arms reached out, and his hands tickled me. I giggled out loud as he commented on my laughter. "It's alive!" he exclaimed like a mad scientist.

A roar of thunder echoed after a few more moments of him tickling me. My father's attention gravitated towards the gray clouds. "A storm's coming! Let's go ashore."

He grabbed the front end of the boat and swam towards the direction of the windmill. He pulled the boat onto shore as a few drops of rain began to fall. He swept me up and carried me inside the windmill. There was hay laid all across the floors as he floundered in dripping wet. Father climbed the ladder to the second floor and came back down with a few towels. I unfastened my lifejacket, and he dried me off. I gripped my towel to finish drying while he dried himself. As I had almost finished, a trapdoor caught my attention. I had never noticed it before because it was shrouded with hay. A dark iron ring nob gave away its location.

"Daddy, what's down there?" I pointed.

He threw the towel over his head like a spooky ghost in a sheet. He rose slowly to his feet. He enacted his low-toned scary voice and said, "A crypt to the under-passages of the dead. Beware; for they are fearless, and therefore powerful. Thou shall not disturb the dead." He jumped-scared me by flailing the towel away with his eyes wide with horror. I screamed in terror, but he stopped, laughed, and hugged me tightly.

He kissed my forehead and said, "I love you."

98

Chapter 10

Once I say those three words, I can't speak. I'm speechless, and an overwhelming emotion takes over me. I want to cry and pry out the pain. That's the only time I can remember my father saying those words. He had changed over time as I grew older. Something in his brain had altered him. Was he pretending when I was little? I shove my head into my palms sobbing. I've never told anyone about that memory.

"It's a beautiful memory," Ionel says.

He stands up from his chair and walks over to me. Behind me, I hear another pair of footsteps coming toward us.

"Hey, you're both still out here? It's almost three in the morning!" It's Viviana's voice. "What's wrong Alice?" she asks, seeing me weep.

"We were just sharing childhood memories," says Ionel. I look up at him, water fills my eyes, and he jams his hands into his pockets.

Viviana's hands rest upon my shoulders from behind. She grips them to comfort me and speaks, "Well, it's late. The fire is finally out, and she needs sleep."

I laugh inside my head as she is right about my need for sleep. I haven't slept in days and it's showing. I can tell by Ionel's face, his expression of empathy, and how his eyes stake my soul. Briefly, I wonder if he has feelings for me, but at this moment it isn't a concern. My body aches and my vision blurs from the mixture of tears and the lack of sleep.

"Yeah, she does. You got this sis?"

"Oh, yeah. She'll stay with me. I don't mind."

"What?" I exclaim.

Viviana's voice stutters, "Uh, if you don't mind of course. We're adults."

I'm in shock—speechless. I've never shared a bed with anyone before. At this point, I don't care at the same time. A nice comfy bed sounds nice and my body longs for it.

"It's fine," I mutter in exhaustion.

"Okay, come with me." She squeezes my shoulders, signaling me to move.

"Thank you for our conversation, Ionel," I say sincerely while grabbing my journal.

"Of course, it was a pleasure. Goodnight you two."

As Ionel departs with his guitar from Viviana and me, I ask, "Where's your brother's room by the way?"

Viviana chuckles, "His room is in the basement. It's pretty decked out, but for now let's get some sleep."

When we arrive in Viviana's room, I observe what she wears to bed. It's nothing but her panties and a large, black Alice in Chains t-shirt with the image of their album Dirt.

"Fan of Alice in Chains?" I ask, sleepily.

She scratches her head and sits on the stool by the mirror on a table that's in a corner as she removes her makeup. "Oh, yeah! I love Layne Staley. His tormented voice is alluring, and I can relate to him as far as depression goes. Sometimes, depending on which sabbath, I'll play his song 'Angry Chair.' The drums and the guitar, how their rhythms syncopate in time with some of the formal rituals."

I lie upon the right side of Viviana's bed but not underneath the covers.

"Oh, what kind of formal rituals?"

Viviana finishes removing her makeup, shuts off the mirror light, and bounces over to the entrance of her room. "Hmm… You should come with me some time to celebrate Samhain. Maybe, you'll find out " She shuts off the main light and I hear her bare feet creak on the floorboards.

"Leaving me in suspense?"

"Oh, yeah. You'll get a better experience that way than me trying to explain it."

The sheets ruffle next to me as we get underneath the covers.

"Nite," she says.

"Nite," I reply.

My eyes fixate upon the ceiling in reflection. The Alice in Chains album Dirt runs through my head. The front cover of the album features a woman lying upon the dirt, drugged, wasted, and covered in mud. The image is one of the most disturbing looks at a wasted life and is one long slide down to the bottom of Dante's *Inferno*. Its frightening image of the woman's eyes speaks its intensity and its mastery of a world shrouded in depression's shadows. I feel like an Alice in chains. It makes me think about my nightmare of being bound on the pink pentagram. I shift to my side. Funny, that there's a pentagram rug by this bed. This bed is comfy; more than mine at the apartment. Maybe it's because someone who cares for me is sleeping next to me? My eyes shut and blackness swallows them.

My eyes open, blurring in and out of focus. My body is motionless as if in a sleep-like paralysis. The ground is grassy, tall, and wet as thick heavy rain pours down violently. I don't know how long I've been lying there. No matter how hard I try, I can't move anything but my eyes. The moisture hangs thick and the wind howls. My body is ice cold from the rain. I must have been unconscious for quite some time. I grunt and beyond the darkness I see a glimpse of the windmill in the far distance. I stare at it, slowly realizing it's the one from my old home, and I gather the adrenaline to move towards it. Finally, I'm able to move, but with difficulty. I feel weak; my body, sore and heavy, crawls. I inch forward as a roar of thunder cracks and lightning blinds me. My eyes are fixated upon that mill; I have to get there. Streaks of lightning illuminate the dark sky and the visage of the windmill.

The blades of the windmill are rotted, and some are even broken off. The wheel rotates, but loosely as if the wheel of the mill will fall. It creaks and wails in the storm as moss shrouds the wood tower. Water drips from my hair and into my eyes. I shut them to get the water out of them and crawl. I find the stairway that leads up to the tower. The front door opens ajar and slams again and again from the wind. The step-boards creak with every inch. Hand to knee, I go up. The wood feels wet, slippery, and flimsy. One of the boards snaps and breaks through. My left arm falls through and my forehead slams against the step-in front of me.

"Ah, dammit!" I cry. I continue to climb and grab the doorknob to lift myself up. I stand only for a moment before my strength wanes, and I stumble inside the mill. Sawdust and speckles of dirt shroud the wooden floors. I push myself further inside and my fingernails capture a mixture of sawdust and dirt. The inside smells moldy, decayed, and rotten. A stack of hay is laid out in the far-left corner by an uncovered window. My teeth clatter, and water drips from me as I shiver. My nose becomes runny and snot dangles from my nostrils. I sniffle and cough as I turn over my body to lean against the rough, wooden wall.

The hay crunches from my body weight as I breathe short breaths from my mouth. The rain outside heavily pounds the roof as if it plays a melodic lullaby. The door continues to creak and slam from the wind like my own heartbeat. My body is tired, and I slowly shut my eyes and listen to the sounds around me. I feel and hear the thump of my own heart and it drifts me to a deathlike sleep. Those deathlike slices of sleep jolt-start me awake.

The morning light shines upon my face from the uncovered window. The birds chirp and all is quiet. The summer air feels warm and slightly humid. My body flinches as I slowly close and re-open my eyes. The light from the sun feels soothing upon my face, but I still feel weak from the night's storm. My body is stiff, and my skin is pale. My stomach growls.

"Ugh… Hungry." I mumble. I study my surroundings and I see specks of dust fluttering in the air through the sunlight. Cobwebs fill the ceiling corners of the mill and a post runs through the floor to the ceiling by the wall facing me. I look left and observe that the front door of the windmill is wide open.

It's unsettling to be inside an empty room filled with silence. I slowly muster myself to rise up. I look up to see through the cracks of the ceiling and see another floor above me. This *has* to be my childhood windmill. I'm curious to explore my surroundings to make sure, and I sluggishly drag my feet. My damp, flat heels scrape against the wooden floors. I look down at myself, and I'm wearing a black strapless dress. After scuffing a few inches, my feet tap against something hard. I look down and discover a large, rusted iron ring attached to the floor.

"An opening to a cellar?" I say aloud. "No…" I shift to the side and bend down to lift the ring. It's the trapdoor. My stomach knots and I feel nauseated. A small wooden ladder follows down, but darkness completely opaques the bottom. I stare into what feels like an eternal abyss. I shake my head, quivering, and shudder. I don't want to go in. I ignore it and turn. I tread over and climb a ladder to the right of the entrance of the windmill. The second level consists of a storage area full of barrels, but that didn't seem right. What happened to my father's equipment and tools? I open and look inside one of the barrels and see it is filled with ashes. They run like sand through my fingers back into the barrel. I turn my head away from the smell of the ashes, like rotted corpses, and slam the top shut I hyperventilate, my breathing unnerved, and mutter "Ashes, ashes; no more…"

In my panic, my eyes catch the glimpse of a certain object. Against the wall is an old rustic lantern hanging from a hook mounted upon the wall. It calms me as it reminds me of my mother's old-fashioned oil canisters upon the mantel. I grip the lantern and swing it from its hook. Oil swishes inside.

"Very little oil…But it's green."

An old trunk below where the lantern hangs grabs my attention. I open it and find oil stored in containers which comforts me, but there is also a layer of ashes. I grab the oil aside. Terror chills and curdles the beatings of my heart. Am I meant to find something else in this trunk? I run my fingers through the ashes, touching shards of broken glass, and a wooden frame. I take out whatever object this is and discover an old faded black and white picture.

It's a picture of a couple; my parents. My father is wearing a suit and tie with fancy buttons on it. My mother is wearing a wedding dress and her beauty is apparent. The picture has the handwritten year 1988. I cling the picture close to my chest and a wave of grief conceives in my emotions. "Why did you have to die?"

A bloodcurdling scream replies. It jolts me as the picture falls from my hand, breaking the frame. A breeze from the second-floor window sweeps up and flutters the picture away to the first floor. A baby cries. I rise slowly. The baby continues to cry, but the first scream I heard is not from the baby.

My breath is short as I falter and my flat heels crackle glass. I look down and see it's not glass, but shards of broken urns. As I peer down to the first level, I hear a woman weeping and the sound of my father's voice calling my mother's name. It's coming from the cellar of the mill where the darkness resides. The sobbing continues to wail, shrieking in pain and sorrow.

I, at an uneasy pace, climb down to the first floor and crouch. I stare into the darkness of the cellar.

"Hello?" I call.

My father's voice elongates a short sob, and everything stops.

"Are you down there?"

Silence.

I lick my dried lips as my palms begin to sweat. I lunge my body forward to the edge of the trapdoor. My head and neck stick out while my body becomes stiff from my crouching position. Cold dry air blows gently from the darkness of the cellar.

I sprout up cautiously, turn around, and my father's pale face with white eyes stares at me. I scream and fall backwards into the darkness of the cellar. I crash into a rotted ladder that breaks as I fall. The sound of my ankle snaps, crackles, and twists. I wail and scream in agony as tears water in my eyes. I thrash and pound one fist into the ground while gripping my ankle with the other. The pain shoots like daggers as I scream and wallow in it. I look up, but no one is there. Different colors of spots consume my sight from the darkness. I clutch my right hand in a fist and grind my teeth. The pain becomes unbearable and throbs. I crawl on the floor full of dirt and reach out with my right hand, but there's nothing to touch but empty darkness. I go on, crawling about as tears roll down from my cheeks. My right-hand scrapes against a stonewall. Specks of stone crumble off; my hand becomes rough and touches something mounted upon the wall. It's sturdy enough that I try to pull myself up to hop. As I try, the object twists to the side and clicks. The sound of stone shuffles and crumbles.

Breathless, exhausted, and sore from all the crawling and constant motion, I stop. I look forward and finally see a light. It revives my strength to crawl forward, and I exclaim, "A light! I see a light!"

The light illuminates upon the ceiling ahead and reveals a surface body of water. My body is weak, heavy, and my throbbing broken ankle is as hot as fire. I stop at the body of water and stare at my reflection. Blood streams down my face and drips from my hair and I try to wipe it away

"This isn't my blood?!" I cry.

While looking at my own reflection, a figure ripples within. A beautiful young woman with long, jet-black hair, eloquent pale skin, and soft ruby lips. She wears a dark purple dress with short sleeves that expose her arms. . I'm mesmerized by her beauty. I lean closer in a trance—a deathlike sleep. All the pain I feel is now numb to me. I reach out to her…my hand barely touches the fluid surface. The woman's icy green eyes open and I jolt. Her eyes fixate upon mine and I fall…

Chapter 11

"Unable are the loved to die. For love is immortality."
~ Emily Dickinson

A woman's curdling scream rings inside my skull and my eyes whip wide open. As they open, I catapult straight out of bed.

"Mama!"

The image of the young woman's piercing icy green eyes are inside my brain. An outward force keeps me from moving forward and someone presses against my shoulders.

"Alice-Alice-stop!" shouts a voice. I frantically jerk my neck to look around. I breathe heavily and soon realize my surroundings. Viviana's eyes meet mine as it's her in front of me.

"Alice, it was a dream. Just a dream…"

"But it was so real!" I exclaim. My hands pat my face maniacally—the blood.

"Alice, it's just sweat."

Viviana wipes my brow as my hands grasp hers. My head throbs, my skin is hot, and my breath is short. I stare into her eyes and a wave of calmness seeps into my soul. The only word to describe my growing feelings for her escape from my mouth.

"Sublime."

"What?"

"Huh?"

"What do you mean sublime?" Viviana bites her lips after she asks that question.

"Uh, nothing."

"Are you blushing Alice?"

"What, I…" My face feels warm. I usually don't blush.

"Well, I'm curious… You think I'm cute or something?"

Viviana's voice is silvery and smoky, but I can't tell if it's honeyed in such a way that is false or flirty.

"Hmm… Do I think you're cute? I have to think about it…" I bite my lip; my eyes glare to the ceiling in thought and I stall. "According to my literary skills… Cute is not a strong enough diction to describe you."

Viviana's eyebrows pique, her voice becoming fruity, as she asks, "Well, what diction would you use then?"

My mind is wobbly, racing. This is it.

"In a Romantic Period, literary term… Sublime. In other words, your level of cuteness is on the level of beauty that conveys to what English romantics would identify as 'a realm of beauty beyond the measurable.'"

Viviana's mouth drops and her chest deflates as if my words steal the life from her heart. She blinks as her breath is strangulated, tremulous. "Aww, Alice… That is so sweet! Thank you, are you just talking about my face or the rest of me too?"

There's no going back now. My heart bleeds impulsiveness as the words rush into my mind like a ravaging storm, "When I use sublime, I'm applying it to your beauty beyond measure from not only your face, eyes, smile, and physical appearance, but who you are as a person, how you carry yourself—everything, and how you treat and care for me."

Suddenly, Viviana latches her arms around me. Her warm embrace startles me. I'm not prepared for it, as that intimate moment I had with Camila flashes before me.

"Alice, that is so kind! Thank you…"

She squeezes me and after a few moments, my arms wrap around her shoulders. In my embrace my chin rests upon her right shoulder as I speak, "You're welcome. I've never used the word sublime before. You're good to me."

Her voice is soft spoken and gentle, "Aww…" She squeezes me against her again tenderly.

We break our embrace and gaze at each other, "I've gotten sexy or beautiful in the past, but I've never gotten sublime. So, that means a lot!"

Butterflies take over. "It's the truth. That's how I feel about you."

She smiles at me warmly. "I really appreciate your deep thoughts and feelings Alice. I do care about you. I think a relationship could potentially work at some point, but I don't want to make any big promises, if that makes sense."

My heart sinks as my eyes turn downcast in confusion. Viviana's eyes never stray from me. She delicately rests her hands upon my shoulders, and her voice is firm, "Let me reiterate. I do care about you, but like I said before, there's a lot more to focus on than just this, but perhaps something to keep in the back of your mind. I will be honest with you, especially, with everything going on, I am only interested in being friends right now. So, I am fine with talking, but I don't want to create any false expectations or thoughts that I will be looking for a relationship soon. I am aware of your feelings, but that is where I stand."

Her words wither the cockles of my heart as my words croak small, "I don't mean to put pressure on you. Nor is it my intention to put it on you…"

Viviana crosses her arms and sighs, "Well, I'll be honest, I am most comfortable keeping this at a friend level in terms of communication. To be honest I am fine, but emotionally I feel I need friends most."

I flash a little smile, but it withers, "Is it your mom?"

"Yes, partly. But I'll be honest, I lost an ex-boyfriend to suicide and it was not a good situation. I don't take suicide lightly at all."

My forlorn heart rots as my words are almost brittle, "I'm sorry you lost someone you cared for from suicide. I know it leaves a scar…"

Viviana shuts her eyes, reopens them, and scratches between her eyebrows. "Suicide is never a good option. No matter what the moment seems like, it's never a good choice. My ex committed suicide not long after we had broken up…" Her voice becomes frail, guttural, and the room fills with a dead silence. She sighs to push through her words."I had known about his suicidal tendencies from the beginning of meeting him, since he had been in a severe episode of depression. I don't know the details and didn't have a way to find them out, and really don't ever want to. But he was making things even worse for himself long before I had met him… I learned a lot in that relationship." A thunderous shrill roars throughout the house.

"Antonia!"

The wallowing screams of despair trigger the cries of my voice for my father inside the burning house. My breath is short—fire, ashes, shards.

Viviana races faster than a bat out of hell. "Papa!" she cries. Her footsteps are frantic as every board wails and I listen to shrieks of pain, sorrow, and grief. They are Mr. Dragomir's cries. I follow Viviana like a ghost from a haunting distance. My ears ring of more footsteps below with Ionel's voice shouting, "*Matka*!" Over and over again, "*Matka*!" He's sobbing.

Viviana speaks, "*Co stało*?"

Despair fills the atmosphere. It reminds me of when my father was around in my old home. Viviana weeps as I wait at the bottom of the stairs. Mrs. Dragomir's door is open. A harrowing weight grips my legs, and I know. Death had wrapped her in a cloak so lithe.

Viviana's cat Revenant flashes within my mind. My heart mourns for their pain. I don't know whether to depart or stay. A part of me thinks to leave so they can grieve as a family. I've had much experience with families in mourning. The funerals held at my house, dressed in a black strapless dress. Flashes of memories seep into my brain of past funerals of the community.

Our parlor where the funerals were held, me standing by the archway, hands clasped, dressed in mourning . My father giving heartfelt speeches of the deceased, their elegies said, attendees with obituaries read, and the cemetery where the flowers wither dead. I'd greet the guests, hand them the pamphlets I typed and printed, open our doors. Sometimes, father would allow me to drive our hearse, depending on the needs of the family. Sometimes, the pallbearers of the deceased carried the caskets out.

At other times, they wanted the hearse to travel down the dirt gravel path to the cemetery.

Viviana bumps into me, breaking my sequence of memories. Her feet stomp against the steps in syncopation with her sobs. Her door slams. Ionel is by the front door motionless, his greatest fear now realized.

Mr. Dragomir's distinct voice is talking, "My wife has passed. Please send someone."

I gaze at Mrs. Dragomir's picture mounted upon the wall. A life once lived. I stagger to Ionel as I embrace him. His body jolts as if I had taken him from a somber slumber. He cries and trembles like the leaves of an autumn tree whisked away. He whispers brittle, "I'll drive you home."

We break our embrace, and my eyes linger with his. "Are you sure? If you're not able to, I understand. I'll get a bus."

His eyes stray away from mine. "No, driving helps clear my head."

I probe him. "You need to grieve with your family."

Ionel's upper lip presses onto his bottom and into a thin line; his voice putters in a grind against his teeth. "I will, but don't tell me how to grieve. People grieve differently and let me grieve in mine."

I freeze, my eyes wander with shock, and my brows sparse. I've never seen him this way, but I don't pry or push further. I suspire to let it go.

The drive back to Bedford is deafening. The engine caterwauls the entire way and the fumes of gasoline are acrid. My insides rot. I don't want to be alone. The leaves flutter with flight as the car strolls through Downtown Bedford. There's a dead calmness but charm to the town. Old-fashioned green light posts stalk the sidewalks and every building huddles together in rows like Bedford Falls from *It's a Wonderful Life*. We stop at a red light between Broadway and North Park Street. There's the Bedford Falls cafe.

"That's the place I work."

"Ah…"

Silence.

By his agitated tone, I unbuckle my seatbelt, and unlock my side with a push of a button. "Alice, what are you doing?"

"You can drop me off here. I feel you need time to yourself." Ionel's flashers click repeatedly as I pry open my door and press the chair to eject forward.

I snatch my bag from the back as he says, "I'm sorry if my demeanor is uncomfortable. I just lost my mother…"

"I understand, which is why I feel you need time to reflect and process alone." My tone is quick and strong as I want to leave. I swing my bag against my shoulder, slam the door, and traverse promptly into the cafe. No one is behind the front counter as I grab a seat by the window. The smell of the cafe eases my mind to process everything—my dream last night, the confession of my feelings for Viviana, and the sudden death of Mrs. Dragomir. I don't know how to process these feelings as I grab the journal which Viviana gave to me to reflect:

Am I a shadow? I wonder if I too will become one of them. A shadow which spreads like wildfire and turns everything in my path to ashes. Viviana is fire, and she fuels the shadow of my being. Will this fire burn me down into ashes? The smell of smoke still lingers around. All are but fragments and shards, a seemingly hopeless pile. What secrets do they hold?

"Alice."

My eyes peer. My boss.

"I am surprised to see you here, but it's good to see you. I was going to call you about what happened a few days ago." He sits across from me. "I've signed you on the schedule to start on Monday, November 2nd and Thursday the 5th. Are you alright?"

I've never heard my boss ever ask that question. He's so focused on his job but yet here he is asking if I'm ok. I want to share my thoughts, but they're scattered, broken, and non-coherent. The words mumble, "Yeah, I'm better."

My boss silently studies me, his eyes quench, and he grips his teeth to clench the inside of his lip. "Ok, I'll see you then." He walks away back behind the counter. I don't think he believes me.

I glare back down to my journal and re-read the scribble I had written. Poor Viviana. She's full of life, but I know she will need time to process everything. How can I give her space with these feelings I have for her? There must be a way I can support her without appearing gloomy, overbearing, and my affections infested like death. I don't want what happened between Camila and I to happen with Viviana. I don't want my inner darkness and demons to destroy something as beautiful as her, brimming with life. For now, I should go back to my apartment and distract my mind on academia.

Chapter 12

*"What other dungeon is so dark as one's own heart!
What jailer so inexorable as one's self!"
— Nathaniel Hawthorne, The House of the Seven Gables*

October 30, 2019

Time passes and I'm nowhere closer to discovering the meaning of my dreams. Long hours and nights staring at a computer screen to distract myself. Sleep terrifies me. More nightmares. In one of them, I stand in the corner of an empty room, a first-person view. The room is very old, and it's made of cobblestone that has been scratched by human hands all over the place. The atmosphere feels as it did in the cellar I fell through. A pain throbs where my ankle was broken. I'm unable to move. In the middle of the room there's a chair, an old chair, and it's empty at first but then...A woman sits there. It's the same woman from the water. She wears a dark purple dress with short sleeves. Her hair is in a low ponytail and her face molds to a cold, serious gaze. The lady just sits there with her hands on her lap as she holds something wrapped up in a blanket. It's like she's not focusing on it. She's just holding it for a minute in silence. The woman sits there.

She turns her head slowly towards me, and she's smiling. She stands with her eyes staring into my soul. She slowly raises her right hand, presses a finger in front of her mouth like a hushing impression. The thing she holds in her hands is not there; she's still smiling, and lurches towards me. It's unnerving and creepy as she lurches, and her head slithers like a snake side by side. Her left hand is behind her. I can't move. The desire to shout is strong, but there's no sound. I struggle for so long to move, but nothing happens. She's suddenly gone. I stand there awhile, unable to move, in silence. Her face flashes in front of me, screaming. It rings in my ears and I watch as her face changes, decomposing before my eyes, and then I bolt from my slumber.

The last one is honestly the most disturbing for me. I'm locked into a first-person view in the foyer of my old home, but yet it looks like a room I've never seen before. There's the grand staircase in front of me, pictures hanging on the walls of past family relatives, much like how they were standing in person in the attic dancing with my father. Yet, the pictures are worn, molded, and I can't quite make them out, but I know it has to be pictures of my family relatives. The wallpaper is old, peeled, complimenting the rotted wooden furniture. It's like I'm standing in the front door looking in, frozen. From my viewpoint, all manner of disturbing entities trapped in the walls seep out to torment me. From the paintings and pictures, thousands of tiny little shadows pour out and come together, chattering teeth to form a giant version of the little ones...It shambles towards me with its head vibrating left to right, too fast to make out anything other than its shining, sharpened, grinning teeth. Eventually, it wanders out of my field of view and then something prowls backwards down the stairs; some kind of girl in a dress covered in mold. It pulls at its hair; strands of it fall out in mats with the scalp attached.

Eventually, it's standing in front of me, clawing at its still hidden face. I wonder if it's the same little girl I've seen before in my dreams. Viscera falls out and the stench of its rotten dress congests my nose. I never see its face as it moves in triple time back up the stairs as if it's missing frames of its natural movement. At this point, I see vines with thorns protruding out from my view above my head; it's almost like they will crawl into my eyes, ears, mouth, and skull.

I recall what Viviana had told me. That I can't be afraid of the shadows. I fear these nightmares will affect any relationship whether it's with myself or others. It's five in the morning, and I feel as if I'm still in these nightmares. ~~In my apartment~~ my body convulses with the idea in my head of someone standing next to my side of the bed. I can't see them, but I know they're there. Sometimes, I wonder if they talk to me, say my name, and I wake up, seeing the shadow of someone still there or walking towards me. This is similar to what happened during the thunderstorm ~~a few nights ago~~. With my sleep problems, it's often hard for me to fall asleep due to anxiety. So, I have to lie there—in the dark—where my imagination burns wild. I'm a twenty-seven-year-old, and I'm still convinced that there are monsters in my room at night. I'm trapped. I'm sitting at the kitchen table with my laptop and journal; my heart is pounding—I'm paranoid—constantly thinking about the staircase. I'm being watched. The feeling of powerlessness makes me even more maddening.

I worry. I haven't heard from Viviana since she fled into her room. The silence is dreadful…Should I reach out to her? Is she that kind of person, or does she rather confide in solitude? Maybe reactivate my Facebook to find her? I haven't been on it since I came to Ohio. I'm sure nobody on social media cares about my online existence. Camila was the only person who really texted me on Facebook. I wonder if she would message me if I reactivate Facebook? There are people from school, and some from the Boydton community who knew my father, but they're just there, and their lives used to appear on my newsfeed. It made me ill; their illusions of happiness, the pictures, and the smiles. It's why I deactivated it because it's something not real.

I haven't heard from Ionel since our ride back to Bedford…I feel horrid about suddenly leaving—monstrous as if I'm a Camila. I wish him not to feel what I did in my time of need. I wonder if he likes me, or if he knows my feelings for his sister. I wonder if she told him-would he be ~~sad~~ angry-disappointed? I should tell him if he does.

AR

I'm my own vampire. I render stiff as one at least. The sun is about to rise, and I haven't rested. These walls shall burn my insides slowly. This place feeds upon my weary and vulnerable subsistence. I need to get out. My mind is erratic; it races with the clock, deafening in its silence. I space out in this manner for some time, endeavoring a bodily intellection and to ease the weight upon my brain:

> 'The Horror not to be surveyed—
>
> But skirted in the Dark—
>
> With Consciousness suspended-—
>
> And Being under Lock—'

Emily Dickinson wrote powerfully about loneliness and solitude, and perhaps nowhere more movingly than *The Loneliness One dare not sound*, a poem about a loneliness so profound that I can't even bring myself to confront it for fear of being overwhelmed. This is my horror, the dark, and my own being under its crypt. My body jolts; my phone vibrates with impulsiveness.

"Hello?"

"Alice, it's Ionel… I apologize for calling you at a sudden notice, but you are invited to attend my mother's funeral this afternoon. My sister, father, and I would appreciate your presence."

"Of course, where will it be held?"

His voice croaks, "It's at the historic St. Peter Church in Cleveland close by to CSU."

"I'll be there."

The call disconnects. I'm puzzled—why a Catholic funeral? I'll probably find out. I search the address of the church. My eyebrows lift seeing how close it is, only a few blocks away from CSU located on E. 17th Street. I lock my phone, place it on the table, shower, and look through my closet. My black strapless dress—I haven't worn it since—since my father died. It's the same dress I see myself in during my dreams. Random voices of the Boydton community ring inside my head echoing the words they had said at his funeral:

"Paul Reaper was a good, honest man!"

"Mr. Reaper always put others before himself."

"You'll be okay Alice, your father is at peace."

I plummet onto my knees with my dress in hands gripping onto it like something died in my arms as the voices repeat their words to me. I bury my face into it; my screams muffle, and father's face flashes before me in clips. From my childhood when he said he loved me to the moments when we grew apart. His abandonment of me, the disdain, the loathing. The shadowy omen which possessed him and the solitude. Nobody knew him like I did. When I re-open my eyes, tears fill them and I think I see an orb of blackness from the corner of my eye. It churns like smoke, but as my eyes blink to rid the tears it disappears. I convince myself it has to be from not sleeping.. I flash my phone; an hour and a half till the funeral.

The autumn air is melancholy but picturesque. The leaves of red, orange, yellow, and dried brown flutter around the luscious and frost bare breeze. The soles of my shoes scrape the indolent sidewalks with the St. Peter Church to my left. Its architecture intimidates me even though it's beautiful. It's a towering gothic presence, built from dark brownish-gray bricks and stones.. I read a plaque that states it was founded in 1853. I step up its steps and pull the heavy brown finished door. My flat heels click and reverberate upon the gray stone floors. I'm in awe of the pure white marble stone and painted stained-glass windows as massive as I've ever seen. Wooden chairs in rows to the left and right side. A podium with a microphone is facing to the left side before the altar. A white stone table is centered upon the altar. Flowers of all types surround it, and the casket lies in front.

Mrs. Dragomir's body holds a rosary of some kind but I can't make out her appearance from the distance I'm standing. As I wander in through the main entrance, I see numerous pictures of Mrs. Dragomir's life. I turn my head facing the altar to find Viviana, Ionel, and Mr. Dragomir standing by the right front row of the chairs. They're chatting with the priest.

Viviana sees me standing; her eyes meet mine as a wave of emotions consumes my internal being. Her black heels click as I observe her and it feels as if time slows down. She's gorgeous. Her short blond-hair parts from the top neatly and flutters down from the back. She wears pearl earrings and a light-tint of red lipstick. Her dress is fashioned in an A-line cocktail with an illusion scoop neckline, semi-sheer long sleeves, a ribbon-defined waist, and a knee-length tulle skirt. Her despondent eyes radiate in the solace of my arrival. She embraces me lightly as I wrap my arms around her. I touch her bare back from the prominent cutout in the back of her dress. Our embrace warms the cockles of my heart and her touch speaks more words than what I can describe.

"I'm happy you made it…" she says brittlely.

My voice croaks: "Of course…" I want to cry.

We break our embrace and she studies me.

"You look wonderful."

"Thank you." My eyes wander timidly.

"What's wrong?"

"This place…" I whisper quietly. "It scares me."

She chuckles under her breath. "I think it's just the architecture, but it's still beautiful."

"Indeed, but I would never have thought…"

Viviana interjects as she smirks, "We would be at a Catholic vigil?"

"Yeah."

She shakes her head, "It's not what I believe in, but my mother was a Catholic and so is my dad. It's why, if you noticed, that the living room is not as decorative as my room because I respect my father's space. He finds my Wiccan beliefs strange and sometimes terrifying. Though he respects me and I him. I remember…" she laughs under her breath, "both of my parents were freaked out when I ordered a mourning gothic statue from Amazon. It was a prayer wall sculpture…" She pauses by biting her lip to think, "about twelve inches?" Her eyes focus back to mine. "Yeah, it was a black and white finish of a hooded maiden with tears in her eyes. The statue was stunning for a candlelit spot of quiet meditation with a gothic-style rosary to reflect, in my opinion, and balance energy. I loved the statue because it was based on my favorite artist Anne Stokes."

She groans quietly with a shrug, "Alas, my parents hated it. Especially, my mother… She didn't see it as an artistic-subcultural gothic work, but a horrifying sacrilegious statue. She said to me, 'That! That is the Virgin Mary dressed in black! She has tears of blood in her eyes. I don't feel comfortable with it in the house.'"

My eyebrows grow wide, and my mouth forms a 'wow' expression. "Huh, I imagine… You got rid of it?"

"Yeah, I wasn't angry at my parents or her because I respect them. I was just sad because it spoke to me differently. I felt hurt because I took it as a way of them not accepting me. To me, it's something that is a part of gothic culture such as various forms of literature. My mom didn't discourage Ionel or I from reading gothic literature like *The House of the Seven Gables* or something…" She laughs about the memory but in a cheerful manner. I nod my head to acknowledge her to let her know of Ionel and Mr. Dragomir approaching us. Viviana angles her head towards them. I smell her perfume as she turns, and the scent of lilac eases my mind. Ionel hugs me and releases me.

"I'm glad you're here."

"Thank you for coming," chimes Mr. Dragomir.

Both of the men have on dark identical black-charcoal suits with a silver-gray dress shirt and black tie. We walk over to the rows of chairs and sit together upon the right side as other spectators wander in. Perhaps they're previous friends of hers from Playhouse Square just by overhearing their conversations. Mr. Dragomir, Ionel, and Viviana are greeted by them with their sympathies and condolences. I shift restlessly but stiffly because each greeting triggers the memories of my father's funeral:

"You'll be okay Alice; your father is at peace."

From where I'm sitting, I observe Mrs. Dragomir's corpse. She has frail-worn and long-golden blonde hair, curled and wavy past her shoulders. Her skin is white as snow with dangling silver earrings, pink-soft lips, and narrow shoulders. Her dress is like an A-line princess scoop neck and floor-length, dark navy blue. She's as glamorous and awe-inspiring in life as I would imagine.

I don't miss the funeral business. I glare to my left and high above is the cathedral organ. White silver pipes crowd together within the balcony.

The vigil begins with those in attendance offering prayers and condolences and listening to the scripture through readings and reflections. Some people speak eulogies and Ionel plays his guitar and sings. This isn't new to me as various strangers and people of Boydton held such ceremonies at my home. My father welcomed it if the grieving family didn't want to use the church.

I sit in silence observing as I've always done at funerals. Sometimes I would speak a few words, other times I'd participate or witness. Mr. Dragomir, and only a few others, partake in receiving communion. Ionel, Viviana, and I don't. Instead, we cross our arms during the ceremony while in line. The last segments of the ceremony are coming to an end. My eyes fixate upon Viviana next to me. She bites her lip and her eyes quench sorrows. Tears stream from her eyes and she sniffles. She clutches her left hand into a fist and squeezes it as if she's squeezing a stress ball. I break my gaze to slide my hand near her. I don't look. I don't *want* to look but her hand falls into my palm and I inhale a deep breath of comfort. I'm happy to be here for her and her family. She squeezes my hand as if thanking me for the comfort. Then she lets go.

Chapter 13

After the funeral, there's a small luncheon at the Dragomir's estate. A few of Mrs. Dragomir's friends stay but they depart afterwards. I grab my coat ready to leave and catch the bus.

"Wait…" says Viviana. I freeze and gaze upon her. "Could you stay just a little longer…?"

I warmly smile and nod my head, and remove my coat. I pace to her as she embraces me in a fragile manner, as if I'd shatter into shards.

"Thank you…" she whispers softly. She sobs, and her body falters forward as she's been suppressing her emotions. Her hands grip my dress.

"Is there anything you'd like to do?" I gesture.

We break our embrace; her tears stain her makeup, and she wipes her eyelids. "I can't really think honestly, but I redecorated my room a bit. Would you like to see?"

"Sure."

As I agree, an accordion plays a sorrowful tune. I swing my head where the sound is coming from. It pours through the open door of Mrs. Dragomir's room.

"Music nurtures my father's soul. I'd let him be at peace." Viviana clears her throat as I follow upstairs and into her room.

My eyes blink as I notice the change, "Purple drapes?"

Viviana stands next to her purple draped window, "Not exactly purple, but aubergine. I haven't hung these drapes in years since I attended university. I used to hang these in my dorm room window for all to see." Her hand and fingers brush upon the drapes in reflection as if she thought of a memory. Her face conveys a tenderness by her gaze. A sincerity.

"What is it?" I ask, crossing my arms together.

Her body jolts as my words disturb her trance. She doesn't answer me straight away. She lowers her head and wanders over to her bed, sitting down. "The last time I saw and hung these drapes, my ex-boyfriend was alive. I took them down after his passing because of the pain they brought me, but now I look at them, and they don't bother me anymore," she breaks a quick laugh, "now these remind me of something about myself I had lost and forgotten."

My eyes blink rapidly as my eyebrows crunch up and then down as I walk to her and sit. "What had you forgotten?"

She laughs. "Funny, I don't quite know. For one thing, I used to love the color dark lilac. I was obsessed with it. Dark lilac drapes, violet contacts, dark lilac-colored nails and toenails." She

132

turns her head to me and smiles, "Even a hoodie in dark lilac. I was so different at the time; lost, but so was he."

I bite my lip, "What was his name?"

"Oscar Waldo."

My eyes wander and I try not to laugh because of his name. I grit my teeth as my lips sink into my mouth, "Oh…"

"It's okay. I know his name sounds charming but yet tempting to laugh at, in a good way. He brought me so much joy despite his own darkness. He made me see beauty in it, and beauty with the darkness within myself even though I never knew what tormented him. I'm still glad I don't, but he opened me up. He was my first love." She stares back at the drapes, "It's why I took them down because lilac has the representation of a first love. I look at them now, and feel peace because life, despite its hardships, is worth living. He—my everything—died but it shows me that life cannot exist without death as death cannot exist without life."

The room fills with silence. The accordion melody is still playing but is slightly muffled. I don't know what to say as I never thought about life and death as opposites that attract each other. My hands convulse. I stare at them as my fingers bend slightly into my palm to stop the shaking. I exhale a muffled groan.

"Alice, I would like to tell you something…"

My eyes gravitate to her in earnest. Her gaze is serious and molds into a despondence.

"I-I haven't told anyone this except my brother. My father and mother do not even know about what I'm going to tell you, but I feel I need to share it with you because I know of your feelings for me. I would like to tell you why I feel not ready for a relationship and why I don't want to make any promises. Just keep this between us."

I'm terrified. I wonder what secret she keeps to herself as when she speaks, it's like revealing a burden she concealed within herself for years. She breathes a deep breath:

"I got pregnant but couldn't carry because I was on chemo, but not for cancer. Oscar left me alone to handle everything because of his depression and the situation. We were grieving and I was emotional."

A pain festers out of my soul; my mouth agape, moans a rigid breath, "I understand."

"I'm at peace with everything that's happened. I've forgiven him, myself, and my baby. Oscar, who got me pregnant, wallowed in his solitude. It tore him and me apart and we broke up soon after. Then, he committed suicide. Even though I'm finally at peace, I often wonder what my baby would have been like. I think it definitely plays a part in me wanting to be alone. I know now I could be a single parent and raise a child alone because I lost one alone. I chose to have an abortion because my doctor told me that if my baby made it full term, it would have such severe deformities because of the specific chemo and medication regime I was on. My baby would be born in pain and likely die within a few days of birth. I couldn't—I couldn't do that to my baby, so I made a decision alone and went through the process alone. If my baby had lived and died in pain, I wouldn't be here today. I couldn't handle that. I wish things had been different, but it's not how life and death are. I've worked through it and I'm happy where I'm at in life."

Neither of us say anything. I space out, only catching glimpses of the words that follow after, "I'm sorry to lay this on you. It's just my mom passing away had made me recollect my past and it's why I brought out these drapes to face it. I am content to say I have conquered my past though it will never be forgotten." Viviana rests her head against my shoulder, cries, and I wrap myself around her to fall, snuggle, and nothing more.

Everything is black. A wet, thick substance drips upon my face and trickles along my cheeks. My eyes open to a very dark place. I lie in this dark deepness. My body is damp and chills my bones. There's a weight to my chest and I can't breathe as if I took a deep dive and decided to lay out to dry, but there's no sun. Only a deep, black, deathlike reign of the dark. In the distance, there is a natural light, but it hasn't reached me yet. I feel I've been here before, except it's completely black and gray with a dense opaque layer of mist. They shroud the grounds and me.

Above me, I begin to see drops of red as my eyes wave in and out of focus. I panic and roll my body over to the natural light. It's a body of water, the same one as before. No woman is there this time, only my reflection. Whatever trickles down upon my face drips off and into the water. Blood mixes with the water as it dissolves before my eyes. I dash away from the pool, horrified.

A childish laughter echoes as I turn my head to its source. I catch a glimpse of a little girl, but she's so quick that I only observe her molded dress and black hair. Her feet scurry in triple time as if she's missing the natural frames of movement. I stand, slowly. A breeze from where the girl runs sweeps across my body. Specks hit against me, snow I think, until I catch it in my hand— ashes. The wind dies down as an orb of shadow hovers and churns like smoke. It fades away as I follow the trail of ashes that are swept in. I find a spiral staircase. It winds down farther into the darkness and into the pit. I've no idea what I'm looking for, but it seems urgent, so I go down to see where it leads. When I reach the bottom, I discover a long corridor that looks like it's dug out from the earth. I finally scuttle to its end and recognize my surroundings.

The preparation room of my old home—the pet cremation chamber. The chamber is in ruins. There's no house, only the open air as I'm standing inside its ruins. The chamber's heat resistant bricks remain standing as other bricks from its structure have fallen out. My shoes crunch against shards and ashes of what's left of my house. The clouds in the sky are gray but are painted bottomless. Ashes seep and flutter across the sky. My teeth chatter; my arms squeeze and huddle against myself like it's the heart of winter.

An object inside the cremation chamber grabs my attention. Amongst the ashes, bone fragments, and soot is a book. The moment I see it, I rush to snatch it, and I know this is what I'm looking for. Still, something feels very wrong and off. It's the book my father had given to me, Poe's stories and poems, but it's charred. I open the book to find that all the pages are completely empty and wrinkled as if it was left to dry. At this point terror fills my heart. I panic, more horrified than I'd ever been.

Suddenly, out of nowhere, a flap of wings rustles in the wind. My eyes fixate upon a bird soaring and landing upon the little girl's shoulder. She's been standing behind me for I don't know how long. The bird doesn't nibble on her face this time, and the girl looks a lot like me as a child.

I speak to it, "Have you ever wanted death so badly, you've longed for it to come to you?"

She stares at me and says no words, but her face speaks so much to me. The dismay and the sadness. It's mine. She looks right through me in a consoling way and we embrace. The bird cries, takes flight, and soars away, but immediately after, this dread comes.

The cremation chamber and what's left of it crumbles to the ground. There's this terrible ringing. My eyes fixate back to the little girl, but she's gone. She vanishes like the thing which was held in the woman's arms.

I think I hear the little girl speak, "Can you hear it breathing? I can…"

There's a terrible noise—a wailing scream. This lithe, naked woman duel wielding both vibrance and decay is hovering, clawing, and scratching herself violently. She cries and wails and at some point, I hear her scream:

"You don't belong here."

She has long, straight flowing blonde hair; wet, like she's in water instead of outside in the air. Her eyes are replaced with large black holes that look like they're concave and will never end if I stare into them.

I scream loudly, hyperventilate, and flail my body about. The dream really gets to me. Something that feels wrong—like something terrible has happened—or will happen. It's the weirdest, strangest feeling that I've ever felt. My entire body is numb, and I shriek. Footsteps reverberate down the halls and suddenly someone is violently shaking me.

"Alice-Alice-Alice!"

My body shatters to the ground. Tears fill my eyes, my skin is hot, and my aching head pounds relentlessly. My heart beats rapidly, savage, and burns.

"What is going on?" shouts Mr. Dragomir horrified.

That woman! Her hollow eyes flash in my vision. She's nocturne; her words ring inside my brain,:

"You don't belong here."

As these words ring, I scream, "I belong! I belong!"

Arms embrace me, enveloping me in lilac. The ravaging sensation declines and the touch of Viviana's hair lingers upon my fingertips. I sob, unable to speak, buried between Viviana's neck and chest.

"You aren't alone. Alice, you aren't alone," she whispers as her breath tickles my ears.

I think about the woman hovering… Is she my image of death itself?

"I wish you everything you deserve," says Viviana to me with her chin resting upon my head. My forehead tingles from the pounding and pressure. I look into her eyes. I don't know how to process what she means. These words. I can't express, talk, speak; my emotions threaten to overflow as if nature itself destroys the dam.

Viviana searches my eyes, seeing the lost confusion as she speaks, "The ultimate blessing, or the most cryptic spell, depending how you've lived your life." Her fingers run through my hair and my head falls gracefully upon Viviana's chest. Her heart sings a lullaby.

The hours pass. I don't know when Mr. Dragomir left as my thoughts have been consumed with my nightmare. What does it all mean? By this time, I lie upon Viviana's bed in reflection. She's asleep next to me. My thoughts begin to focus. I know the little girl is my own self, but the woman of nocturne disturbs me. As I think about it, the more I think, I realize perhaps I've seen her from somewhere and then it clicks. I snatch my phone from the floor; the light flashes at my face as the cord falls out and shows three in the morning. The sun will rise in a few hours, but I don't care. My heart races, my mind is erratic, and my palms sweat.

After the longest time, I reactivate Facebook on my phone. It has been two years since I've used it. It updates and after signing in, I see nothing much has changed. Sure, the setup has changed but the people on it haven't. I access my messages and find Camila's chat. It's the same message I read before everything changed. My last message to her reads:

Oct 28, 2016 AT 7:45 AM
Things I love about you since dating:

1. Your laugh
2. Your smile
3. Our snuggles
4. Kisses
5. Hugs
6. Your affection
7. Your loyalty
8. Your honesty
9. Your love
10. Your emojis
11. How you include me with your friends
12. Our adventures
13. Going on hikes together
14. Your obsession with coffee
15. Your support
16. Your eyes
17. Your silly singing
18. Your dancing
19. Your acceptance of me, my imperfections
20. Your nicknames/pet names you give to me
21. Your respect
22. Our tickle wars
23. Our pokes calling each other "boops"
24. Our conversations and discussions
25. Sharing music together
26. Your love for animals
27. Intimacy/sex
28. Your back scratches/massages

Oct 28, 2016 AT 9:55 AM

Awwwwwwww Babe!!! This made my morning!!! See ya soon! 

That was the afternoon she had abandoned me in that bookstore. A book date. Her picture strikes me as I tap on it to view her profile. The page refreshes and reveals a horrifying truth. Her profile picture is of her standing in a sunflower field. She smiles brightly with her long straight flowing blonde hair. The sunlight makes her green eyes appear emerald but her hair. That hair! I imagine her without eyes, replaced with those black concave eyes. They're both similar in hair, face, and body. She's the only one I had sex with, and I knew her body well. Her vibrance. I scroll to see her wall…My eyes read a post from a friend of hers on the timeline:

Sam Thatcher

October 30 at 2:11 PM

Can't believe I said my final goodbyes to someone I've known and loved my whole life. What I would do to go back and see you one more time. My heart is broken, I just talked to you too. In your 26 years of life you loved with all your heart and made so many people smile. Rest easy Camila Hayes

I gasp, my fingers grow weak, and my phone slips and smashes against my face. It falls, slides off the side of the bed, and thuds loudly against the wooden floor. I roll over my body rapidly to grab it. The phone is facedown upon Viviana's pink pentagram rug. Flashbacks of the hands flood my vision, how they grabbed me, gripped their dirty, bloody, and decayed fingernails into my skin. My chest tightens and burns as I think that my eyes deceive me. Viviana's door is open as I think I see an orb of shadow looming at the entrance.

"It's not real—it's not real!" I utter in whispers of madness. The shadow churns like smoke. Am I awake, or still in a nightmare? I don't know—sleepless nights make it impossible to determine. My body lunges out of bed. It's the most grueling exercise. My body slams, and it startles Viviana.

"Huh?"

I feel paralyzed. My body tries to budge but to no avail. I'm on my knees, on Viviana's rug, and my body has ruled against me. I can't move no matter how hard I try. I glare to the doorway—it's there, it's there—in my reach—if only! My arm reaches out, and I fall forward. My arm catches my fall, and I push my hand up to reach. It's there—still there—

"Alice?" Viviana calls. Her bare feet creak upon the floors. She sees me kneeling, rushes to switch on the main light. I look at the door, and it's gone.   The light blinds me. My face hides against my forearm.

I groan. "Shadow."

"What?"

I point at the doorway. "An orb-shadow."

Her face is hidden from me. I don't look, but her voice trembles. "I can burn incense."

Fire, ashes, shards— "No!"

A madness possesses me. A frenzy consumes me. The thought of smoke—I dart and flee her room.

Chapter 14

The moon is bright, full, and its light shines upon the house's porch and steps. The air is crisp as I try to ease my mind by breathing in the cool air. I need to get a hold of myself. I sit upon the porch's stoop, clutching my body close to me, holding onto it. My head pounds from my left temple. The tension pulsates as my heart races from dashing out. It's on a night like this in which all I knew withered to ash. The screen door creaks behind me. I know it's Viviana.

"Alice, what's gotten into you? Are you okay? Talk to me." She sits next to me.

I don't look at her. I gaze upon the moon, "The wondrous moon. Its fullness is as bright as it was when the smoke engulfed and swallowed it."

I gaze at her. "I can tell by the look on your face, you're wondering what happened and why smoke and fire terrify me. Since you were so open to me about your past, it gives me the courage to tell you mine. I haven't found peace like you have, but I admire you even more for sharing such darkness with me."

"You don't have to, if you don't want to." She slides her hand over. I stare at her hand as mine ladles and caresses into hers.

"No. For once, I want to."

As I answer this, Viviana strokes my palm, I grasp her hand, and begin my tale.

It was the first evening of November. I was nowhere close to finishing the final paper of my undergraduate career. For a break, I was reading the collection of Poe poems and stories that my father had given me earlier that morning for my birthday. I was by my mother's grave, dressed in a black dress as the sun shone its unique dying colors of a blood red, pinkish sky. I was enjoying the crisp air and the rustle of the leaves as they swept around and brushed against the grave. As I finished reading the last stanza of Poe's poem, *Spirits of the Dead*, the wind tickled my hair, and I glanced at my mother's gravestone. I smiled, thinking and imagining it was her playing with my hair as a means of affection. My fingertips graced the carvings of my mother's name. It had become worn and rough over the years of my existence. I flashed a warm smile, and my eyes fluttered with solace. All at once, my heart harrowed at the sight of her date of death. My birthday. I had become twenty-five and I had never known her. Moved with emotion, I thought about the poem's last five lines:

146

'And the mist upon the hill

Shadowy, shadowy, yet unbroken,

Is a symbol and a token.

How it hangs upon the trees,

A mystery of mysteries!'

At the time, I had thought about myself, my aloneness in the cemetery. How the spirit of my mother transitioned between worlds, awaiting the moment her soul would pierce the veil and enter the next realm—if such a place exists. Now, reflecting— these final words are different for me. They symbolized the veil between life and death, that which separates us from the ultimate mystery of beyond. A mist between two realms of consciousness—waking consciousness and the subconscious. In the shadowy realm of the subconscious lies our hidden memories, which bubble to the surface as symbols in our dreams and fantasies. For as long as I could remember, I had desired to explore my subconscious mind, to know what exists. To know how my mother existed since my father didn't speak of her. What she was like. I desired to know how I existed within the love Camila had for me, if she had any. I hadn't known at the time and desired beyond my being to know its secrets. The love Camila had for me, the love my mother had as she breathed her last, and my father's love. There were times I wanted to cry, shout, and scream at my father. To ask how he sees me, how he loves me. All I had held onto was our day fishing when I was a little girl. As I had grown in the shape of my mother, the similarities of dark raven hair, green eyes, and pale skin took form. I knew my father shunned me because of my appearance. The pain he must have felt was but a shadow of what he had loved. Was I but a spirit to him?

The light had dissipated enough for me to stop reading. I padded back inside. My father was nowhere to be found, and I knew he had secluded himself in the preparation room. The room's door was unlatched as I entered the house. White light loomed from the doorway. Various objects clinked, clanked, and scrubbed. He was reorganizing and cleaning after the funeral we had held earlier that afternoon.

Death had often made me reflect on my own family. Their stories, their lives, and existence. What were they like? In the darkness of the house, I shuffled to my room, and left my book upon my bed, and exited towards the attic. I flicked the switch and the light above the stairway shone. As I approached the top of the stairs, the light above the ceiling grew dark. I had thought about running back down to replace the light bulb, but to do that I had to creep into the basement. I didn't want to go there. I didn't want to see the despondence or pain in my father's eyes considering it was my birthday and the day of my mother's death. Upon one of the shelves was an oil lantern. A box of matches was next to it. I removed the glass from the lantern, twisted the peg to raise its wick, and struck the match.

My hands cusped the handle, the light glowed and began to burn. My wrist shook the match, the flame died, smoke rose from it, and I disposed of it inside a tin can. I gripped the glass dome of the lantern and gently put it in its place. The handle creaked as I wandered the room, looking for a box of photos and framed portraits of our family relatives. I wanted to find them, look at them, and reflect upon them. I knew they were stored inside a trunk and soon enough, I found it.

After opening the trunk and setting the lantern down beside me, I took out the pictures shrouded in dust. Time fled from my mind. I was lost in all the memories they had, and I imagined what my relatives did, the lives they had lived. Their smiles, graduations, weddings, babies they held at birth, holidays, family gatherings, past pets, and so much more. I held a picture of my parents together, at their wedding.

At that moment, my father's voice shouted "Fire! Alice, fire!" His scream curdled my blood, chilling my frame to the bone. It broke my trance. I darted from the floor, dropping the picture. It shattered across the floor, my foot knocking over the lantern as I bolted. My breath was short, and my heart palpitated to my footsteps pounding against the floorboards. In my heightened state, my feet stumbled and I missed a few steps from the attic, snapping my ankle after crashing upon the landing. Blackness swallowed my eyes, and I lost consciousness.

My vision blurred in and out of focus. My ears rang, and a wave of black smoke fluttered around me as I breathed its odorous poison. I coughed brutally. Rising to my feet was a grueling exercise. I angled my head to the top of the stairs, and the flames roared high like a slithering snake.

"No!" I croaked. My body attempted to lunge forward into the flames to save my family pictures before they withered to ash, but the flames spewed, and the ceiling crumbled. Debris blocked the stairs as I crawled hastily down to the second floor. It rolled as if it was chasing me and had been reanimated to life because of the flames. The house wailed and groaned, as if it were dying. The ceiling above me started to split. I crawled into my room and snatched the book I had left upon the bed. I turned my body, reached, and gripped my hand onto my dresser in an attempt to pull myself up. My book was in my other hand, my weight compressed against my unbroken leg. I hopped along, using the walls as support to reach the stairs. Flames sputtered and grew like vines among the second floor. Smoke veiled the entire floor, and the heat was unforgiving.

My father's voice screamed in agony as he called my name, "Alice! Alice, where are you?"

"Dad!" I cried.

By this time, I had made it to the grand stairway. The flames snapped, crackled, and popped, chasing me. The top of my head was sprinkled by tiny specks of debris and ash. My free hand gripped upon the railing as I hopped along the stairs going down. The house let out another groan and chunks fell from the ceiling. One piece landed upon the railing causing me to fall and plummet into the foyer. Smoke and crumbled walls shrouded the archway into the parlor as I heard my father's screams coming from inside the room. The front door was left opened wide as the sliding door hinge held its place. I slid my book with great velocity, as strong as I could. It flew to the outside of the house and onto the dirt path.

"Dad!" I shouted. My hands gripped onto the black and ember rubble to get him out, but it was too hot. My hands were near them and felt the heat.

"Get out!"

The flames were getting bigger, swallowing the room.

After hearing my father's voice, I bolted into the library because I wanted to save my dog Viktor's ashes on the mantle. I didn't care about the excruciating pain in my ankle. The curtains in the room were ablaze, and a wooden beam had fallen against the shelves of my mother's library. All the books were burning. It horrified me, and I couldn't save them. The old-fashioned oil lamps had fallen from the mantle and oil covered the fireplace.

My shoes ground on broken glass and I snatched Viktor's urn. I gritted my teeth. The pain was unbearable, and I fought against my body to not give out. The house continued to crumble, splitting the ceiling and a chunk fell in front of me. Its impact teetered my movement, and my body gave out from the strain of the pain. I fell, and the urn shattered into pieces.

As I screamed, my father's flesh burned, and his screams rang my ears. Fire, ashes, and shards were all around me. I scraped up Viktor's ashes and the shards of his urn. I wanted to save them. The palms of my hands filled with dirt and blood. Shards sliced the inside of my palms, mixing with ashes. I coughed, the poisonous odor wavering my vision. I thought I was going to die. I wanted to die. This house was my life—my home—a place of memories and years lived. I didn't want to watch it burn. That would be too hard. As my vision blurred, my ears muffled to the sound of my breathing and heartbeat. My breathing wheezed and waned, and my heartbeat thumped as if drifting me into a deathlike sleep. It slowed gradually; my body drained, and all of my surroundings were churning into shadows. A shadowy figure appeared, and I thought it was death coming to wrap me in its cloak. It swept me up so lithe that when it carried me out, my last thought was of my father who had carried me in his arms as a little girl.

Chapter 15

"The night before, it was a bonny home. The morning after, an ashen wreck. Even looking at it, even recalling the flames—it didn't feel real for a while. It still doesn't." As I finish my tale of the night, Viviana's eyes never leave me.

"Alice, you can and will rebuild, naturally. You'll build a new house right here and in time perhaps be at peace with how you came to raise it up from the ashes of the old. I guess it helps to picture that new place, that new home, as if it waits for us in the world of future time."

"What do you mean?" My eyes wave as if searching for an answer.

Viviana squeezes my hand, "Flames rise into the night as if they challenge you to stop their consumption of what was your home and place of sanctuary. Yet, fire is impatient, and you will breathe eons and moments as if they were one. A new house will rise because you will build it with your own hands and toil. Remember, in your reading? The moon was in your present and yet look how it shined so brightly upon this porch."

I gaze upon the moon. It's still visible, but the morning light revives the sky.

"You must face your fears that are haunting you. You must face them in order to cut through what is deception and what is illusion. I feel you are getting to the heart of the matter in opening up to me as I once did to you. I believe in you. I will not abandon you, but you are the only one who can face them."

A wave of tranquility reigns. I relax my posture. I listen to Viviana chuckle as I feel her warm embrace from behind. "I'd say fuzzy slippers, a glass of wine, and a good book for you."

I laugh and gaze back at her. "Perfect."

I desire to kiss her, but as I hesitate to bite my lip, she vibrantly jumps back. "Well, let's get right to it then!"

"What?"

My eyes bat and wander.

"It's my favorite day of the year and perfect for you!"

The rising sun shines upon her face and her teeth glow as she smiles at me.

"Huh?"

"It's October 31st!"

I laugh, "Halloween? What's special about that? Trick or treating?" My voice is silvery and smoky.

"Oh, nothing wrong with Trick or Treating. You old Mari Lwyd!"

"What, are you calling me a horse head? Is this a trick?"

Viviana shrugs her shoulders with a smile. "It's my favorite day and holiday because it's Samhain! The time of the year when the nights grow darker, there's a chill in the air, and there's a thinning of the veil between our world and the realm of the spirits. For many pagans such as myself, this is a time of reflection and spiritual growth."

"Oh…"

She snatches my hand and pulls me up with great force. "Come on. Let's celebrate!" We rush into the house and I chuckle under my breath trying not to laugh out loud. Her energy, excitement, and happiness for her holiday is contagious.

"How?"

"We can decorate the altar in my room!"

I laugh as I trip over my feet on the treacherous stairs. She releases my hand as we make our way. Our feet stomp the stairs, "Oh, come on. You're a bit of a Romanticist! Use your imagination." She respires breathlessly as we approach the narrow hallway. "The leaves have fallen, and most are on the ground. This is a time when the earth is going dark, so reflect on the colors of late autumn."

I huff out air. "So, decorate your space with deep colors like purples, burgundies, and black, as well as shades of the leaves with their tint of gold and orange."

Viviana laughs. "Yes, 'tint of gold' I knew you to be a poet."

We rush into the room and Viviana strides in towards the closet nearby where her altar stands.

"We can use the shades of harvest as colors." She whips her closet wide open.

"Cover my altar with dark cloths, welcoming the coming darker nights. Ooo-candles!" Her excited breath breaks apart the word 'candles' as her emotion makes me smile and happy.

"What kind of candles?"

"Well, why don't you pick them out!" She steps aside and gestures with her arms, presenting her closet. "There should be candles of all kinds in a box which display deep, rich colors, or maybe find an ethereal contrasting touch with white and silver."

I dive onto the floor. I crawl farther to the closet and see a brown worn box on the floor inside. Suddenly, a blare of music echoes in her room. I jump. A live crowd cheers and applauds as she turns down the volume from her phone. I glare back.

"Music, this early?"

"Ha-ha, I turned it down hopefully enough."

After she says this, I recognize the band. The voice on the record speaks. "Good evening. This is off our first record. Most people don't know it."

But I know the song.

"About a Girl… Nirvana."

Viviana smiles warmly and shrouds her smile with her hand clasping over it.

"Yes, one of my favorite bands! I'll be right back. Pick out the candles, cloths, or anything else that catches your eye!" She flees out of her room almost as madly as I did hours before.

I smile while going through her box. It's amazing how in going through a box, there's much to be learned about a person. The objects they contain. I find a figurine as the music switches to the next song. The band's song "Come as You Are" plays. The figure I hold is a grim reaper dancing with a woman in a white dress with a mask shrouding her eyes as she dances with the reaper. It's a dance with death as the reaper has black wings. The reaper gracefully holds the woman with a white rose in her hair and her ginger long hair waves as if the wind blows it. Her head rests upon the bony chest of the reaper and the reaper's gaze upon the woman is of tenderness and affection. It strikes me. My emotions ember with my feelings for Viviana. Her inside joke about my last name, 'Tell us of a Reaper's tale' rings in my head. In an objectionable way, I feel I'm the reaper and Viviana is the woman dancing with me. At the same time, this feeling is so beautiful! The detailing is remarkable. I love this so much because it really stands out.

I sit the figure on the floor next to me and scavenge the box like a vulture. Viviana's footsteps scurry back.

"Ok, I'm back!"

I glance back and see a picture frame of some kind in her hands. She places the frame upon her altar. She turns to me and sees the figurine I placed on the floor and picks it up.

"Oh, this is by Anne Stokes; a good choice! Samhain is the time of the dying of the crops and of life itself. So, skulls, skeletons, grave rubbings, or ghosts will work well for the altar."

I lift the box and carry it to the bed. I don't speak but I understand why that figurine would make a good fit because it's a symbol of death. It shows the relationship between life and death like how I feel about Poe's poem 'Spirits of the Dead.' However, I also see the figure as an allusion to her and me. I'm death and she's life. I shudder at this thought because I don't want to lose her because of me. Life gives, but death takes. Each gift life gives, death takes it and the gift is no more. I don't want to become a shadow—an entity which withers the love she gives to me. This thought deflates the energy I had earlier. Nirvana's song, "Something in the Way" plays and it affects my mood even more. The nocturne creature of my dream flashes before me as a phantom. Camila was my first love. I don't want this connection I've come to endear with Viviana to decay as Camila's did.

"Alice, you okay?" asks Viviana.

Her words disrupt my deep thoughts. I flash a smile as if I'm still in a trance.

"Yeah, just tired." I'm drained from not sleeping but the response is also a veil to cloak the thoughts of my feelings. I change the subject.

"What's the picture you brought up?" I point to it upon her altar.

"Oh, a picture of my mom holding me. It's a close up of her and I facing each other smiling from when I was a little girl."

"Oh…" I walk over to it.

"Some people choose to add representations of their ancestors to their Samhain altar. So, I chose to do this in honor of remembering my mom."

I envy that photo. It's something Viviana has but I don't. Even though she lost her mother, I never had one to recall memories of or enjoy pictures like this one. I know Viviana is grieving as Ionel's words ring in my head, 'People grieve differently—let me grieve in mine.'

I flash a smile to her, "It's a lovely photo."

My words crease a smile upon her. It spreads check to check, "Thanks Alice," she says. "Come on. There are other things we need to prepare for the harvest tonight."

"Other things?"

Viviana's voice croaks with vitality."Yeah, no pagan celebration is really complete without a meal to go along with it! We should celebrate with foods that symbolize the final harvest…" She bites her lips as her teeth grit them inside her mouth. "Hmm… I should make my soul cakes or maybe a Pumpkin Spice Cheesecake!"

I laugh. "Ha, didn't know you like to bake. What are soul cakes?"

Viviana's eyes meander as I ask this question. "Oh, you'll love them! Soul cakes are traditionally baked as a gift for the spirits of the dead. From what I know, beggars who came around on All Souls' Eve offered to say prayers for the family's departed. One cake given, is one soul saved. Other times, these cakes were given to the costumed entertainers known as mummers who made their rounds at Halloween."

"Mummers. They sound like trick-or-treaters."

"They do. We'll need to check and see if we have the ingredients to bake them and perhaps a pumpkin spice cheesecake!"

My eyes devour her altar, "What about your altar?"

"We can decorate it as we go along. I trust you in how you think it should be decorated."

My brows lift apart. I can't believe the trust she places in me to change her altar. With or without her present she trusts me. She sets the dances with death figurine upon her altar by her Freya statue.She bounces to her makeup table, grabs her phone, deactivates the music, and checks the time.

Her eyes quench in the light. "It's almost 8:30. My brother should be up." Her head turns to my direction. "I've asked him if he could run some errands for Samhain. I'll look in the kitchen and make a list of what we need."

We pad to the kitchen. A white cat sits upon the table by the black candelabra. Viviana grins and her voice changes pitch. "Hello, Mr. Wednesday!" Her hands caress the cat's ears as she rubs them. The cat purrs like a motorboat.

"I rarely see that cat," I say as I recall only seeing it when I first arrived at the house.

"Yeah, Mr. Wednesday is very shy and withdrawn. My brother accidentally left the side door open late one evening, and Mr. Wednesday vanished. He was nowhere to be found when I had awoken in the morning. I checked everywhere and found the side door open. I was horrified. I panicked and searched everywhere in the backyard but nothing. I barged into my brother's room and screamed at him because I knew he was late coming home. He felt horrible and Mr. Wednesday was gone for a whole year. One day my brother and I came back from CSU and saw Mr. Wednesday out on our porch. He was healthy but we noticed he was missing his right eye, and we were shocked that he was able to live outside for a whole year."

As Viviana finishes her story, her rule about what she told me the last time I was here clicks. "Oh, that's why you have that rule about shutting doors."

"Yeah, I don't want Mr. Wednesday or Revenant to wander outside." She nips over to the kitchen sink, grabs a yellow prescription bottle of some kind. She pops open the bottle and jiggles it for pills.

"Help yourself to the fridge or there are bananas over there." She reaches for one of the kitchen cabinets, grabs a glass, and fills it with water. The pill she has in her other hand is red and oblong. I'm curious as to what she's taking. I bite my lip as I mooch over to grab a banana. A part of me thinks not to ask. I peel the skin off as I observe her swallowing the pill and chasing it down. Seconds pass; she gulps the water and lets out a deep groan after finishing. She's breathless and quick.

"Blah, okay… Let's see what we have here." She scouts the kitchen cabinets and the fridge. I think the medication makes her nauseated by how she groaned. It's like she just swallowed vomit.

My mouth mumbles, "What do you take?"

She doesn't hear the words. "We'll need more butter and I have everything else."

"Ok…"

"Hmm… Ionel is still downstairs. Can you go check on him while I start preparing?"

I wander over to the entrance to the side door and shut the door behind me. Something doesn't feel right. I'm not quite sure if it's Viviana's excitement over the holiday or if she doesn't want me to see something. She's quick, hesitant, like she wants to shoo me out of her way. Perhaps, I'm over thinking. Maybe, it's my mind preying upon me. I haven't slept in a while and Viviana didn't get much sleep either because of me. This thought depresses my emotions. My shoulders sink, sullen. I don't want to think that it's all me that makes her feel this way.

Chapter 16

"Happiness is like a butterfly which, when pursued,
is always beyond our grasp, but,
if you will sit down quietly, may alight upon you"
— Nathaniel Hawthorne

Sound effects from the basement door break my mellow thoughts. I walk down the steps and stand before it. I knock. The sound cuts off.

"It's open!"

I twist the knob and enter upon Ionel's room. I'm in awe. The walls are scarlet red; next to me on my right is a picture of a mysterious figure shadowed with elongated horns which curve inward. It disturbs me. The sound effects and music resume from what I heard earlier.

"What is this figure?"

The sound effects cut off again.

"Hmm? Oh. That's a picture based off the tarot card The Devil depicted by Victoria Iva. She has a tarot card deck called The Black Tarot."

My eyes squeeze together as I beat them confused and turn towards Ionel. His hands are gripping a gaming console controller while his thumbs twist and tilt the control-sticks.

His eyes drift out to space in deep concentration to the screen facing him and the lights dance upon his face.

He speaks, "Not to worry, the devil is not what you think. I'm not into tarot cards, but the picture is a gift from my sister. I did a one-card reading with her once and The Devil is what I drew. It really grabbed my attention because it reminded me of my shadow or darker side and negative forces that contain me and hold me back from being the best version of myself."

I mosey over to him as I speak.

"Hmm… I've never seen Viviana with *The Black Tarot* before. May I ask about your tarot experience?"

Ionel exhales a deep breath and puts down his controller. His eyes meet mine.

"There's not much to it but yeah, she has the deck. She never uses it on others who come to a reading. She consults the deck as a reserve for only when she does tarot readings on herself. I'm the only other person she used the deck with because she felt I needed to consult the deck specifically." Ionel's eyes downcast as if reaching within himself to scrape out the memory from his skull. He shuts his eyes, shakes his head, and speaks.

"For a time, I trapped myself between short-term pleasure along with a longer-term pain I've experienced. I remember Viv told me: 'The Devil speaks about duality and choice just as The Lovers card, however, with the Devil, you are choosing the path of instant gratification, even if it is at the expense of your long-term well-being.' I'll never forget that because she made me realize that I was tricking myself into thinking I have no control over my shadow or these negative forces, that I could never break free from their hold. I believed I needed it and I must have it, even if it means going against what I knew to be right to obtain it. Deep down, though, I knew it was to my detriment, and I was only doing myself, and often others, a disservice when I caved into these lower needs and desires."

I long to know what it was. My mind is feverish to know the shadow which haunted him and tormented him in order to understand mine. I bite my lips, my eyes wander, and my hands grip my knees and rub them.

"You like my sister…"

His words echo in my skull as if I heard the Bells of Poe. My eyes are wide, horrified, staring into his countenance. His eyebrows rake as his eyes devour my soul. I'm speechless because it's true, and he knows it. He bites his lips and laments a short groan out of his breath,

"It's fine. I know you like her because I saw you reach your hand out to her. I observed your expression of tenderness when she grasped your hand during my mother's funeral."

"You're not mad?"

"No, just disappointed but also content. I-I have mixed emotions about it."

"I'm sorry." My breath deflates after my words.

Ionel breaks a grunt through his laugh.

"It's how you feel, and no one can take that from you. I respect my sister and you. Thus, if your heart truly desires her as she does you; then go for it. My sister deserves all the happiness especially after what she's been through."

"Oscar you mean?"

"I see she's told you some things." Ionel's mouth is agape like he's about to speak of something but he stops and sinks his lips inside. "I met Oscar through my sister. I'm a gamer and so was he and that's how he and I mostly bonded." His head turns to the direction of the TV. "In fact, the game I'm playing right now was a game Oscar loved to play."

I chuckle at the delight. "I haven't considered giving video games a try. I was too absorbed into literature and exploring the outdoors. What's the game you're playing called?"

Ionel flashes a smile. "The Ultraborne. This hard copy was Oscar's, but he left it to me after his death, but now thinking about it; it might be something you'll like because it's dark and mysterious."

My mouth widens and I nudge Ionel by playfully pushing him. "Oh, I'm dark and mysterious? It's not just because of my last name is it?"

"Well, only part… Let's be honest, I don't think anyone has heard of Reaper as a last name especially with its association with death. Yet, ironically your family has worked in the funeral business from what you've told me."

I cross my arms but begin to think, "Yeah, I guess it does sound dark and mysterious if you put it that way, but there's more to me than that."

"There is to everyone. I overheard you scream from your nightmares as my sister calmed you down. I know it's not my business but if you ever want to talk, I'm always happy to listen."

His voice is sincere, mellow, and calm. It gives me a solace that I've never had. Not once have I ever heard someone say, 'I'm always happy to listen.' He and Viviana are so kind to me.

"Alice?"

He breaks my thoughts.

"Sorry, it's just thatI've been veiled for so long, I don't know how to get out of my shell. It's been a crazy few days as I'm fighting sleep deprivation and long periods of it."

"I understand. I feel that you're going through your deepest, darkest places-whether or not you're ready."

"Yes, it's a path I'm taking consciously, but I'm afraid." I grip my hands into a fist as they tremble and shake.

"Hmm… But you need to take your path with strength, confidence, and courage. Maybe sharing with you my inner demons will help find your way. I don't know what Viviana has shared with you."

"She told me about her baby."

"Ah, that's about the time I was going through my shadows. She's never told anyone about the death of her baby except me. She puts a lot of trust in you which is good. I think she really likes you." He stands up, "Alexa, shut off TV." The cube box glows blue as she replies, 'Ok' and shuts off the TV.

He stretches his arms above his head and pushes his toes up. "Welp." He says with a short breath. "I'm sure my sister would like me to get going and get what she needs." Behind us are connected leather couches as he walks toward it and grabs a leather jacket. The jacket hugs against his shoulders as the collar flips up. "Let's take a ride. I can tell you more as we go."

We make our way to the driveway by exiting the side door. The leaves rustle gently across the sky and the clouds continue to churn and swirl with hints of blue. The gas from Ionel's car waves endless fumes and we are off. He stops at the Marathon gas station to fill his car with gas.

"Come out with me," he says, gesturing his hand. My body doesn't want to budge. I'm in a dream-walk. Everything around me is hazy and wobbly. My stomach aches sickly and my head pounds with great anxiety. I don't want to see the shadows. I don't want my mind to play its tricks upon me. I lean against the car for support as he configures the gas pump to fuel his car.

"What I am about to tell you, Alice, is only something my sister knows. When my mother first became ill and bed-ridden, her beauty, life, and light began to fade. She was not the same independent free-spirited woman she was. After I came home from New York is when I started to take notice of my mother. It shattered me as I began my study during my undergraduate at CSU. My mother, throughout her life, had a slow progression of lupus which developed sometime after I was born. The progression of the disease changed rapidly after the birth of my sister. As my sister got older, my mother's behavior changed, and she'd let her anger get the best of her over little things. She experienced many headaches and dizziness at times where she would lie in bed and in the dark. It wasn't until she started experiencing strokes and seizures that she became bedridden. I was alone at this time because my sister went off to college somewhere else while I stayed with my dad and struggled with my mother's condition. My mother developed several memory problems and had difficulty expressing her thoughts."

Ionel pauses as the gas pump stops with the price of twenty dollars and eleven cents.

"I remember once my mother mistook me as a younger version of my grandfather because my eyes are like his. At least that's what my father told me after that experience. At times, like that… She didn't know who I was. I would hear her calling me *tată* which is 'father' in Romanian."

The holster for the gas pump clicks as Ionel presses the button on it for no receipt. He shuts his gas cap and panel. His shoes scrape against the concrete as we crouch into the car. He starts the engine and continues his story.

"I didn't know how to cope with my mother's illness and the absence of my sister. Usually, my sister has my back, but this was the first time I felt like an only child. I was twenty-three at the time, going to parties with friends and such. Alcohol became my friend and I'd carelessly given myself away to at least three women at the time. Two of them really liked me, wanted a relationship, but I couldn't commit to either because it wasn't fair to them. I just wanted to feel whether it was through alcohol or sex. To feel I existed. It's how I became interested in English literature and why I switched over from music. I became fascinated by Wordsworth and Coleridge. The poem which really touched me was Wordsworth's '*I Wandered as a Lonely Cloud.*' The way my professor recited and broke apart the poem gave me a feeling of peace and serenity. I felt a sense of isolation in the poem but as it went on, the daffodils heralded a renewal of rebirth and new beginnings. The poem made me want to take more notice of nature, that I should take my time, look more closely, and marvel at the natural world's incredible variety of forms. It made me see that what I was doing in contrast to myself was blinding me from this experience. How could I marvel at the natural world when my sensations were masked by short-term pleasure?"

We are at a red light as Ionel pauses to breathe thinking about his past. His eyes flicker like each movement triggers flashbacks. He squeezes the wheel as a feeling of sympathy flows through me. I will never know what a brother and sister bond is like, but in his feelings of seclusion and his desire to feel in order to exist I can relate.

"I relate to what you feel as far as a sick parent and feeling isolated. My father had lung cancer, but it wasn't the disease that killed him. It was a house fire and all I knew was reduced to ashes."

"Ashes… That reminds me of a quote by a poet I found online once. The poet's name is Atticus."

"Atticus?"

"Yeah, Atticus said in their work *Love Her Wild*, two things which I think you might want to hear. One is that 'We are made of all those who have built and broken us' and 'She conquered her demons and wore her scars like wings.' Like everyone, we are built upon our experiences and even broken by them whether we want to be or not. What matters most is if you conquer the ashes which are left by these experiences and grow from them by meandering in flight with wings."

All is silent as an image of myself with wings filters into my brain. The image makes me recall Viviana's life and death statue. The grim reaper has black wings around the woman it loved and desired. My heart sickens. I sputter my words, "My wings are broken because the ashes around me are quicksand." The light changes green and we drive onward.

"No, you're letting yourself think they are. It's easier said than done, but you can overcome it. When Oscar died it left my sister and me grieved. I was broken because he, his friends Marcin, Mitch, and I used to hang out together. After Oscar died, it just wasn't the same and sometimes when faced with suicide, the consequences aren't clear. I went back to drinking and my sister started to notice. I'd push her away, but she stood by me despite her grievance and that's when she gave me that tarot card reading of The Devil."

Shortly after this, we pull into a parking lot. As Ionel stops the car, and shifts it to park, he glances over at me. "Just before Oscar died, he sent me an audio recording of himself. It was his

174

reflection on his life, his love for my sister, and the inner darkness he was not able to conquer."

My eyes are wide and my lips curve.

"Does Viviana know of the recording?"

"No."

"What, but why?"

"It's because she told me she wishes not to know about Oscar's suicidal tendencies. I have shown the recording to Oscar's friends but no one else. I think I should share this recording with you."

My heart jolts at Ionel's words as I shake my head slowly. "No. No, I don't think it's right."

"Alice, I'm worried about you. You look like death infested. I know these signs because Oscar looked as pale as you did before he killed himself. I don't want the same to happen to you or the same pain."

Rage seethes inside my aching corpse. "Oh, and you don't think I can overcome my darkness!"

"No, I'm not…"

"No, I can prove you wrong that I do belong!"

As I say the word 'belong,' it triggers the nocturne image of the woman in my dream and her words 'You don't belong here' ring in my head.

Ionel's mouth is moving but his words are muffled; the ringing becomes insatiable, and I clasp my hands against my ears. I shut my eyes as flashbacks of the fire, ashes, and shards flash simultaneously. Tears stream my hot cheeks and as they dry, they stain them. I whimper and feel Ionel's touch upon my shoulder. I'm frozen and overwhelmed.

Chapter 17

My eyes gaze above at the gray sky as it churns and swivels like smoke. Ionel had left his car to go shopping inside the store as I lay in the back of his car staring through the open sunroof. There's something at work within me that I can't scrape out of the walls of my internal self. I understand Ionel's fears about losing me because suicide is a darkness that I've faced before but it's always there. People one way or another face this darkness. It never truly goes away. No matter how hard I try, it always comes back with a hellish vengeance.

Maybe listening to Oscar's recording will bring me peace. It might be good to know the darkness he faced because his voice, like many others, are now silenced. Being suicidal is often considered attention-seeking. Confessions of such thoughts are often met with avoidance, irritation, or even dismissal. As though the afflicted would never actually follow through.

I've been guilty of avoiding my darkness. I feel irritated, I pretend the problem isn't there, and I convince myself that I'll never do it.

I almost came close, but close doesn't count. I don't seek the attention of others because I'm afraid of their judgments. To be open with such a burden is scary and horrifying. It chills my heart to its core. Even the strongest people have their limits, their breaking point, and I'm close to reaching mine. I desire peace, but dread to face the shadows in order to find it.

Vulnerability is difficult. It's as fragile as shards. It takes forever to piece back together but only seconds to destroy. I still feel as if I'm there in my old home scraping the shards and ashes to mold anew. Blood flows from my lattice veins and seeps out a red consultation. As the blood drips, so does my weary existence. Not sleeping… And dreading the deathlike sleep. The bloodstains dry upon the surface and every passing day a corpse molds to my image. I don't recognize myself. The chirping birds and the churning of the clouds lull me as my body sinks into the unknown.

A figure looms beyond the flames. The fire towers and hums an inflaming passion. My surroundings are shrouded into black, but everything feels familiar. In a chair, I sit across the flames as Viviana sits in a chair opposite from me like the night I first met her. She flashes a warm smile as my heart embers vivaciously. I reach my hand to her; my arm extends and feels the heat of the fire. I hesitate, but the flames tremble and fear grips my heart. My father's screams wail from the darkness. As his screams ring, I shut my eyes, and a bird cries. I reopen my eyes as the morning light shines upon my surroundings.

The sky is a clear gray and blue dawn. The fire is out but the smoke before me shrouds my vision. To my left, I catch a glimpse of a black bird. It stares at me. The bird has a large, thick neck. It's all black, right down to the legs, eyes, and beak. It swoops down; its wings ruffle and echo. I hear its talons roost. The smoke dissipates and I see she's no longer there. The chair is empty. The bird is in front of me upon the stones of the fire pit. In its beak is an obsidian stone. It's the same cut as the one Viviana wears around her neck. The bird stares at me; it tilts its head to the side and back to face forward. Its head bows down and drops the stone into the pit among the gray coals and ashes. It flies away and my dream ends.

For once I open my eyes without horror or dread. The dream was so vivid, real, and lucid. The breeze plays a cool melody upon my cheeks. The leaves meander with flight across the sky. My head is hazy from the dream and my body is stiff from sleeping upon the leather seats. My body desires more but my mind can't rest because of my dream. Was the bird a raven? What does it mean about Viviana? I've never dreamt about her. I'm terrified because those in my dreams like the deformity of Camila as the nocturne figure are dead, but Viviana had not death's hue. She's lively across the fire. The car door suddenly opens and startles me. I jolt and sit upright.

"It's ok Alice. It's just me," says Ionel rustling bags. He places a few bags in the front seat. "How are you feeling?"

"Still drained. How long were you in there?"

"Not too long; I'd say almost an hour."

All is silent. Ionel sits in the driver's side and inserts his key into the ignition.

"Ionel?" I mewl.

His car beeps with the key inside.

"Yeah?"

"I would like to listen to Oscar's recording. I think I can learn from it."

"Ok, are you sure?"

"Yeah, send it to me on Messenger."

I fish out my phone to download the Messenger application. Ionel grabs the key out of the ignition and stares at me. "Promise me, you'll never show this recording to Viv and anyone else."

"I promise."

He nods his head, starts the car, and drives.

When we arrive back at the house, Viviana and Mr. Dragomir are conversing with each other in Polish. Ionel opens the gate to the back yard and there are two picnic tables lodged together horizontally between the fire pit and the house. Beyond the fire pit is an outside altar. It's the kitchen table that's shrouded with the black cloth and the gothic candelabra upon the center of it. Pumpkins of various sizes and colors of white, orange, and dirty brown circle around the table upon the ground. Leaves veil the top of the cloth and framed pictures surround the candelabra. A grated and lattice-metal birdcage illuminates a thick red candle inside; the candle embers.

My eyes catch Viviana and her dress. It's a gothic ballgown with an eloquent and vampiric choker. It laces around her slim neck and the tip touches her chest. The dress is fashioned as a princess line—stunning, enchanting, and original. It's crafted luxuriously with a midnight black crushed velvet style as if ideal for a medieval or renaissance themed ball. It is floor length, and the sleeves are a medieval style fashioned from a beautiful embroidered black tulle with a breathless garden meadow flower design worthy of woodland kin, for that extra touch of elegance. The front is laced with black satin ribbon of a corset style, and it presents the ability to fit Viviana's figure comfortably

"You two are back, excellent! Alice, can you take and unload the groceries inside? Ionel, there is something I need to talk to you about." Ionel hands me the bags as I falter into the side door. Before I go in, I overhear Viviana talking to him, "There is one more stop I would like you to go before it closes." As she says this, I go inside and shut the door. I assume it's something more than likely for Samhain. I giggle under my breath at how bossy she is during this holiday. I know she wants everything to be perfect.

All the bags in my arms weigh down as I crowd them upon the counter. I hear the door creak open.

"Hello there! How are you feeling?" My ears tingle with the warmness of Mr. Dragomir's voice. I smile at him with my hands clasped.

"Better than last night, I suppose."

"It can always be worse, but I am glad to hear you are in better spirits, it seems. I will help you unload the food." He walks over to the crowded bags and unpacks them.

"Are there other guests coming?" I ask, rinsing my hands under the faucet.

"Yes, there should be a mix of my daughter's and son's friends. I think they need this especially after the funeral."

"How do you feel about it?"

His eyes light up and sparkle, "Oh, I am looking forward to it. Solitude is good, but sometimes friends are better. Some of them I have not seen in a while and so I hope they will come."

The door shoots wide open as it slams against the wall. My attention rapidly goes to its source.

"Hey!" chimes Viviana vibrantly. She dances and twirls around towards my direction. She shuts the door behind her and snaps her fingers together, flashes a bright smile, and her eyes gleam like glitter.

"I made you smile!" she says to me. I raise my eyebrows, and my hand cusps my mouth. I don't even notice the smile which shines upon my face.

"I think you'll like what I'm thinking to do for tonight." She's smoky with her mouth slightly open and her voice sonorous.

"Oh?" My eyes pique with curiosity.

"Hmm… I know that tone. You know I worry every time you do this," interjects Mr. Dragomir. His lips sink under his mouth, gritting his teeth.

"Papa, it will be fine. I've done this for years."

"I know… But it has been a while and you know how it almost gives me a heart attack every time I see you do it."

My anticipation enflames ecstatically as my mouth dries. "Do what?"

"Oh, you'll have to wait. The anticipation is murder," She playfully taps her finger on my nose.

"You are not going…"

"To perform in this outfit. Nope." She sways her shoulders side to side and asks me, "Have you ever heard of the band Liliac?"

I laugh as my eyes meander from the word, "Like the flower?"

"Oh, I see why you're laughing because I have a motif for lilac. No, and besides the band name is spelled differently. It's spelled l-i-l-i-a-c not l-i-l-a-c."

"Ah, so what's the difference?"

"I'm happy you asked you English scholar!" She winks and clears her throat. "It's Romanian. The word liliac means vampire bat."

"Of course, they would be from Romania…"

"Hey… No, they aren't. They have family roots there, but they are a Los Angeles family band. They have a sound they like to call Vamp Metal."

I cross my arms and my eyebrows rise with interest, "Oh…"

"Besides, I would like to do this for my mother who was Romanian."

I flash a smile. "I get it. What better way than to use a band from Romanian origins."

"Exactly!"

My phone vibrates a notification which startles me. It's something I never get and I'm curious to what it can be. My hand jolts into my inner-jacket pocket. I flash a quick smile to hide any implications which may cause Viviana to ask questions.

"Anyway, enough chatting! There's a celebration to prepare especially for our guests coming!" She hands her phone to me, "Pick out some music! You're going to help me bake and cook!"

My entire body shudders in terror. "Uh, umm… I."

"Never cooked?"

"Yeah…"

Viviana bursts out laughing. "Oh, Alice. I think I will enjoy this too much."

"How do you live on your own?" chimes Mr. Dragomir astonished. He glares at me like it's a talent not to cook and live on my own. His bushy eyebrows rake apart as I'm able to observe his eyelids between his brows. "I think I am more terrified about you cooking than my own daughter's intentions tonight."

Viviana bursts out with more laughter. "Papa, be gentle with Alice."

"Well, let's get this started. I'll wash my hands." I operate Viviana's phone on shuffle with her music as I stride to the faucet and scrub my hands with soap and water.

"She knows the first step!" chimes Mr. Dragomir jokingly.

"You got this Alice!" follows Viviana. With my hands rinsed we all begin the preparations.

Chapter 18

All is warm and cozy. The oven radiates with heat and delights the senses with the smells of cinnamon, ginger, and other spices. The sunlight from the window shines inside but dwindles with the approaching darkness to come. My apron is messy, smudged with batter and dough from the pumpkin spice cheesecake. My head throbs from the heat as Viviana bounces to open the window. A dizzy spell falls upon me, and the room spins. I rub the temples upon my head and shut my eyes. As I open them, the corner of my eyes catches a blurry wave of shadow. It is an orb and churns like smoke. I shut my eyes again to get rid of the image and combat against my frail body. My legs tingle numbly, and a chill runs down my spine. I shudder a groan and my teeth clatter. I know it's still there. My body jolts, my eyes open, and the shadow is closer; its shape is humanoid, and its hand spreads to my direction slithering like a snake. It's beckoning me. I pull away, turning my head, and I feel the delicate touch of Viviana's hands grasping upon my shoulders.

"Alice, are you alright? You look pale."

"Just feeling dizzy," I say, clasping my hand against my forehead.

"Well, I'd sit outside if I were you. You were a great help in the kitchen. This heat won't help you."

I wobble away from her, untie my apron, and hang it on the back of a kitchen chair. "I think you're right. I'll get some air."

All is still a haze and my feet drag heavily. As my vision wavers between black and blur, my heart palpitates out of my chest. My breath, short, struggles from the tightness in my chest. My hand presses against my heart. The weight of my body failing triggers the fire, ashes, and shards. Death is in my company, in my own shadow, gripping me, and whispering in my ears. They ring. Nature can't comfort me. No sounds or sight from it. I sit upon the bench at one of the tables in the backyard as my father's last words echo, *"Get out!"* His screams wail, and I shroud my ears by pressing them. All is numb, tingly, like static and fragmented shards. Water fills my eyes; the pain, and my eyes wane between darkness and light with the sun.

My father's image flashes in my brain. He reaches his hand out to me like previous times from my dreams. His image boils my blood; anger seethes from his abandonment. Guilt, despair, and sorrow seep into the fiber of my being. My mother—her death— is because of me. I never asked to be born. I never had a choice. If I were never born, my mother would be here, and my father would be happier; I'm sure of it. There was nothing he loved more than her.

The pictures of our family memories flash before me. They were all in that trunk but now are forever gone. How happy he was in his wedding photo. Voices echo. They come from the driveway as I hear footsteps crunch upon the grass and dead autumn leaves.

"Alice, here, this will help."

It's Viviana with a glass of some kind of green drink.

I grasp the drink and observe a green powder upon the top.

"It is matcha tea. It will help with your sleep deprivation."

"Caffeine?"

"No, better. It has l-theanine, which alters the effects of caffeine, promoting alertness and helping avoid the crash in energy levels."

The voices from the driveway grow louder as two figures walk towards us.

"Viv!" shouts a familiar voice.

I sip the tea. It's smooth, grassy, and sweet without tasting like dirt. Vegetal notes, but not astringent bitterness.

"Cai, Tessa! You made it."

Viviana sprints towards Cai and embraces him. My vision perceives his figure, but the blur and shadows distort his image. It horrifies me. He's like a shadow fading in and out. Seeing Viviana embrace him terrifies me; her body is against a shadow. From their appearances they're all like shadows—Cai, Tessa, and Viviana. Her embracement of Tessa from my view makes it seem like Viviana's appearance switches back and forth from shadow to non-shadow. I shut my eyes and rub them to get the horrid image out.

"Hey Alice!" shouts Cai's voice.

"Hey," I call.

"I'm sorry about the last time we saw each other, and that Tessa and I did not get to spend much time with you."

I reopen my eyes, and everything is normal.

"It's cool. I know you and Tessa had obligations to attend."

"Would you two like a drink?" chimes Viviana.

"Yeah, I can go for a beer," clucks Cai with a smile.

"Sure, follow me."

Viviana and Cai go into the house and it's just Tessa and me. The silence is awkward as her piercing eyes scowl at me. Her mouth forms a frown as I stare at her. Finally, she speaks, "Why don't you slip into something a little comfier, like a coma?"

"What?"

"You look like a corpse."

I know she doesn't like me, and for what reason I've no clue. Her comment brews anger and rage.

I slightly pound my tea against the table, "Sweetie, if you're going to be two-faced, at least make one of them pretty. What did I ever do to you anyways?"

Tessa bites her lips at me, and her eyebrows narrow, "All I hear about between Viviana and Cai is you. It agitates me. Cai scolded me for him and I not spending the time to get to know you. Then I see on Facebook that you and Viviana baked together. Her comments are all about how amazing you are. Anyway, I don't care what you think of me, because it can't be half as bad as what I think of you."

Tessa's words ring in my head as I recall what Ionel told me about Tessa being a spoiled brat. My hand caresses my chin. "I'm not an astronomer, but I'm pretty sure that the earth revolves around the sun and not you."

"Mature."

My breath jolts and I laugh. "Mature… I feel you're this way towards me because you aren't the center of attention. You silently judge others from afar and determine that they're all under you. You're an old cliche of a spoiled brat."

She says nothing to me, but her face says it all. Her face burns red, but her eyes flay in shock.

"Yeah, I'm not afraid to bite back." I sneer, reaching and sipping my tea.

Tessa's hand balls into a fist and she bites her lip as both Viviana and Cai pace toward us.

"Babe, you okay?" Cai purses his lips against the rim of his beer bottle.

Tessa's face beats red like a blood vessel in her skull might burst at any second. She flounces quickly, moving in an exaggerated manner and towards the house.

"What was that about?" chimes Cai, squinting his eyes to see in the far distance.

Viviana bites her lip as Tessa disappears into the house. The side door slams, and Viviana's breath perspires. Her eyes anchor in my direction. "What happened?"

"Oh, well…" My voice croaks and is smoky, "Tessa shrewdly said I should slip into a coma because I look like a corpse. So, I told her how it is and that she's a cliche of a spoiled brat." There's silence. It's dreadful as I murmur, "I'm sorry… Cai."

He doesn't speak to me, but his face turns red, and I know this is the moment he'd rip into me. Instead, he bursts out laughing and asks, "You actually called her that?"

My eyes flicker like a flash of lightning. My body is motionless like a deer in the headlights.

He laughs again. "Wow… Finally, someone said it."

"Wait, you're not mad?" pings Viviana dazed by Cai's reaction.

Cai roars a brassy sound from his nose and throat. "No." He waves his hand in a downward motion. "Listen, I love her, but man…Tessa needs to get off that pedestal. She needs to understand that life is way too short to treat others as if they are dirt because we will all end up in the ground somewhere or dust."

"That sounds like something from experience?" I chime sipping my tea again.

Cai's eyes cast downward, and he groans, "Yeah… I lost two dear friends of mine. One last year who died from a seizure and this year back in March. The strange thing is, they both died almost a year apart from each other and they were good friends together. I miss them and it made me realize that I need to do better in keeping in touch with my friends. Sure, I see them on social media, but they're just there. I don't communicate with them, and they don't with me. It is sad because everyone is so wrapped up in their own lives that they get lost, and then one day, a friend of yours is no longer there online because their timeline is bombarded with sentiments and condolences…You realize that you've had all this time to reach out to them because they are always online, always there, but now they're gone."

Cai sips his beer and stares into space. Viviana touches his shoulder, and he jolts from her hand clasped upon him.

"The veil grows thin at the time of the dead," says Viviana. "We'll say a prayer for them tonight and in honor of their passing I shall do a performance."

Cai's eyes light up and he remarks, "A performance like a sending from Final Fantasy X?"

Viviana's lips sparse apart to mouth a 'wow' expression. "What a dweeb..." jokes Viviana. Cai laughs knowing Viviana understands his reference. "If that brings you comfort, then I suppose," she adds.

I don't know what they are talking about. I've never heard of this reference. Cai catches onto my silence. "Do you like FFX?" he asks.

"Eh, I don't know what that is..."

His eyes jolt in shock. "You've never heard of FFX?"

Viviana gasps, her mouth agape, and she's about to speak until her eyes wander to the gate. Something catches her attention.

"Marcin!"

"Merry meet Vivi!"

Viviana lunges toward whomever greeted her. She embraces the guest vibrantly. "I can't believe you're here!" She breaks her embrace.

"Of course, I wouldn't miss celebrating the harvest with you."

"Come, there is someone I'd like you to meet!" They sashay toward my direction and I observe her guest. Viviana's guest blossoms with pink dye in his hair. The sides of his head are shaved as one side illustrates a tattoo of the waxing crescent and the other side the waning crescent. His eyebrows are thin and naturally curved. His eyelashes curve like wings; he has a nose ring tucked in his right nostril and dark purple lipstick. A thick silver chain wraps around his neck with a pentagram as a pendant. His shawl illustrates a diverse range of shades of purple and his dark-blue jeans have slits with stitches of white shrouding the holes against his thighs and kneecaps.

"Marcin, this is Alice. Alice, this is my dear friend Marcin!"

"Blessed be Alice!"

"Hello…"

I shake his hand as I greet him. My hand jolts from his touch; it's cold as if icicles impale every inch of my hand. Numbness seeps into my hand like a thousand needles dancing inside it. Fear jilts in my heart for the loss of feeling. Is it from not sleeping?

"I'll let you two get acquainted while I get ready for the performance tonight. It will be dark soon and then we shall feast " Viviana clasps her hand upon my shoulder and strokes them. My heart palpitates from her departure. Though at the same time, my heart's unnatural rhythms are not from her leaving. I groan out a short breath.

"Are you alright, Alice? You look like you haven't slept in a while and it seems like anxiety grips you."

I don't answer Marcin as I clasp my hand over my heart. It is on fire, burning, and it is like I am suffocating. Suffocating among the smoke. Flashbacks cloud my sight. I see the shadow which carried me away from my burning home.

"Here take these…"

Marcin's words break my trance. In his hands are gummies.

"What are these?"

"Gummies. These will be helpful for quelling anxiety and insomnia."

His words echo inside my hollow skull, and my head wobbles around on my neck. Every few seconds it falls forward and then snaps back up. My eyelids feel weighty and I can barely keep them open. An intense itchy sensation engulfs my senses; it's the only thing keeping me awake. It's as if I'm burning alive, trapped inside my burning house. I have no idea what Marcin is talking about, and frankly I don't care. I wobble back as I ignore his words and clumsily sit upon one of the picnic benches. I rest my head against the palm of my hand. The itchiness becomes unbearable as I scratch at my thighs like the little girl with mats and viscera seeping out of her from one of my nightmares. I jiggle my legs, stamp my feet to make the itchiness go away, but nothing is working. Paranoia fuels me. I'm sure the people around me think I am weird, but I don't care. There are shards stabbing me in my legs, and I'm afraid.

I do not stare at anyone and focus on the beauty of the outside altar. I try to concentrate upon it, but when I look at it, something strange happens. My father. His image wavers like a burning flame with hazy smoke. My eyelids no longer feel heavy as I stare at him, wide-eyed with shock.

"This is impossible," I mutter to myself. He looks so real. I am witnessing something magical—he's here! I glance left and right toward everyone, but they are all engaged with each other and completely unfazed. My eyes fixate back to the altar—he's gone.

"What just happened?" I mumble. Then, Viviana enters the backyard. Her outfit is different. She wears a black tank top with shorts. She walks near the front of the altar with a hoop in her hands. A shadow waves around her as if it will devour her. Something bad is about to happen. I can feel it. I glance around to everyone, but no one seems worried. They're all fixated upon her. I even see people I do not know nor recognize who came to the party. One guy is near Ionel and Marcin. I do not care to observe them anymore; I should do something, anything, to stop this shadow, but I stay still. I watch in horror as the shadow swallows her. Fire appears and burns a ring around the hoop she grips in her hand. Music starts to play. The song "Dancing in the Dark" by Liliac rings my ears. I don't know whether it's the music or the shadow possessing her to dance and move. She sways her body back and forth as if the shadow is murdering her. I spring up, my legs slam against the picnic bench ready to run to her, but I blink, and everything is normal again. There's no shadow. Viviana is completely unharmed and continues dancing.

There is no shadow.

Chapter 19

The fire waves, hisses, and flares andViviana is in her element. She twirls, sways, and twists in and out of the hoop of fire. Her eyes wander seductively, in her own trance. The night is black with the candlelit altar behind her and embers like fluttering ash. The smell of smoke is faint but lingers.

I am mesmerized. She's beautiful in the way she dances with shadows everywhere as fire illuminates her complexion. I catch glimpses of her blue eyes. They sparkle with the light of the flame, but nobody is there. The smoke, fire, and her image remind me of my dream where she sits across from me and the pit of fire is between us. The raven. Emotions of comfort, sorrow, fear, serenity, and panic devour my being. My brain can't comprehend them. An ill feeling takes over me, but I stare frozen. Her beauty lures me into a trance. I don't want to lose her like Camila. She's dead, not Viviana. *Please don't take my Viviana from me.*

She is fire and I'm shadow. Shadows cannot live without the fire that fuels them and radiates heat and light.

She spins, kneels down, and the hoop falls, surrounding her as the music abruptly ends. Her eyes are shut; sweat trickles down from her pale skin. Her dark eye makeup shrouds her eyelids, and her eyelashes are thick and black. She opens them and her blue eyes seethe in my soul. My heart aches as she smiles. Mr. Dragomir sprinkles the hoop with a hose to put out the flames. They die and smoke rises around her. Viviana steps and walks out of the hoop of smoke. She strides with confidence as she grabs a towel to wipe the sweat. From a distance, she buries her head into the towel. Her shoulders shrug up and then down. I sense her emotions overwhelming her. She must have thought about her mother as she danced; wishing those who have passed to prosper in their journey through the veil.

Everyone is silent. Viviana sets her towel down and stands tall and strong.

"This is the night when the gateway between our world and the spirit world is thinnest. Tonight, I have honored my ancestors. Spirits of my fathers and mothers, I call to you, and welcome you in for this night. You watch over me always, protecting and guiding me, and tonight I thank you. Your blood runs in my veins, your spirit is in my heart, your memories are in my soul. Antonia Dragomir of my blood and spiritual ones of family and friends who have passed, with the gift of remembrance and the sending; I remember all of you. You are dead but never forgotten, and you live on within me, and within those who are yet to come."

Marcin steps forward in front of the altar and speaks words of his own, "The veil grows thin at the time of the dead, as we honor our long-gone ancestors, in whose footsteps we tread. Life retreats into the bulbs and the roots; the time has passed for the flowers and the fruits. As leaves fall thick and carpet the ground, the Dark Mother waits in silence profound. Now is the time for the apple feasts; time stands still for humans and beasts. Seek the wisdom of days gone by, to deal with the past and let it lie. Face your shadow and accept your faults; look now to the future and seek your results."

"Blessed be," replies Viviana.

"Let's eat and celebrate!" chimes Marcin clapping his hands in excitement. Everyone gathers around the picnic tables. Mr. Dragomir hands out the plates, Ionel opens a bottle of wine, and Viviana opens the different kinds of food that was cooked during the day. I stand there reflecting upon Marcin's last words of prayer, "Seek the wisdom of days gone by, to deal with the past and let it lie. Face your shadow and accept your faults; look now to the future and seek your results."

Facing my shadow is difficult and the past cannot die. I desire peace but the steps to take for such peace is always a work in progress. It's driving me to insanity. Every little thing is agitating.

I don't want to be alone and yet I cannot stand a crowd. The thought of my father before the altar a few moments before flashes in my mind. What wisdom can I seek from him haunting me? I know but can't tell. I must tell, I must let it out, pry it out— screams, death, darkness—all the answers I seek are within me. My head throbs; my body is heavy again—blackness—now here—bench. My mind rambles and scrambles…Scatter—the premonition of the raven—mind—stop, mind—stop! Nothing.

The roar of water runs along a dark and narrow stream. The night is black, and my eyes can only comprehend figures and shapes. A massive tunnel is before me. I stare at its abyss and discover a feminine, shadowy figure. Hair dangles from its face but in moments, I see red eyes. I'm frightened but I scuttle toward it. It just stands there in a stance of furious rage. Its hands grip into fists and it's still staring right at me. The loose rocks and stones crackle under my feet. The water roars louder and the figure's eyes never leave its gaze upon me. The tunnel has thick black bars like a cemetery's gate. It contains the shadowy figure before me. Its gaze never leaves me. Terror strikes my heart, and I move aside to avoid it. I do not face it, and then, I appear at my apartment. The low yellow streetlights only illuminate the room and surrounding me are all the friends who I know: Ionel, Viviana, Marcin, Mr. Dragomir, Cai, and even Tessa. They're all there, but an ill feeling consumes my entire body. Dread. I know the figure from the tunnel followed me here. I can't escape it. It's outside—its red eyes catch my sight as all those around me change. It's as if the figure possesses them, taking them one by one. Ionel and I escape and drive away in his car. The figure is still there—I can feel it—its eyes red and burning flames. The shadow stands before us, Ionel slams on the brake, the car spins and flips. Shards of glass spread everywhere; weight compresses against my chest and I cannot breathe. I watch Ionel die next to me.

I bolt up in pain and scream. However, I don't scream loud enough for anyone to hear me. My heart palpitates and sweat rains from my forehead. I'm inside Viviana's room catching the looming scent of mugwort. My nose whiffs the scent, and it smells like mint toothpaste. Its scent doesn't frighten me. I glance over to Viviana's altar and find a cup with a mugwort bundle in it. My eyes see its tiny, strong, dark green leaves. It burns and embers its dying smoke. I look over next to me and find Viviana asleep. How long was I out?

I'm hazy and fuzzy, and I touch the back of my head. My hair is soaked, and I touch a bump that is hot. I must have passed out. I look around the room for my phone; I want to know the time. It's still dark. A small streetlight reflects upon Viviana's mirror. I look around her makeup table and find my phone. My phone lights up, blinding my eyes, but they see the time.

"3:02 A.M. It's my birthday, November 1st," I whisper to myself. My breath inhales a sharp pain. It's the anniversary of my mother's death and the evening when my house burned into ashes. Before my phone's light vanished, I observe the notification of Ionel's message from Messenger that I had received earlier. I know it's the audio file of Oscar Waldo. I scour Viviana's room to find something, anything to quietly listen to his story. They must have the answers and the wisdom I seek. Ah, perfect. I find earbuds.

My bare feet tiptoe upon the floorboards. They wail and creak. I'm still in my black dress I've been wearing…I will definitely need some new clothes. It doesn't matter; I desire to know Oscar and his story. I unlock the front door, shut it behind me, and sit upon the porch swing. It creaks as I sit, the clouds shroud the moon, and a breeze plays upon my cheeks. This is it. This is his story and Viviana must not know. I plug in the earbuds, put them in my ears, and press play.

Chapter 20

As the recording plays, Oscar's voice takes over:

Who says video games aren't therapeutic? I mean, they can be better than real people sometimes and be able to help ease the hardships of life. How great is my life? It's just as great as a brown paper bag with nothing in it but a pile of dog crap. Seriously, whether people know it or not, in life you just have to eat crap, take it, and say thank you, may I have another?! Ugh, more often as of late, I feel that being part of a video game universe would be a heck of a lot better than living in the current reality of the present. Since childhood, I have indulged myself in the pleasure of playing video games. Out of all the video games I have played, my all-time favorite and most treasured is "The Ultraborne."

It is a dark fantasy RPG game that tells the story of Gaden the Ultraborne who has the ability to absorb powers and utilize them as he chooses. He can become anything he desires because he is an Ultraborne. Depending on the player of the game, the choices made will result in Gaden becoming either good or evil. Thus, there are several alternative endings to the game. I've played through all the possible endings there can be which are the good ending, the bad ending, the tragic, and the happily-ever-after ending. My most favorite ending is the happily-ever-after ending where Gaden ends up with the love of his life Cora, retires from being an Ultraborne, and Sadie, his ward, ends up becoming an Ultraborne! I guess it's my favorite because I too wish for a happy ending for myself.

Oh man, if only I could live in the Ultraborne universe, I'd be so much happier than existing in this awful world. I would love to be with Cora. I daydream often about romantically being involved with her and being a part of the Ultraborne universe. I would be an Ultraborne myself if it were possible. I would be involved with many of the characters from the game for they would make better friends and family because I feel they would understand me. I have a bad tendency to stay up all night and play video games. It's just something that happens, and I know it's a problem, but I don't know how to fix it. Since I can't sleep, I tend to sleep during the day instead. I feel bad about it when I wake up around the evening time, but it's just that my high time is during the night where I'm more active.

Unfortunately, this problem has cost me in maintaining a job. I worked at a video game store, but they fired me because I'd show up late to work sometimes, or I didn't show up at all. I feel awful and there are moments where I just lie in bed all evening and don't come down from my room that's in the attic. Even my best friend Marcin is concerned for me. All seems hopeless for me. I have no direction for life, or know what I want to do, and it's difficult making friends because of my many problems and issues. I've been to a shrink and everything, but nothing has changed.

Until one day, Marcin recommends I take a trip somewhere to get away. He thinks that maybe a change of scenery will inspire me or help me find a path for myself. He, my parents, and I have a sit-down discussion about my issues and the solution that my best friend proposes. My parents believe it will help, so they save enough money for me to go to school at Timber Creek University within Woodhaerst. A part of me doesn't want to go because I'd be a stranger in an unfamiliar area and also because I'm shy, but at the same time, I think it's better than staying where I have been because nothing has changed.

Weeks later summer finally ends, and I am prepared to start my new journey. Marcin and my father decide to drive to Woodhearst with me to say their goodbyes and to make sure I settle in just fine. It's close to noon when we arrive at Timber Creek University. It is strange to see that fog shrouds the entire area, and the air is thick as if the fog itself suffocates my lungs.

"I guess they don't call this place Woodhearst for nothing…" states Marcin.

My dad, Marcin, and I are parked in a small parking lot where nearby there is a small waterfall streaming down.

"Hmm, almost reminds me of the many metro parks I used to explore in Ohio when I was your age, Oscar!" my father says as he observes the area.

"Yeah…" I answer.

Marcin swings his arm around the back of my shoulders like any good friend.

He inhales a deep breath. "Ah, don't worry about it, bro. I think you'll love this place! Just think of the many adventures you'll have like Frodo and Sam!"

"Yeah, except I'll be like a Frodo without a Sam…"

"Oh, come on man, you'll be fine without me and besides Timber Creek doesn't have my major."

"Yeah, I know."

"So, don't fret my friend!"

Marcin wraps his arms around me like a giant bear.

"Bro hug!" he glees vibrantly.

"Ha-ha, thanks for that!"

Soon my father, Marcin, and I carry my luggage and belongings up the road that leads to the university. The entire area is covered with trees and woods as if we are in the Dark Forest from the *Harry Potter* books. There are no birds chirping or anything. Not even a hoot of an owl and all that we can hear is the slight breeze of the wind. The sun does not shine. Instead, it's dark, and cloudy and it reminds me of going deep into Alaska to visit my grandparents. Gosh, how I hate to visit them out there because they have no electricity which means no video games, but family is family. Speaking of video games, I'm fortunate enough to bring my Samsung flat screen HDTV with me along with my gaming console. For my luggage, I have a long, thick, and wooden storage trunk. Marcin holds onto one handle of the trunk while I grip the other because of how heavy it is.

My father carries my flat screen TV that is stored inside its original box and eventually, we begin to see Timber Creek University within the distance. The university has a massive and overpowering presence and it feels like the college stands strong and proud showcasing all its glory, history, and heritage before us. The architectural layout of the college is a late nineteenth century structure. There are well-kept open fields around the university and in front of us is a massive rectangular stone sign that reads, "Timber Creek University." Slightly below the name of the college, the year when the university was first founded, 1891, is etched upon the stone.

We set down my luggage to look at where my dorm hall will be. My father takes out the map of the university grounds from a lettered envelope.

"Let's see…" he putters while studying the map.

There is a moment of pause until he finally speaks, "So, we go straight from where we are and at the crossroads before the university, we go left until we find Salmon River Hall."

Nobody says anything as we pick up my luggage and set off to find my dorm. A bit farther down and past the rectangular stone sign are the crossroads. Between the path in front of us and the one to the left is a lamp-lit posted sign that shows which way to go around campus. We take the left path on the crossroads to get to Salmon River Hall. Along the way, we see Badger Residence Hall, and finally much farther down the path after crossing a small bridge that stretches across a creek is the residence hall where I've been spending my fall semester, Salmon River Hall.

Salmon River Hall is structured almost like a mansion of some sort except just like any modern standard dorm for students, it's just a bunch of lofts stacked together. The check-in office is inside the residence hall on the first floor. The layout of the first floor is almost like a lobby of a hotel. Nobody is at the desk as I ring the service bell. I ring it once as nobody comes. Then, I ring it twice in a row, and there is still no answer. I look at both my father and Marcin. Marcin shrugs his shoulders and my father seems just as annoyed as I am about not having anyone there at the front desk. Soon, my father loses his patience and hesitantly rings the service bell over and over again. As the bell chimes repeatedly over and over again, a voice shouts out to us in an obnoxious manner.

"I hear the bell!" cries a woman. Soon, a woman waddles out from the doorway behind the desk while wagging her hand around with her index finger and says, "Was that you sir, ringing that dang bell?"

My father is at a loss of words, "Uh, um yes… Yes, it was."

The woman has a stiff upper lip about her along with a hairy mole on one side of her cheek. It's rather difficult to pay attention to her because of the mole.

"Didn't you see the sign over there?" she asks pointing over to it.

We are all dumbfounded that we didn't see the sign that reads, "On break until" with a clock indicating the return time.

"I apologize, we did not see the sign" says my father.

The woman sighs calmingly, "I'm sorry too for getting in your face, it's just that today has been crazy, this morning with all the students coming back along with the new ones. It's just been stressful, and I just got on lunch break too."

It becomes quiet as I catch the woman's scent that reeks like cigarettes.

"Well, since y'all are here, we might as well get right to it!"

The woman clenches her hands into fists, and we hear the bones from her fingers crackle. She then wakes up the computer and logs into the system.

"Name and student ID please?" she asks politely.

"Oscar Waldo Apple," I answer.

"Mhm, and your ID please?" she adds typing away.

"736241723"

"Thank you, do you have cash for your deposit?"

"Yes, one-hundred and fifty dollars."

I hand her the money, she counts it, and grabs the safety deposit box from underneath the desk. The woman unlocks the box, places the cash inside it, and grabs a piece of paper.

"Ok, so this is your agreement stating that you have placed your deposit and that you agree to the terms and conditions of staying within the residence hall."

I glance at the document, and with a pen, I sign and date it. The woman takes the agreement and gives me the pink slip of paper that is underneath the paper I had just signed.

"Here is your receipt and please keep it for your records. Now, bear with me one moment please while I get your key to your room." The woman leaves to go back through the doorway, and in moments, she returns with a keycard. "Here's your keycard to your dorm room; just follow the signs if you please."

I take the keycard. "Thank you," I reply.

We follow the signs to my dorm room,417, which is on the top floor according to the elevator we take to get there. The hallways after getting off the elevator are long and narrow, but very moderate.

"Hmm… well, Oscar, by the looks of this residence hall I'm assuming that this building is very new," states Marcin as we head down the far right. The three of us go down the hall and eventually discover my dorm room, the very last room on the right-hand side. I swipe my keycard. The door unlocks, and I slowly turn the doorknob hoping the room will turn out like it displays online.

"Nice," says my father, seeing the loft before him.

My dorm is a two-bedroom loft with an ultramodern design and layout with walk in closets, but a bathroom to share. The space within the room is plentiful enough and I actually become excited. "Oh wow, this is awesome!" I exclaim.

Soon, a toilet flushes, and water flows and roars out of a faucet. In moments, the door opens from the bathroom.

"Ah, welcome. I'm Mitch. Nice to meet you!"

Before me is a guy who has short brown hair, blue eyes, a maroon button-down shirt with the sleeves rolled up, and a pair of dark blue jeans with a brown standard belt around his waist. He holds out his hand for a handshake.

Awkwardly, I shake his hand. "Oscar Waldo, but just call me Oscar," I say.

"Cool beans man. I believe your room is the second bedroom," follows Mitch with a smile pointing out the doorway to my room. It's a white door with a bronze doorknob, and I walk up to it. I open it and smile. My room has the WIFI box sitting right there on top of a desk. In front of the desk is a window that has a backside view.

My room is very spacious, yet very empty, but I know that will soon change.

"Great room bro, what more could you ask for?" pings Marcin with excitement. The three of us set my luggage and belongings on the floor of the room.

"Well son, we'll leave you right to it," says my father, giving me a hug.

"Thanks Dad, take care!"

Marcin and my father say their goodbyes and shortly leave to go all the way back to Ohio. I anxiously and eagerly set up my TV and gaming console on the floor near a corner between where the desk is against the wall and the walk-in closet. I decide not to wait. I switch everything on and set up the WIFI on my gaming console because it will be better to have some time to myself before I explore the campus grounds and be familiar with where my classes are going to be the next day.

Chapter 21

"No man chooses evil because it is evil:
he only mistakes it for happiness, the good he seeks."
— Mary Shelley, Frankenstein

Well, at least that's what I think the plan will be. I've done it again…Here I thought that I would only spend a few hours playing my game, but instead I lose track of the time. It's now a little after midnight, and I will have my first day of classes at nine in the morning. I go to bed soon after I realize the time, but I can't get myself to sleep, and I end up wasting an hour in bed. *Ugh.*

I can't take it anymore and I decide to be adventurous and go explore the campus. I take my brown leather coat and set off outside. The night is cool, dark, and there is a slight breeze of wet mist that makes the air thick. The pathways around campus have lampposts to light up the path just like any suburban neighborhood with streetlights. There is no sound of any kind. No crickets or nightlife, which is rather strange, but then again, it's extremely late and everyone on campus is more than likely sleeping. After crossing the bridge that stretches across the creek, I wrap my leather jacket tighter around my body because I feel unsettlingly ill.

My chest is tight, my stomach knots, and my heart aches as if I'm being watched. I keep my eyes forward. I do not want to look back, I will not look back, and I do not… I quicken my pace and hum loudly to distract myself. I continue to do this while going down the path. I don't want to turn around, and then that's when I hear it—crying and weeping. I stand and stop for a moment only to find something within the distance at the crossroads. It's a shadowy figure sitting with their back against the lamppost while clutching their own body into a ball. I walk at an uneasy pace and realize it's someone dressed in a dark lilac hoodie. This person's hood is over their head while the front of their face is hidden because their knees are shielding their face.

Soon, I am close enough and ask, "Are you ok?"

As I am asking that question, I notice this person is a girl wearing shorts that match her hoodie. She is barefoot, and has her toenails painted in dark lilac. While extending my hand out to her, I notice she has her fingernails painted dark lilac as well. She neglects me when I try reaching out to her and at the same time, the light from the lamppost above us flickers.

"Go away…" she mutters in a cold and unfriendly manner.

I squat down. "I'm sorry, I'm only trying to help… I'm Oscar Waldo."

"I said, go away…" she replies once more.

It's silent for a moment as she continues to weep, and I stand on my feet. I scuttle away and decide to head back to my dorm. As I am walking away, I hear buzzing from the lamppost that is at the crossroads. I turn around to see that the light from the lamppost flickers completely off for a moment and then comes back on. The crying stops and the girl sitting underneath the lamppost is gone.

"So much for the adventure," I mumble. There is no point in trying to go to sleep because of the time and knowing I have class at nine. So, I decide to pull an all-nighter, which isn't the best thing to do, but I think after today is over, I'll be tired. I shuffle out of my room like a hermit turtle from his shell and I look like a zombie because of the dark circles under my eyes. Soon, I smell black tea from inside the dorm. I go inside the kitchen only to find my roommate Mitch holding a bowl of hot black tea. It's rather strange seeing someone with a bowl of tea instead of a cup of tea.

"Ah, mornin' there Oscar!" he glees cheerfully, holding his bowl of tea.

"Eh, morning Mitch…" I reply dimly.

"Jeez man, you look worse than a hangover. Who shit in your oatmeal this morning?"

"Ha-ha, very funny…" I answer in monotone while fixing up a bowl of oatmeal. I place my bowl into the microwave and remark, "You seem more chipper than when we met yesterday."

"Yeppers, a bowl of tea keeps the guarantee!"

I chuckle as I go over to get some bread and place it into the toaster.

"Meaning?" I ask.

"Meaning, that tea will start your day better than a cup of coffee!"

There is a pause as I stumble over to one of the upper cabinets to grab a jar of Nutella.

Mitch slurps from his bowl of tea. "Besides, tea is much healthier than…" Suddenly, Mitch doesn't finish his sentence and quickly squeals like a giddy schoolgirl.

"Oh my God, is that Nutella?"

I glance over and see his eyes are huge and wide with vitality.

"Uh, yes, why yes, it is…"

Mitch gasps with excitement. "You are officially the coolest dude roommate ever… You have… Nutella! AHHHHH!!"

"Whoa, easy dude…"

"Sorry dude, it's just I freaking love Nutella and I put that shit on everything from bread, toast, crackers, potato chips, and even French fries!"

The microwave beeps, indicating that my oatmeal is ready. As I go over to the microwave, Mitch continues his rant on how much he loves Nutella.

"Nutella is the best freaking thing on this planet. It's essential like water; it's the nectar of the gods…"

I listen and I reply with "Yeah" the whole time.

Mitch rambles on about Nutella. "It's like an orgy or an orgasmic explosion inside your mouth!"

"Yeah."

"Or… Or, like a bear with his honey!"

"Yeah."

"No wait, it's like two energizer bunnies in heat!"

"What?"

Mitch emphasizes and expresses his voice by using the melody from the song, *Sexy and I Know It.* "Yeah, it just keeps on going and going!" Ends Mitch with a smile and a little laughter while coming up to me for a high five.

There is an awkward moment of silence, and I just give him a high-five for the heck of it.

"Yeah, alright Nutella is dope! I'll see you later," squeaks Mitch chugging down the rest of the tea from his bowl. Mitch leaves and my piece of bread flies out from the toaster. I spread Nutella onto my piece of bread, and while doing so, I shake my head in disbelief from what I just experienced.

After breakfast I snatch a can of Monster from inside my fridge to help me stay awake during the day. I take it with me while on my first set of classes for the day, my bag strapped around my shoulder. On my way to the first class, according to the map, I have to go by Foxrice Hall which is a girl's dormitory on campus.

All I have to do is to stay on the path I am starting from my residence hall, then when arriving at the crossroads continue straight, and eventually, to the right will be Foxrice Hall. Then, from Foxrice Hall just continue onward until I find the science and mathematics college building.

The weather outside is better than it has been. It's just cloudy, but there is no fog, and the temperature is moderately cool. A few college students roam past me while on the path. Some students have earbuds in their ears listening to music while some are diddle-dawdling on their phones, and others are chatting with their friends. It's pretty normal, just like any college campus, but then something grabs my attention after I arrive at Foxrice Hall. As I continue onward, I see in one of the windows from the top floor of Foxrice Hall, decked in dark lilac drapes. All the other drapes from Foxrice Hall are all beige and ordinary except for a window on the top floor; it's dark lilac. Suddenly, I see from the window a face staring and then I feel myself bumping into someone.

"Ugh, look at what you did to my blouse you stupid jerk!"

"Oh, I'm so sorry I wasn't paying attention…" I utter, seeing that this girl I bumped into caused my Monster drink to spill on her blouse. My Monster drink didn't just spill on her blouse, but the spill is on her breasts causing them to be somewhat exposed from my drink soaking through her blouse. I cannot help but stare at her chest—not because I'm a pig, but because I can't believe what just happened. She catches me staring and becomes extremely flustered.

"Ugh!" she cries angrily and the next thing I feel is a strong and stingy slap across my face.

My face feels warm. I press my hand upon my cheek where she slapped me, and then she loudly screams at me.

"Why don't you take a picture? It will last longer, you perv!"

Next, she waltzes by me like an exploding volcano. I turn around still having my hand pressed against my cheek and I stumble over my words.

"I'm sorry… I… I didn't mean to…there's this face I just saw…" I look up at the window where I saw the face and can't finish my sentence because the face isn't there.

"Humph!" remarks the girl, and she storms off like a mad hatter.

I heavily sigh as I check to see how much Monster I have left and not even a drop is left.

"Ugh well, there goes my Monster…"

The first day of classes go by just like any ordinary first day. The professor or instructor hands over a syllabus, goes over regulations and material we will cover, and blah, blah, blah… What is interesting is when I have a break from my schedule and have lunch in the student center cafeteria. The student center is decorated with several unique pieces of art and artistic expression of the university's mascot, "The Woodwind Witches." The university's most cherished sport is lacrosse, but there are other sports too like wrestling, fencing, and swimming. There are a couple of trophies on display from past championships ranging from the lacrosse team, wrestling, fencing, and swimming team. Inside there is the university's cafeteria and it's called the Wolves' Den. Within the Wolves' Den are several restaurant stands, along with plenty of chairs and tables for anyone to sit at. In the far back of the Wolves' Den is a grand hall with long bench tables just like in the medieval times and at the end of the hall is a round table.

It is crowded throughout the cafeteria, and so it takes a few moments to find a place to sit down and eat my lunch. Finally, I find a spot to myself and start to chow down on some food from a place called "Dog's Tallow" that is inside the cafeteria. I'm eating a sub from there called the "cry wolf" sub. It's basically a sub with black forest ham and hot jalapeños that is spicy enough to make me howl and cry wolf. After devouring my sub, I look through my phone until somebody comes up to me.

"Excuse me, but is someone using this chair?"

I glance up, seeing this guy asking if he can take the chair to the other table so he can sit at an empty table.

"Nope, it's all yours," I answer.

"Thanks," he replies, taking the chair to his table. I close my eyes from a slight sudden pain in my head. I reopen my eyes after the pain subsides. I glare over at the guy who took the chair with his group of friends as they are all laughing and having a good time. Were his friends there before? I do not know and he's sitting there not speaking to them. Then someone from the group asks about a girl sitting alone.

"Hey, who's that girl sitting there all by herself?" the guy inquires.

"Oh, that's Viviana; she's not like other girls."

"Oh, is that a bad thing?" another girl from the group chimes in with her thoughts.

"Oh, wait. Gabby, doesn't that girl come from a wealthy family?"

"Huh, oh yeah. I can tell just by the fancy dark purple drapes hanging from her dorm room window! She's such a snobby bitch and thinks she's just better than us by how she is sitting there by herself."

Then the guy who asked about her speaks, "If that's the case then never mind. I was gonna see if she wanted to hang out with us."

"No, don't. She's just a disdainful human being."

Next, I look over to the girl that the group is talking about and instantly it reminds me of the girl I saw earlier today staring at the window. Studying her more, I notice that she has long dark lilac hair that touches past her shoulders. Her hood shrouds her face, but the natural light shows her violet eyes. She also has a light delicate touch of dark lilac eyeshadow that sharpens the color of her eyes. However, by looking at them, I feel an emotion of despondence from her.

Suddenly, she emotionlessly glances over to me and out of reaction, I quickly turn my head away. For a moment, I feel her stare. I'm uncomfortable and unnerved. I drum my fingers against the top of the table thinking about what I should do. Thinking about it, I sort of understand her feelings of sadness because I too have social issues. Next, I peek over to her and notice she stopped staring at me, and she looks like a hollowed vessel. I take in a deep breath and hold it in as I get up to go over to her. My heart races with butterflies, and the jitters control my stomach. I don't know what to say or what to do. I'm not an expert at making social conversation. This is the part where I say in my mind, "Curse my introverted self!" Soon as I am contemplating myself to death in my mind, I'm at her table and do not realize it until my foot lightly taps the chair across from her.

My hands touch the chair that my foot tapped, and I look over at her noticing that she still doesn't seem to know I am there.

"Uh, um…" I putter quietly while having my hand on top of my head. I hesitantly and nervously place my hand back at my side with a stammer. "Uh, I um… I…" Then, I exhale and finally ask, "May I sit down with you?"

She finally glares over at me and replies coldly and in an unfriendly manner.

"Why?"

"Duh, I uh, well, because I thought you wouldn't like to sit alone…?" I stutter awkwardly scratching my head. My nervous scratching causes a few flakes of dandruff to fall onto my shoulders. She doesn't say anything to me as I end up sitting down across from her. We just sit there together and don't say a word to one another for I don't know how long. She is just embittered, withdrawn, and I think maybe she is resentful of my presence or perhaps my kind gesture of asking to sit with her. Still, I sit with her, but she does not say a word. I'm losing my mind for I don't know how to strike up a conversation until I bluntly say without thinking, "The dark lilac color suits you! Is that your favorite color?"

God, was that a dumb question? Well, duh Oscar. Of course, that's her favorite color. I mean dark lilac hair, violet eyes, dark lilac eyeshadow, and painted fingernails in dark lilac…

"Eh, I'm sorry…That was a stupid question. I'm never that great at striking up a social conversation and I'm just shy… I'm not from around here. My parents and best friend brought me here and I'm sort of unhappy because I'm in an unfamiliar town and it's just in general hard for me to make friends. And well, if it's hard for you to talk and make friends then that's ok too. I won't judge you."

There is still no answer from her, and I just give a sigh.

"Alright um, if you wanna talk or hangout sometime I live over at the Salmon River."

I leave the student center and come back to my dorm. Since there isn't really that much homework, I stay inside my room and play video games for the rest of the day.

Chapter 22

Glancing at the time, I see it is past midnight once more.

"Ugh, I did it again… Damn it… Oh well, at least I don't have to be at the university until around noon."

I shuffle out of my room to go inside the bathroom that Mitch and I have to share. I brush my teeth and nothing but the nightlight is on inside the bathroom. I study myself in the mirror before glancing down to grab my toothbrush and toothpaste. After putting the toothpaste on my brush, I stare at the mirror and there is something standing right by the tub behind me. I drop my toothbrush, startled. I don't know what it is, and I hesitantly flip on the light switch above the sink and below the mirror in front of me.

Whatever it is, it's gone and no longer by the tub. I exhale, deeply relieved and pick up my brush to start brushing. I make funny faces while brushing my teeth and keep the main light on. Afterward, I finish, rinse my mouth out, and flip the main lights off. Suddenly, in a flash, what I saw earlier reappears and I drop my toothbrush on the floor.

Quickly, I switch on the main lights again and then turn them off again to make sure I'm not going crazy from not sleeping. It reappears once more but this time it's closer behind me.

I do not want to turn around. I cannot look behind me, and with a little squeal, I flip the light switch on again. In seconds it disappears, and I shrug my shoulders after I turn around to see that nothing is there. I pick up my toothbrush from the floor, rinse it again with water, and not even with a second glance at the mirror, white eyes and a white mask that only conceals the face's mouth surfaces. I jolt, shut my eyes, and slip onto the floor.

I can't breathe. I look behind me, but nothing is there. I need to get out! I check myself and everything seems to be fine as I give a sigh of relief.

"I'm ok…Ugh."

I clench my mouth and decide that I can't go to bed. I think strolling the night away again will help me sleep. I turn off the bathroom lights, creep into my room, get my earbuds, and put on my brown leather jacket. I snag my phone, connect the earbuds, and listen to music.

Outside, it's pitch black, the path barely visible except the lamppost lights guiding the pathways. I listen to my favorite song, "Jessie's Girl" by Rick Springfield. It's my most favorite tune because it's a song I can relate to back in high school when my best friend Marcin and I liked the same girl. So, instead of singing the chorus as, "I wish I had Jessie's Girl" I sing, "I wish I had Marcin's Girl." It's a tune that makes me happy because it also recollects the good times Marcin and I had in the past and still do. I mean getting drunk together, watching The Lord of The Rings trailers, and saying drunk-like that it's the best freaking movie trilogy ever... Yeah, good times!

I'm halfway through the song on the second run through of the chorus, but there is static. I notice it quickly and as soon as I do, I feel something oozing. Out of the reaction of what I'm feeling, I violently yank out the earbud from my right ear. A white bubbling foam curdles from the earbud and the foam changes into a red liquid. I press my finger into my ear canal and notice a dab of blood on my fingertip. From within the darkness the sound of humming looms in the air. I do not recognize the melody, but the words, I think, are from somewhere before:

> *"Lilac falls beneath the ivory black,*
>
> *It wails underneath the insomniac.*
>
> *Little raven kraa to the paranoiac,*
>
> *Anima infects within the amnesiac.*
>
> *Crypt's call to lure the cardiac..."*

After these words a chill runs down my spine with a cold breeze down my neck. The humming is louder; it stops, and a voice calls in a whisper.

"Oscar...".

The very breath of my name tickles behind my left ear. I turn… Nobody is there.

"Oscar," the voice quickly shudders.

My heart races and the streetlamps flicker and go out. I twist my body in all directions and the voice giggles.

"Oscar." It calls again but in the far distance.

"Hello?" I cry.

The sound of my name crawls within my skull. The voice echoes repeatedly in tones and voices… The voices. I shut my eyes, clasp my hands over my ears, and they call my name. I need to get away… I need—to —I run! My legs thrash into something cold and hard. I scream aloud in pain and for the voices to stop. I keep my eyes shut. I do not want to open them for I know I'm falling, but to where I do not know…. But finally, the voices stop, and my eyes catch the glimpse of the girl in dark lilac.

"Ouch!" she cries. "Why did you run into me like that?"

She rubs her head.

My voice croaks and my words break, "I-I'm sorry-so sorry…"

She rolls her eyes, paces away, and that's when I speak, "Wait, stop!"

"Why? You'll think I'm disdainful like everyone else!"

"No, they mistake it for shyness. I know you're unhappy in unfamiliar surroundings!"

She halts but does not face me.

"Is that why you sit alone in the dining hall? People think you're cold and unfriendly, but you're not."

"How do you know? You know nothing about me…"

I lunge up from the ground and plead, "I don't but I want to. I would like to know more about you because like you, I need a friend. I am unhappy in a place I do not know."

She turns slowly and her eyes fixate upon me. I know then what she desires is a friend. I want to give her that because I too am lonely.

That night, we stroll among the campus grounds in the moonlight and the lamplit pathways. Viviana and I talk the night away. Viviana tells me she was dressed in lilac when she arrived, and she brought with her other accessories of the same color. Although many of her fellow dormmates ask her to explain her apparent obsession with dark lilac, Viviana always demurs.

Being a stranger and shy, as well as unhappy in her unfamiliar surroundings, Viviana struggles to make friends among anyone except me. They sense that she is different from them, but her oddity only strengthens my affections for her. They think she is rich because she is foreign, weird, and strange because of her passion for dark lilac. I want to probe into her love of the color but I feel there is a deeper meaning to it like she might not be ready to share about it.

She and I reveal that we've never had a significant other. I am foolish and fall in love with her melancholy because it's what I can relate to and understand. She is dark and mysterious, gentle and sincere. One night as I escort her to her dormitory, she gives me my first kiss. She stares into me; my heart trembles, and her violet eyes embed into my soul. The darkness swallows her face and all I see are those eyes. Whoever said, "Eyes are the gateway to the soul" was on point.

Viviana never looks at me directly in the light, instead, always keeping her hood up to shroud her face. Whatever she is physically hiding doesn't matter to me because of what her eyes implore to me. She wants acceptance, love, and companionship. What do we have to lose? It all happens in a flash; her lips against mine. Her lips are very fragrant, but slightly bitter. They have a distinct lemony taste with floral, pungent overtones which linger upon my lips. That's it for me! I want her and no one else. She darts away into the seclusion of her dorm. I stand outside dumbfounded, in shock, and I smile. My lips smudge against each other; my most cherished memory and the highlight of my life. She is, was, my only love.

Our newfound love makes me forget my own darkness; it mends me anew. I have forgotten in a few seconds the mysterious figure which I saw inside my dorm. Sleep does not come for me, but a high dose of delight does. Love that makes me feel I exist and is that not worth dying for? To die for love, to know, and feel my own existence.

This feeling only lasts moments as I wander the pathways of the campus grounds. The gloom of my dorm triggers my uncanny experiences. I cannot recall if I slept or not; my days blend. Extreme fatigue weighs upon my being and I begin to reflect. I never reflect because my mind stays distracted by video games and daydreaming. As I traverse to my room, a wave of despair looms over me. Like a replay button, it relays over and over again Viviana's words, *"You'll think I'm disdainful like everyone else!"*

It wallows inside my skull. An ill despondency seeps into my brain, a feeling that something is going to go wrong and ruin what's newly well. Loneliness creeps up on me; I can do better, I think…

Why am I thinking this way? What is the validation to feel this way because this is the best thing in the world; a new relationship? Am I not as great as I think I am? It can, possibly, even be that I can't pinpoint the issue. This struggle in my brain is a great burden. I lie in the complete darkness of my room, no video games this night.

Chapter 23

If there is one friend, I wish I paid more attention to, it's Mitch. He frequently checks up on me because most days, I stay in bed with the blinds, curtains, door, and lights shut. His mechanism to cheer me up is to crack jokes. One day, he cranks up "Cotton Eye Joe" by Rednex. He's hootin' and howlin' like an old-hillbilly redneck. His yelling drives me mad, and the beat-that rhythm of the damn song wires me nuts! It gets to the point where I bolt up, snatch open my door, and there he is! I want to scream at him to shut up but seeing him dance idiotically and squatting down is hilarious. No words form and my demeanor alters from angry to a plain-blank.

His jeans are tight to a point where I think they will split open at any second. He holds his comb in his hand while mouthing the lyrics, staring at me wide eyed. His eyes cross as he sways his head side to side to follow the rhythm of the song.

Other times, Mitch plays songs from a band called The Native Howl, a thrash metal bluegrass band that identifies themselves as thrash-grass.

I will regret not spending the time that could have been, but as I am speaking, it is only a matter of time. The room I am in recalls a treasured memory of my time at Timber Creek.

It is the first night that Viviana smuggles me into her dorm room. Foxrice Hall does not allow men in the dormitory, but one night Viviana and I rebel against university rules. The rain is heavy and pouring. She tells me that when other girls drop in to visit her, she seems so cold and unfriendly that they eventually stopped coming. Truthfully, many of the girls only come out of curiosity to see the pink pentagram rug she brought with her and the odd little figurines on her bookshelves. Odd figurines from an artist she admires like Anne Stokes. I recall one statue of a grim reaper and a woman dancing together.

Viviana tells me her roommate ultimately found her living situation unbearable and asked their housemother if she could move out. The housemother granted the roommate's request. Viviana sobs to me that nobody else wants to be in the same room with her. This makes her increasingly aloof and irritable. I want to make her pain go away and so I offer to stay with her through the night. I depart early enough to not get caught by the housemother or any of the fellow girls who stay at Foxrice. I'll never forget what Viviana had said to me.

"I love you; you're so sweet and kind. You're getting me out of my shell, and it would mean a lot for you to stay."

"Are you sure we aren't going too fast?"

"No, every couple is different and each one goes at a speed they are comfortable with. Do you want us to slow down?"

I clear my throat and stare into her eyes. She still has her dark lilac hoodie shrouding her head, covering her face in a multitude of shadows. I desire to caress her cheek. I withdraw because I'm not sure why she still hides her face from me.

"I like the speed we are going together. I just don't know what to say because saying 'I love you' is more than just words. They have meaning and many misuse these words."

She grips my hand and strokes it. "I understand, but these words are true within my heart. You're the first person and man to not judge me for what I am, how I dress, look, and carry myself. I know it's only been a few weeks since our first kiss, but I want this with you."

I flash a smile and my heart aches, "I do too…" I whisper romantically and stroke her hand tenderly. I stare at our hands and summon the courage to ask, "Why do you shroud yourself in your hoodie, if I may ask?"

Viviana squeezes my hand and jolts suddenly from our grasp. She clutches her hand into a fist and croaks, "I-I am… Ashamed. Self-conscious. Monstrous."

"Monstrous? I don't believe you to be monstrous because I love you too. I accept you for you, but I also understand if you are not ready to reveal yourself to me."

Silence. She ponders in thought by playing with her hands.

"May I say something to you first?" She mutters.

"Of course."

"I know you are fighting against something in your head. Your face shows me by how you linger in deep thought with a blank expression as if nobody is there. Your eyes have red and dark circles. Sometimes, you jabber on and on without pause and not making sense. A part of me wishes to know why but other times, not. You don't sleep because you wander the campus grounds at night like I do. Whatever it is you are going through, I hope I am enough. I hope that you won't do anything to hurt yourself and others. Your friend Mitch seems funny and how you talk about Marcin is special."

"Sometimes, I don't even know why I am this way. I know I have a good life, good friends, and you but I just don't know why I continue to struggle with my mind and inner-self."

"I get it and I am here for you. Actions speak louder than words and thus I will reveal to you my face to prove how much I love you and want you here."

Viviana's hands pull back. She stops briefly, and stares into my eyes. She pulls the hood back. I gasp but conceal my emotions.

I understand now why she shrouds herself. She does not look at me as her eyes are shut because she does not want to see my reaction.

I take a deep breath and speak, "Look at me…" I putter softly.

Her face is shrouded with a red, puffy rash. It resembles the shape of a butterfly's wings unfolding across both cheeks. She opens her eyes, terror filling them, and my hand caresses her cheek.

"You are beautiful."

My words break her into a sob. She cries and kisses my lips. We embrace and lie upon her bed. The rain dances upon the windows and flashes of lightning illuminate the entire room. Our kisses deepen into a hungry passion. Emotions of all kinds are swarming within me. Deep, sincere, and passionate emotions rapture between her and me. By the end of that intimate moment, we wrap ourselves around each other and under her purple blanket, completely naked and vulnerable. Her head rests upon my chest and we both snuggle to the rhythm of the storm.

The comfort of Viviana's body against mine melts my heart, but it isn't enough to gain sleep. I just cannot sleep. My mind races at an abnormal rate that I can't keep up. Some thoughts I think are petty and others perhaps reasonable.

Viviana's words of what she wanted to convey to me ring in my head about how she does not want me to hurt myself. I appreciate that she does not press me, but it makes me reflect again. I have no reason to feel and act this way because there are amazing people in my life. My parents, Marcin, Mitch, and now Viviana. But what about life itself?

A crack of thunder and lightning disrupt my deep thoughts. My head jolts to the window and through the light I hear footsteps echo up and down the stairs. I glance back to Viviana and notice she shifted over to her side and is no longer upon my chest. I dress, investigate the footsteps, and go down the stairs. In a hallway, a young woman appears. She wears a lilac dress and carries a purple parasol walking wordlessly up and down the halls of the girl's dormitory bathed in a purple glow. This apparition ultimately departs the residence hall and disappears from my view as she passes through a gateway outside. I sneak back inside the dormitory and Viviana is sleeping soundly in her bed. For a moment, I think the young woman I saw is her because of the dark lilac, but how can that be if she is right here? I think myself mad as I have been running on unrestful sleep. I do not feel safe in this dormitory after this encounter.

Apparitions do not exist! This is my mind playing tricks on me; this is because of no sleep but still it's as if I saw her doppelgänger. I did not get to see the young woman's face directly. Why dark lilac though? So strange.

I have to work on myself, I have to get better, or else, I won't be able to love Viviana completely. The figure in my bathroom, the first time I thought I saw Viviana at the crossroads, and now this young woman haunting the halls. They are hallucinations; they must be! This woman before me is real—I know this, I must focus on self-care. I need space—she can't know of my condition; it will be too much for her because of what she is going through. I will not be good enough for her if I can't conquer the darkness in my brain. She needs me though; she is grateful that I stay with her. I-I can't disappoint her. Ugh, I don't know how to keep myself strong and steady. I am on the verge of a complete shut down because my brain cannot comprehend everything. I need help, therapy, and solitude. I am melancholy, bordering insanity.

This is an outcry for help. I am losing everything. I want help but I don't know how to ask. As a man, I feel as if I cannot express this shadow within me because it destroys all that I hold dear. This is a whole new level of depression I have never known before. I am ashamed of expressing this through audio because the judgments and negativity I will receive upon me will worsen my condition. Yet I feel selfish for recording this because of everything going on. This is the most fragile gloom I am in.

Viviana leaves me after only eight weeks. This routine happens again and again as she finds it impossible to live with a surly boy. Finally, the president of the dormitory, who is known for her ability to get along with everyone, discovers me staying in the girl's dormitory. I do everything I can to talk with her, but my efforts are futile. Viviana is embittered as well as withdrawn after the incident, and she seems to resent the presence of my kind heart. Sometimes, I wonder if I misunderstand her embitterment as something else. I don't know. I feel like a burden because of the demons devouring my thoughts and demeanor.

After all my efforts at friendship and romance fail, I am growing depressed and despondent. I pack my belongings and prepare to leave. Just as I am about to depart, Viviana, who does not know of my imminent departure, returns to her room. With a look of defiance, she says, "So you can't stand me either—like all the rest of the stuck-up people here. I was beginning to think you really wanted me to be your friend and lover, but you hate me just like the rest. I'm pregnant; you're the father!"

"Viv…"

"Well, I'm glad to be rid of you! Take your things and go! But I'll tell you one thing, my dear; for the rest of your life, you'll regret leaving this room." I am disturbed by this bitter outburst, but in the midst of my many struggles against my own mind, I soon replay Viviana's prophetic words.

I am a sad boy, abandoned by the one person I believed to be my lover and friend. I form the habit of wandering into rooms where the other boys and girls are congregating, but my presence casts a chill upon the groups, and they soon find flimsy excuses for leaving me alone. Marcin, Mitch, and Ionel invite me back to hang out with them as a distraction for the trauma I am going through, but my mind—my mind always thinks about Viviana and the child she carries—my child! She is nowhere to be found. She is not on campus, not with Ionel, or anywhere. She is like the lady of dark lilac from her dormitory whom I saw vanish at the gateway. I give up calling her and texting her. I wallow in my solitude because it's my only consolation.

Then, with a feeling of alienation from all humankind, I return on campus to Viviana's solitary sleeping quarters, where I wrap myself in her purple bedspread and retreat from the whole world. Her scent comforts me but drives me mad. Lilac; dark lilac! I want her here! The place where we made love—all of this and more, I'm even more erratic. I wait until the lights are out, and then I visit one dormitory after another, never saying a word but staring into space as if I'm in a trance.

The time passes; I take to stalking up and down the halls during the darkest hours of the night. With my student id and Viviana's, I wander both dormitories. Often, I alarm the girls and boys by opening and closing their doors, then hurrying away to resume my pitiful promenade. Now listener, I am in her dorm room speaking to you. I have not appeared for classes or meals all day, I assume my roommate Mitch and others are looking for me. They are too late now as I have been speaking on borrowed time—the deed is already done. This was my life; a life once lived. All spins-round-round-round. This blanket shall be my cloak. May it wrap me in a death so lithe.

Chapter 24

*"She wanted — what some people want throughout life —
a grief that should deeply touch her, and thus humanize
and make her capable of sympathy."
— Nathaniel Hawthorne, The Scarlet Letter*

The recording muffles, statics to its end, and Oscar's story is over. I yank the earbuds out of my ears as the front door wails open.

"What are you doing?" My eyes shoot wide apart, and I jump; it's Viviana. Tears trickle down her cheeks and I wonder how much of it she heard.

"How long were you listening?"

"Not long, but I overheard a voice I have not heard in years."

"I'm sorry."

Grief, anger, and despair grips her demeanor. She shuts her eyes, her body shakes, and she sobs.

"Where did you get that recording? Where did you?"

"I..."

"Answer me!" she screams.

The birds chirp to bring in the morning light. Neither of us say anything. Viviana plummets onto the porch floorboards.

She clasps her hands, buries her face into them, and cries. I walk toward her, sit down, and wrap my arms around her. The touch of her face against my chest is hot and tender. Tears stain my dress and soak upon my breasts.

"Shh…" I say, gracing my hand through her short hair.

The sunlight creeps upon the porch and barely touches us. Viviana sniffles and lays the side of her head against my breast.

"Mitch told me what happened to Oscar. Mitch, as he neared my dorm-room said he noticed pools of red shooting out into the corridor from the room's transom. Opening the door, he screamed and fainted. Girls from all over the fourth floor of Foxrice rushed from their rooms to see what was wrong. Oscar was found on the floor of my room, dressed in my dark lilac hoodie and draped in my purple bedspread, having committed suicide by slashing his wrists. This happened so long ago, but Mitch told me last night that students at Timber Creek each year on the date of Oscar's death shine rays of violet light down from the transom of my old room."

"Mitch was here last night?"

"Yeah, he was standing next to Marcin and Ionel as I did my performance."

"I'm sorry. Last night is a bit of a fog."

I stroke her shoulder and my chin rests upon her head.

"You scared me to death last night!" Viviana's head shoots up to my face. Her blue eyes glisten at me. "You fell, and I thought the worst! Marcin checked your pulse and said you passed out. He told me how strange you acted around him when I left you two alone."

I cling to her tightly for comfort. "I've never done drugs, but this felt like a bad trip, or what I would imagine being on a hallucinogenic drug feels like. I feel horrid because everyone must have thought I was on something due to how bizarrely I acted. I was paranoid and I couldn't be still. Everybody at the party passed in a blur as I was trying to figure everything out."

We groan at the same time together in double stereo. We laugh together and stare into each other's eyes. The desire to kiss her creeps into my mind. I bite my lips as she speaks.

"It's obvious to me that you must have hallucinated, and I know this has happened to you on more than one occasion. I knew during the entire day yesterday that you've been tired and groggy leading up to this, but I thought you had to be seriously sleep deprived to actually see and feel frightened by things that aren't there."

We don't speak then. Our eyes gaze at each other until mine closes. I anchor my neck forward, my upper lip tingles from the touch of her breath, and our lips touch in a tender kiss. I finally got what I always wanted. She shies her face away from me and bolts out of our embrace. My eyes jolt open, confused by the sudden departure. She clasps her forearm against her mouth and coughs. With her other hand, she pries open the front door and rushes inside. I lunge after her with worry and panic.

Her coughing and choking echoes throughout the house. The water from the faucet flows violently. I listen to her spit as I stand between the entrance of the kitchen and living room. She vigorously scrubs her forearm, shakes it, and water splashes everywhere. Trickles of blood seep out of her mouth as she frantically scouts the kitchen shelves for something. I'm in shock; my body trembles with fright and I don't know whether or not to move forward. She grips a pill bottle as the pills jiggle inside, and she twists the cap with great force. The cap falls onto the ground. She breathes wildly and lunges her palm against her mouth. The water from the faucet continues to run and she drinks from it.

A few minutes go by. Viviana still gulps the water, and then pushes the handle back to its position for the water to stop. She leans against the sink; water drops drip into the sink as she catches her breath. She grips a tea-towel to wipe the blood from her mouth, and throws it across the room, shielding her face with her hands. I glare at the bottle and see its yellow color shrouding the redness of the pill. I remember the other day when I first saw her take a red pill.

I walk to her and embrace her. I kiss her head and smell the scent of lilac in her hair. Her arms wrap around me holding me tight. The tightness of her embrace breaks through to my emotions as I sob with her. Viviana stops sobbing and caresses my cheek.

"Alice, it's okay."

"I got what I've always wanted which was a kiss from you and my death infested lips ruined it!"

"Aw, no… Alice, no. That's not true," she strokes my cheekbone and I look into her eyes. They are somber but tender with affection.

"That's your sleep deprivation talking. You're not death infested. You are just you and there is nothing more sublime than that."

I chuckle with my sobs breaking apart. "Good one, using my word." Viviana wipes the tears from my cheeks. She smiles at me and a wave of calmness starts to seep within me.

"I overheard the part in Oscar's recording about my condition when I revealed myself to him."

I sniffle and listen intently to her shallow breaths.

"I have lupus… It's a disease that occurs when the body's immune system attacks the tissues and organs. It's why when I attended Timber Creek, I always shrouded myself in my hoodie because sunlight triggers it. It's something I've been struggling with most of my life, just like my mom. It affected her brain and central nervous system more, but for me, the disease really inflames my lungs. Sometimes, the inflammation in my chest cavity lining makes breathing painful. Blood seeps into my lungs and causes other complications."

My breath shallows and deflates as I learn about Viviana's disease. She runs her fingers through my dark hair as her mouth opens. "It's why I was on chemo and I had to leave university because I did not have the strength to go back. The chemo drugs helped control my overactive immune system, but as I've told you before, I aborted my baby because of the treatments. Since then, I haven't had any physical flare ups, but lately I've been on rifampin because of the infection lupus gave me."

"Which is?" I ask.

"Tuberculosis."

I jolt back from her and terror grips the cockles of my heart with shallow breaths.

"Alice, don't worry… I have latent TB. I haven't been coughing for three or more weeks, but this is the first time I've coughed up blood."

My breathing is loud, and I say with a low moan, "What can I do?"

Viviana reassures me by the serenity in her voice, "You're doing enough by listening. You're good enough, but I advise some space for your safety. Not because I want to be away from you, but because I want to make sure my TB does not change to active.”

I inhale through my nostrils and exhale through my pursed lips. “I understand. You want to protect me.

“I do. You’re important to me.”

“As you are to me.”

She flashes a warm smile. “Good.”

We stare at each other until Viviana crosses her arms to think aloud, “I believe someone has a birthday today…”

Her voice is smoky as my eyebrows lift up to wonder what she is up to. “Before you go home, let me give Ionel’s and my present to you.” She signals me to follow her by tilting her head towards the direction to go. We open the door to the landing with the side door and the entrance to where the basement is. I close the door behind me because of the rules. Viviana knocks upon the basement door. She knocks again.

“Ugh, one second…” says a voice. Moments later, the door opens slightly to reveal that it’s Marcin.

“Oh, hey Vivi. Ionel is sleeping and I just woke up from the comfy couch. What’s up?”

She chuckles by clasping her hand against her mouth. “Too much fun drinking last night?”

Marcin's eyes are despondent but then the light in them clicks. "Oh, yeah… It's why I crashed down here. Hangover." He looks over at me and asks, "Hey, how are you feeling?"

"Oh, I'm better…"

"Eh, still looks like you could use some sleep," he mutters.

"It's Alice's birthday today, Marcin," chimes Viviana.

"Oh, wow… Really?"

Silence.

"Geez, excuse my slow reaction… This headache is killing me. Happy birthday Alice!" He embraces me compassionately. After our embrace he says, "I wish you everything you deserve."

"Did my brother finish wrapping Alice's gift?"

"Ah, I believe so… Let me wake him up."

Marcin leaves and the door stays unshut. We hear him whispering, "Ionel. Ionel…"

"Huh… What?"

"Your sister wants you to get Alice's present."

"Do you know what time it is?"

Viviana rolls her eyes at me. Her eyes squint as she drums her fingers against the door.

"Ionel, I know it's early, but Alice has to get going, please!" shouts Viviana.

He groans and Viviana rolls her eyes while shaking her head. "Alright. Alright, give me a second." A belt clinks with a swooshing sound. Paper crumbles and Ionel opens the door.

"Come on in," he gestures with elongated words. Viviana and I walk inside and sit upon the couch. "Here, you go Alice. Happy birthday!"

I grip the present from Ionel's hands. I chuckle under my breath because of the not so neat and crumbled paper. "You wrapped this yourself?" I inquire while studying the wrapping.

Ionel grits his teeth, "Yeah, I'm not the best at wrapping presents."

"There's so much tape," chimes Viviana, laughing under her breath.

Marcin sits down next to me and watches. Ionel's eyes fill with disgust at his sister's comment.

"At least I know it's you who wrapped it Ionel and that means a lot to me," I chime to ease him.

He smiles. "I'm glad you feel that way about it."

"Well, go on and open it already!" buzzes Marcin lightly clapping his hands.

I rip the paper to shreds and gasp at what it is. I take in shallow breaths, "It can't be…" I mutter.

"You guys didn't… Oh…" I grip the book they had given to me.

"It's *Frankenstein*. The copy from Macbacks… The one I held at the store… You got it?"

I look around me. All of them are smiling and pleased by the expression on my face. Delight takes me over as I observe my copy of the book. It's a cloth-bound hardcopy in gray. Printed throughout the cover are anatomical hearts which display the various arteries and parts of the heart. It is a Penguin Classics edition. Its colorful, tactile cloth with its foil stamped design fuels my eagerness to read it as I grace its surface with the touch of my fingertips.

Viviana swings in to hug me quickly and Ionel runs his fingers across my back.

"She loves it," adds Ionel, withdrawing back his hand and putting it upon his lap.

"I told you she would," follows Viviana.

"Yeah, you were nagging at me yesterday to go get it." Viviana flashes her hands forward to my direction. "Well, see? It paid off to get it didn't it?"

Ionel forms a smile. "Indeed."

"Aye, you like gothic literature Alice?"

My eyes peer over to Marcin who asked me this. "Yeah, of course!"

"Hm… Well." Marcin presses the side of his hand against and under his nose. "I believe one of the pagan shops in Lakewood is hosting an Edgar Allan Poe impersonator!"

My mouth drops open and my eyes are wild with excitement. I inhale, muffle a screech under my breath, and squeal, "Really? When and where?" I grip his shoulders and squeeze them as the excitement and happiness radiates the fiber of my being.

Marcin laughs out loud from my mannerisms. "Ugh, I'm trying to remember, but I know the impersonator is Shawn-someone… I can't recall his last name, but I'll ask around and let you know asap!"

"Oh, I didn't hear of this," implies Viviana.

"Please let me know!" I chime in flabbergasted.

"Okay, okay, I will…" Marcin laughs while waving his hands in front of him. "I live in Lakewood and I spend a lot of time between both shops, so I will ask around. I could have sworn that one of the places is hosting an event where this Poe impersonator reads tarot cards and recites some of Poe's poetry."

Viviana laughs abruptly. "Let me guess… He uses the Poe tarot deck?"

"Now honestly… Viv, you got that Poe deck because of me through another friend who knows the author. That Poe deck is not even published yet; you have a proof copy. Besides, this impersonator used the Moonology Oracle deck last time he was in town. He's got the gimmick down pat in my opinion."

"I'll let Alice be the judge of that," pings Ionel with his index finger pointing up.

"I think it will be good for Alice to meet this Poe impersonator, Marcin," adds Viviana rising from the couch.

"You got it!" Marcin stares at me plainly. "Do you have Facebook or Messenger? I'll give you the deets when I know more information."

"Yes, Alice Reaper!"

Marcin laughs while swiping his phone and typing. "Reaper? That's your real last name?"

"Yes."

"That-is-amazing! Poe meets Reaper... Totally needs to happen. This you?"

He flashes his phone at me. I see my profile picture. It's a picture of Viktor and I together in the woods. I'm sitting upon a rock as he is sitting next to me with his tongue sticking out. Quick flashbacks stream inside my brain. I jolt, grunt, and press my hand against my forehead.

"Yeah…" I answer.

"Wait, let me see!" Viviana snatches the phone. She studies the phone as I remember Camila taking the photo.

"Aw, Alice it's you and Viktor! I love your smile. It's bright, happy, and beautiful. It makes me smile." Viviana grins from cheek to cheek as it's contagious and she can't fight back the urge to smile. Viviana taps the screen. "You look younger too…," she adds, handing back the phone to Marcin.

"Alright, enough eye screwing with each other!" roars Marcin jokingly and playfully.

"What?" I remark.

"Oh, come on! I see how you two stare at each other all googly-eyed. The sexual intimacy and passion are felt from here between you two." Marcin's eyebrows dance up and down after his words.

My face beats red and hot.

Viviana stutters but is speechless.

"Oh, my…" elongates Marcin, deeply changing his voice to a lower tone of tease.

"Okay, not in my room please Marcin…"

"What, they are eye-screwing each other…"

"Dude!" cries Ionel.

Marcin chuckles under his breath. "Well, I better get going. I'll message you Alice!" He hugs me and Viviana but does a small wave to Ionel.

"Blessed be," says Viviana.

"Blessed be," replies Marcin as he shuts the door behind us.

Chapter 25

The side door shuts. The three of us walk back into the kitchen and find Mr. Dragomir sipping his cup of coffee. The light from the window with the dreamcatcher shines behind his figure. His eyes drift into space, and he holds his coffee as if in a deep thought. His hair is tousled from just waking up.

"Oh, good morning!" he glees cheerfully as he hears the door shut. We all smile at him.

"Morning, papa," squeaks Viviana.

"How are you?" I cluck sweetly.

"I am good. I am happy to hear you sound better." He sips his coffee.

"Yeah, I don't recall much of the night…"

Mr. Dragomir scratches his brow. "I am quite sure. You had us worried. I recommend going home and getting a lot of restful sleep."

"Yeah, that's the plan," pops Ionel while searching for his keys. His footsteps echo throughout the house and exits through the living room.

I putter my words out. "I feel bad to go back, especially with it being my birthday."

Mr. Dragomir's eyes grow wide apart. "Oh… Happy birthday. You are always welcome here," he sets his coffee upon the counter, walks, and extends his arms at me. "You have done so much for my children, and I am grateful."

I place my new book upon the counter as he wraps his arms around me. An instant feeling of warmth and comfort forms a smile on my face. The feeling is different from my father's embrace when he gave me the news of his illness. My father's hug was a heavy weight, but Mr. Dragomir's is as delicate as a feather. In this moment, I think of Mr. Dragomir as a second father to me.

"Happy to come back," I chime, breaking our embrace.

"Good. I look forward to it." As he says this, I smile.

"Ah, there's that smile," flirts Viviana with a grin and a sway of her body.

My face tinges red and tender from the sound of her voice. "What's with you suddenly?" I ask.

She playfully laughs and softly runs her fingers in my hair. "Oh… Your head is on fire."

I giggle to fight the obvious. "Well, yes… What do you think is going to happen?"

She smiles tenderly. "We'll see, won't we?"

"Oh, man… I'm going to puke rainbows! Sheesh…"

Viviana steps away from me and laughs out loud from Ionel's commentary in the background. My eyes meander to the floor.

Ionel jingles his keys and promptly walks into the kitchen. He halts at the door ready to leave, and inquires, "Do you have all you need?"

My mouth opens but a crunching sound echoes from the kitchen. My attention follows the sound and both cats are eating from their bowls.

"They have the right idea," says Mr. Dragomir searching his kitchen for food. I go over to the cats and pet them. Mr. Wednesday chomps in his bowl without acknowledging my pets.

"Bye Mr. Wednesday!" I exclaim dulcetly. After I speak, tiny punctures jilt on my bare legs. I glare down and see Revenant climbing my leg. I chuckle. "Ow, that kind of hurts." I pick him up and Revenant nudges my face.

"Oh, wow… He's never done that to anyone before," chimes Viviana with her mouth awestruck.

"I've never seen that cat nudge anyone with affection," adds Ionel impatiently.

Viviana turns to him. "Is that jealousy?"

"No, just want to go before I barf more cutesy rainbows…"

Viviana grins a smirk. "It's jealousy."

"I hope to see you soon Rev," I say with a tiny kiss, and after, I deposit him down near his food bowl. Viviana grabs my book as

I walk toward the door. She holds out the book with a smile and tender eyes. I grip the book and flash a warm smile back.

"I hope to see you soon, Viv."

"Don't worry, we shall, but I would like to ride with you both."

"Very well, let's go," ends Ionel.

I look into Viviana's eyes as Ionel opens the door. As the door creaks, my eyes scan hers and I see something new—fear. Internally, it frightens me, the battle raging in her head. I take the book from her hand and an ill feeling brews. She has never asked to ride with us and that look, that look of dread I've never seen in her discomforts me. I desire to say something and study her expression more, but the door is open. It's time to leave before the cats escape.

We shut the door to the kitchen behind us. My eyes never leave Viviana. She doesn't look at me—there's definitely something. My mind wanders and races—I think about her illness; her coughing up blood. It's a terrifying thing. The way she quickly puts on her leather-fur collar coat fuels my angst.

Viviana jars the door wide open and a cool breeze plays upon my cheeks. Ionel unlocks his car, presses the button for the front seat to slide forward and I get in. Viviana sits next to me and pulls the front seat back. I stare at her. She smiles. The dead silence speaks more than any expression, thought, or word conveyed. My stomach knots and twists to the thought of this being the last time

I'm here. I clench my dress as if I'm driving to a funeral. I gaze upon my bare pale legs. Without notice, I jolt. Viviana's head lays in my lap and her scent of lilac looms in my nose. My heart aches for her touch as I caress and stroke her back underneath her jacket. Ionel's car roars and caterwauls forward to exit the driveway. Viviana suspires a content sigh to my affections and her laying upon me. She buries her face against my leg; the fumes of the car creep into the back. Nobody says anything. Not a word— nothing…

Halfway through the ride, Viviana lifts her head and speaks, "Tessa told me how you got up in her face." She laughs, "I've never seen her that mad to the point she was like a tomato. It doesn't sound like you to sink your teeth into someone harshly."

I nod. "Yeah, everything around me was just agitating— unreal…"

"I bet from not getting any sleep; your mood was quite *moody*."

Silence again. I don't want to go back. Viviana leans down on me again and out of reaction I reach my arm over her. Her head falls against my breast and my hand grasps hers. My heart pounds and anxiety brews. Why is she this affectionate? It's not like her. I urge myself to ask. I squeeze the *Frankenstein* book in my other hand, but no words form from my mouth. I shirk from asking because I don't want this moment to end. She's my everything; my one. At least, that's what my heart desires.

My eyes glance at the rearview mirror. Ionel catches me watching the reflection of his eyes and face. He sees me, but there's no expression from him. It worries me. Usually, he says something when we've been in the car together, but this time he is silent. The car jerks violently to a halt. My hand grips and digs into Viviana's skin. My breath dissipates to empty, and our bodies slightly lunge forward. I gasp hard—almost to a scream. My back thrashes against the leather seat. I feel a smidge of whiplash.

Ionel yells and yowls a raucous rage, *"Głupi palant!"* He pounds his fist; his car horn wails.

"What? What happened?" says Viviana, rising in a daze.

The car in front of us has tail lights that are as bright as blood. It makes me recall my last nightmare—the car crash. I squeeze my eyes shut to fight back the tears as the sensations of my body tingle. The flashbacks of the nightmare trigger the pain which I had felt from the vision. The shards digging into flesh, the pressure of the vehicle crushing us, and Ionel dying right before my eyes. These sensations trigger my brain to remember the feminine shadow within the tunnel. The redness of the car's taillights—the red eyes!

"Alice, what's wrong? Don't cry…" Viviana caresses my cheek in the most delicate manner as if I'm made of shards.

I stare at her and mewl, "The tunnel—the shadow…"

"A nightmare you had?"

I nod.

She embraces me as I study our surroundings. We are in the Maple Heights business district—almost to Bedford. All the stop lights in the district don't change to red. Viviana comforts me until we reach the parking lot of the Glen Valley Apartments. Ionel stops the car and shifts the gear into park. He groans to get over the close fender-bender from earlier. Viviana presses the button behind the front seat. It whooshes forward—she gets out. I follow with my new book close to me as Ionel opens his door.

Viviana and I stare at each other not knowing what to say as Ionel walks over to me. He hugs me.

"Just get some sleep. You'll be fine—don't ever be afraid of the demons inside your head." I flash a smile at him from his encouraging words.

"As of someone gently rapping, rapping at my chamber door." I wink.

Ionel chuckles, "'Tis some visitor' I mutter, 'tapping at my chamber door—"

"Only this and nothing more," I end. We embrace.

"When the semester is over, we should get a reading list going and talk about the books we decide to read."

I break our embrace and stare at him. "Indeed. Text me about what you're interested in."

Ionel straightens his posture, smiles, and flashes a thumb's up, and replies, "Sounds good!"

I stare back at Viviana—her eyes take me in like no other. Ionel takes his leave and I hear the driver's side door slam.

"Sometimes to let go of the past, you have to face it again."

"Face it again? That sounds like a lifetime of a deathlike slumber."

Viviana flashes a warm but a lively smile. She shakes her head. "No, Alice. It's not a deathlike slumber. We're here in each other's lives because it is teaching us how to let go."

"Oh?"

She laughs at my response. "You look like a cute, lost kitten. You'll know what I mean."

"If you say so."

She kisses me without warning; our lips lock. I embrace her and feel the touch of her arms wrapping around my waist. She breaks our kiss away and bounces lively back to Ionel's car and piles onto the front seat.

"I love you," she proclaims.

I bat my eyes in shock, not only from those words, but the quickness of her swooping in for the kiss and then breaking it off. I'm tongue tied—speechless.

"Don't worry, I know," she adds with a lively smile. Ionel's car roars, the tires squeal, and off they go. Smoke lingers behind a trail of rock and gravel—gone.

As the car drives away from the distance, Viviana's words ring in my head, *"Don't worry, I know."* I repeat and mutter, "I know… Know what?"

I look to the direction of my apartment building then back at *Frankenstein* in my hands— I smile with an idea. I stride to my apartment, walk inside it, shower, and change into new clothes. I rummage my dresser into a drawer I rarely open. I dig inside and pull out a random black t-shirt. The shirt's scent is stale as I unfold it. I gasp forgetting I have this.

"Hello, Amy Lee."

The black shirt illustrates the image of Evanescence's album The Open Door. "Eh, hope it still fits…"

In seconds, blackness swallows my eyes from the shirt over my head as I slip it on. The shirt is tight, but fits. I smile as I stand tall and gaze at how well the shirt fits around my body "I wonder…" I mumble, searching through my closet.

"Oh, wow! My old jean jacket!" I eagerly toss the jacket around my shoulders and push my arms through the sleeves—it fits! I glance at the mirror and sway my body from side to side. I observe my jacket; a Levi's dark indigo denim with some discoloration. My hands race through my hair as it falls perfectly upon my shoulders. I smile—for once, alone.

I spend hours working on myself—setting the makeup, making funny faces as I apply eyeliner and eyeshadow. I hum to myself as I finish up—happy. Happy about Viviana's words even though a part of me is worried about her health. What matters most are my feelings along with hers. The way she said those three words are different from Camila—they had to be. I can't even recall how Camila used to say those words to me. I think about Viviana's words, *"Don't worry, I know."* Maybe she knows that I love her too! Maybe that's what she meant by those words.

The music blares as I put all my makeup away, and Evanescence's song "Sweet Sacrifice" plays. Amy's voice sings, *"Fear is only in our minds taking over all the time,"* as the words trigger a thought: my greatest fear lingers in my mind. I snatch *Frankenstein* and catch glimpses of its cover with the hearts. The book's themes about death flash in my brain as I hear Amy's voice sing in a whisper background, *"Our burning ashes blacken the day."* Death—its burning ashes blackened me—it's in my mind— my heart was as still as the hearts on this cover—my clinical death.

Facing this thought, all the happiness I just felt earlier withers and drains me. I gasp for air, clutch my hand against my chest, and remember the final moments I had. The fire, ashes, and shards— the poisonous fumes and smoke drowning me, lulling me to a deathlike slumber. The shadow—carrying me so lithe—and then, nothing….

Yet, I was aware of what was going on around me while in this state—including medics trying to save me, and hearing conversations—trapped inside my body—them, announcing my heart was not beating and not responding to defibrillation. Awakening—my scream—the pain. In the ambulance, I rushed out as the drivers sat in the front while starting the vehicle. They thought I had died after their attempts to revive me. I rushed, escaped through the doors, and saw my old home charred in ruins. My father's remains ran through my fingers—all ashes of a life I once lived—I should have stayed dead—I'm afraid. Afraid every time I sleep—I won't ever wake up.

270

Chapter 26

"The boundaries which divide Life from Death are at
best shadowy and vague. Who shall say where
one ends, and where the other begins?"
– Edgar Allan Poe, The Premature Burial

November 2, 2019

The rest of my birthday was peaceful. I traversed the Bedford Viaduct Park and found a rock to sit upon to read my book. The rock was smooth and large enough to sit comfortably upon with the view of the waterfall in front of me. The scent of water and mist delighted my senses; it was the perfect spot for deep meditation. As I began opening my book, there was a scribble which caught my attention. It was in Viviana's handwriting, "I'll be your Shelley's heart—Love, Viviana." A smile spread from cheek to cheek—I gazed out to my surroundings, reflecting on her little love scribble. How romantic, but cheesy I thought.

I recalled a British Literature course from my undergrad with a special emphasis upon Romanticism. Viviana's romantic gesture was based off of Percy Shelley's death.

His heart survived cremation because of how his disease preserved his heart from the fire and ashes. Mary Shelley kept his heart until her death. I laughed while connecting these ideas together but stopped once my eyes wandered to my right because of a train clicking along a set of tracks nearby. As I observed the train speeding by and wailing its horn, my eyes found the tunnel. Fear jilted because the tunnel in the distance made me remember the tunnel in my dream. The train was gone, but its wheels quaked and rumbled in my ears. I ambled towards the tunnel but there was no easy way of getting to it. I took a flirty selfie with the streaming river as my background and sent it to Viviana. She responded— "Aww, you're smiling!! :) You're so beautiful." That was my birthday...

AR

November 8th

I've been reading Frankenstein—enjoying it! It's nothing like the movie renditions Hollywood has done—they don't do it justice! I've been slowly getting into a groove to get out every day, explore, and read outside. It's been helping but it's still a struggle. The tunnel in the park terrifies me—one second I desire to explore it, but other times I don't. I wonder if it's accessible on the other side. I'll have to find out. Viviana's advice to face it again rings in my head—I worry about her. I haven't heard from her in a few days. I've been busy catching up on school and work. Marcin texted me! The Poe impersonator is doing a small event on November 12th—I must go!

AR

November 12th

So many emotions running through me as I write this…Where do I start? I've been texting Viviana and sometimes calling her, but she doesn't respond. I asked her if she wanted to go with me to see the Poe impersonator, but she never answered. It's not like her—I'm terrified something happened! Ionel has not responded to me either…

I took a bus to Lakewood and traversed the sidewalks of Madison. Lakewood reminds me of Coventry a bit. It has a lively atmosphere on its own with various shops and restaurants up and down the streets. In one of these shops was the place

I needed to be. The building was hidden from the side of the street; its size was small, worn, and old. A dry-erase board stood out upon the sidewalk in front of me. It read, "An evening with Poe and more..." Excitement brewed deep within me as I wandered inside the open door. There he was! Sitting in the back at a creaky desk with a white candle burning upon it. A few people gathered around him as I listened to him scribbling with a feathered and quilted pen. He took a sip of something in a dark opaque beer bottle. The label was scratched out as if it was madly peeled. My ghostly presence wandered in closer, seeing him pass back papers he had written upon to other spectators who came to visit him.

The incense was strong in this place—I couldn't believe it. This Poe impersonator wore a white dress shirt with a black, old fashioned frock coat. A short black cravat was wrapped around his neck; he had a mustache and his hair was jet black. His face was pale, and his cheekbones were slightly sunken in. A small space formed out from the crowd as I blended right in. He glared as his eyes met mine. I said to him, "Hope that's not real alcohol."

He stared only to say, "I have absolutely no pleasure in stimulants in which I sometimes so madly indulge." He paused and studied me. "A fellow Virginian?"

I smiled at him, taking notice of my accent. "Yes, I am."

He nodded his head as I too was impressed by this impersonator's Virginian accent. "What is your name?" he asked, sliding a blank sheet of paper in front of him. He readied his pen awaiting to hear me speak.

"Alice Reaper."

For a moment, I thought he broke character by the surprise in his eyes and by his glare back at me. He bit his lips as if he wanted to say something, but he remained in character. His eyes wandered back and forth between me and the paper. He remained collective and silent. He scribbled. When he handed me the paper, he nodded his head and there was a sympathy in his eyes, but another person gathered in the crowd and I automatically got out.

I exited the building reading the scribble he had written: "Alice, never to suffer would never to have been blessed—Edgar Allan Poe." I wandered aimlessly—why of all things did he write that? I remembered the first name of the impersonator and decided to look up the name Shawn on Facebook. To my discovery—a shock gripped me as it made ~~the~~ sense—the look he gave me as I said my name. Shawn Doyle—A mutual follower on my father's old business page. He has the same sunken face. "You'll be ok Alice; your father is at peace." That memory at my father's funeral—he was there! Professor Doyle from UVA—he was part of the Raven's Society and helped preserve the upkeep on Poe's residence at the university! Maybe he was a friend of my mother when she attended UVA? She dropped out to have me! I'm sure they bonded over books and literature. He saw me! My mother's face and eyes—that's why he broke character and bit his lips.

I scoured his Facebook more thoroughly. He no longer works at UVA but teaches at Oberlin College. I searched for his academic profile through Oberlin and found him! I still can't believe it—I can't process this as I'm writing. I'll have to send him an email—get together to meet—talk. I wonder what he knows of my mother.

AR

November 13th

Professor Doyle responded! It really was him as the Poe impersonator—he said he does impersonations of his favorite literary authors as a side gig for fun. He said he started teaching at Oberlin about a year ago. He heard about the Reaper Funeral Home officially shutting down. I told him how I disappeared off the map and social media for two years. He said in his message that he drove several times between Charlottesville and Boydton to visit my mother. He even drove sometime after my father's funeral to my neighbor's house—five miles down from where my old home was. He wanted to visit me, but I was no longer there when he had arrived. My neighbor told him that I left a note that I had moved to begin life anew. In my letter, I made it clear I wanted nothing to do with my old town and home. Bedford, Ohio is the cheapest—yet farthest I could get away from Virginia. I drove my father's old car here—but traded it in for cash to deposit and live. Though now, I'm realizing I haven't been living. Professor Doyle said we can zoom. I find this professor strange and wonder how close he was to my mom. Still no word from Viviana and lonel...

AR

November 18th

I've been so busy that I haven't written about any nightmares. I sleep, but not restfully. All is black but once my body drifts, it jolts awake. Something in my brain is not allowing me restful sleep. I'm too afraid of dying in my sleep. Ever since my clinical death, I have always felt my soul is in shards. It's like when I cheated death, it took parts of me I can never get back. The pain I felt when I had awakened from death's slumber—this insomnia; it's unreal. I have to fight it— I must focus on self-care. Oscar's story reminds me so. Marcin called me through Messenger. He, too, is worried about Ionel and Viviana. They've not communicated with him. Something is going on—I must—

The zoom screen on my laptop opens to video. I place my pen next to me, fix my hair, and shut my journal. It's time for the meeting with Professor Doyle. I click the audio button from my computer to activate the sound.

"Good afternoon!" he says.

I smile upon seeing his face. "Hello professor!"

He nods as I study his surroundings. The sunlight shines behind him illuminating various stickers and posters of authors and quotes by them hanging on the wall. I know it's his office hours.

"I am just finishing up lunch, so don't mind me," he adds while crumbling wrappers.

"It's been two years…" I say.

"Almost going on three now I'd imagine. When did you leave Virginia?"

I click my tongue to recall and my eyes jolt. "Oh, wow… It will be three years ago this Thursday!"

"Ah, a week before Thanksgiving." There's a pause. "The first and last time I saw you was at your father's funeral."

I bat my eyes to refocus on the conversation. "Yes, you were one of the few who approached me."

"You remind me so much of your mother. You have her eyes, hair, and skin tone. But I also see your father's face there too."

I nod. "Is that why you almost broke character as Poe?"

He leans back into his chair. "Yes, like a specter I thought I saw a ghostly image of Lillian when I first saw you, but it wasn't until you said your name that spooked me." He laughs. "Ah, as the famous words of Poe, *'the death of a beautiful woman, is unquestionably the most poetical topic in the world.'*"

I bite my lips as they sink into my mouth. "Your reaction when you first saw me and how you are speaking with me now—were you close with my mother?"

"Yes, before she moved to Boydton with your father. Your mother and I saw each other as friends, and I would come visit that old house in Boydton before you were born. We discussed literature in her library even though she could no longer continue her education. I was in graduate school so I'd come over once a month because of time and distance. She's the one who encouraged me to go for my PhD."

My eyebrows sparse apart. "Why weren't you around during my time growing up?"

Professor Doyle sighs heavily. "It was your father. After Lillian died, he shunned everyone including me. He cut off all ties of communication and became a hermit. I was no longer welcomed. It wasn't until I saw on the news about the house fire and found the obituary online for your father that I decided to reach out again."

My breath is brittle, and I grip my blue jeans while stating, "I posted my father's obituary as public because everyone adored him in the Boydton community. I'm glad I made it public for you to find it…" I breathe in to control my emotions. "You drove two hours just to attend my father's funeral even though he shunned you?"

He smiles and nods. "Yes, I felt obligated because of your mother. She would have wanted me to go because she would have wanted to know if you were alright. When she was pregnant with you, she wouldn't stop talking to me about how excited she was to meet you."

I clasp my hands together and plump my elbows upon my table; I puff my cheeks while resting my hands underneath my chin. Air deflates out from my cheeks. "So, why did you drive back after dad's funeral to visit me?"

Professor Doyle stares at me plainly. "It's because of what your mother asked of me the last time I saw her alive. In her library, we discussed the last few chapters of *Frankenstein* because that's what she was reading at the time. The book was a nice distraction from my master's thesis. As she and I were wrapping things up, I told her the good news about my master's defense coming up and that UVA had accepted me for the following year for their English PhD program. She told me she would love to come see me defend, but you would arrive sometime at the beginning of November. So, she wished me luck and then she asked me to be your godfather."

My mouth drops. "My godfather?"

"Yes, I was supposed to be. Your mother asked me, and I agreed, but when she died giving birth to you, your father had other plans and made Vincent Reaper and Ophelia Reaper your godparents."

I shut my eyes hearing the names of my family relatives and the flashback of my nightmare dancing with father in the attic—

them turning into ashes. I shake my head to rid myself of the horrid image. "Why didn't my dad want you as my godfather?"

"Because I am not kin of blood."

A knock reverberates through my computer's speakers. Professor Doyle's attention gravitates to his door and his eyes wander off screen. "Oh, yes. One moment," he says with his index finger pointing upward. He looks back at me. "We will speak more, Alice. I am proud of you—stay strong." We wave as I click the button to end the meeting. I shut my laptop, stare into space, and dive my head into my arms upon the table.

Chapter 27

"That it will never come again is what makes life so sweet."
— Emily Dickinson

December 4th

The semester is coming to a close. I've caught up with my workload, but I'm unsure how Ionel is taking the semester. I haven't seen him in classes since October. It worries me with no communication from either of them. I'm despondent. Viviana said she loves me but hasn't communicated with me since she kissed me. I've called, texted, and everything but still nothing. She's abandoned me like my father, she has abandoned me like Camila—she's abandoned me. I've remained optimistic, focused on me and my self-care. Enough! I'm getting too angry—upset—ravage—to write! I need to get out— I'm done!

I slam my journal shut and shove it away. It flies, slams, and slides across the floor. My breathing seethes with rage. I compose myself by rubbing the temples of my forehead. I grunt almost to tears. I pace back and forth. My mind grows restless. It's wracking my brain. My body is growing tired and driving me insane!

The solitude, the confinement of this apartment, and the park. That park—there are days I enjoy it and others when I don't. While pacing, my sight catches a glimpse of *Frankenstein* on my table. I'm almost done reading it, but I'm not sure if I want to finish because it was a gift from her. I've read this story once before but that was my mother's copy. It was the last book she read before I came into this world—before her death. Professor Doyle's words ring in my head. *"She wouldn't stop talking to me about how excited she was to meet you."* Knowing that book was her last read, I have to finish it. I snatch it, grab my jean jacket, and exit the apartment.

A layer of snow shrouds the grounds everywhere, but blades of grass barely peek from its soft white surface. The air is bare, frosty, chilly, but not frigid. It's enough to enjoy a winter's day outside in the park. Tiny specks of snowflakes flutter with grace and fall in the most tender delicate manner. The flakes settle in my long dark hair and a few of them are caught in my eyelashes. A breeze sways to my right side as I saunter down Willis Street.

I turn to my right and see a bridge followed by a small playground. It's the Willis Picnic area. It features a picnic shelter, a swing set, and some horseshoe pits. I walk underneath the bridge and to my right after passing through the Tim Lally Field, a baseball field managed by the city of Bedford. I've never paid attention to this section of the park—it's as desolate and lonely as me.

Beyond the picnic shelter are trees as the ground shows a path between them. I amble through the trees; my feet crunch against snow and the twigs underneath snap. My route diverges to a decline as I shuffle along. I jump down—clump and stagger between the gaps. I falter and teeter while following the path to the right. There are giant stones lodged into the ground. I footslog down and mince the stones. A stream roars as I reach its end and climb down. The ground is rocky as my feet scrape its gravel surface. I look up—the tunnel! I can walk through it, but I freeze.

"This is uncanny," I mumble. My surroundings are similar to my nightmare about the feminine shadow standing furiously inside the tunnel. There are no barred gates of course, but its appearance terrifies me. A chilly wind sweeps through me. Small clumps of ice and snow shroud the rocky walls ahead of me in the gorge. They're so pretty. Next to the tunnel to my left is a spot I can sit and lean my back against. I read the book to finish it.

Time flees from my subconscious. I drown in the words of the novel. My mind, feverish, imagines the ice field through which Victor and The Creature navigate. Snow touches my legs and shoes, but the rest of me is protected by the wall I'm leaning against. I flip the page; it's getting colder as my eyes devour the novel's narrative. My phone vibrates: Viviana!

I swipe my phone and my camera switches on. I catch a glimpse of myself as the screen displays her video feed. It's pitch black. "Viviana?" I mutter.

"Alice…" Her voice is nimble, soft, and hoarse.

"We haven't spoken—"

"I know—I know," she interjects. "I'm sorry, Alice. There were many moments and times that I wanted to reach out, but I wanted you to get better and I too needed space to work on myself before gathering the strength to talk."

"What's going on? Why can't I see you?"

She coughs brittley, "I haven't been well… Alice, I'm scared!" She sobs, "I'm scared—I'm scared!"

"Why? What's going on?"

"I'm not getting any better. I've isolated myself in my room. Ionel and papa don't see me because I am afraid of getting them ill. I went to the doctors and my TB is now active. It's been active—I'm afraid! Alice—Alice—I don't want to die!" she cries.

I bite my lip and fold them inside my mouth. My head twists away; waves of emotions brew and overwhelm the strings inside my heart. "Let me see you, please?" I ask.

"I don't know! I don't want you to see me like this. I want you to remember me as I was—lively."

Silence. My breath shallows and exhales the warm breath out of my lungs. I see it mist away into thin air.

"Does it hurt?" she asks.

I stare back into the black screen. "What?"

"Death; does it hurt?"

"No, depends on how."

"What happens when you die?"

I freeze on not knowing how to respond.

"I know you've experienced it, death."

My eyes squint in confusion at her words.

"The shadow that whisked you away—it was death but in reality, it was a firefighter rescuing you. That night leading into Samhain— you told me about the fire, ashes, and shards."

I gulp the saliva down my throat and suspire out of my mouth. To Viviana, I explain, "You lose your senses—in a particular order: hunger and thirst are the first to go; then you lose the ability to speak, followed by your ability to see. Hearing and touch typically hold out a little longer, but they eventually go too. You might feel like you're dreaming, extremely vivid dreams that sometimes carry over into your waking hours. These dreams, visions, and nightmares take the form of loved ones who have already died. Sometimes, it's frightening and other times not. You might still be aware of what's going on around you for a time. I was officially reported as 'dead,' but I still had a perception of awareness, that is, my brain was still functional—enough for me, in fact, to hear conversations and see events occurring around them which were confirmed by the police and the medical team who were conscious at the present time of my tragedy."

Viviana chuckles. "Sounds like you—death."

The wind rustles and plays with my hair. I close my eyes, my neck straightens, and I inhale the cold air around me. My hair falls upon my shoulders, and I open my eyes to the dark screen. "You're right. It sounds like the dread and fear of my past three years. Life—my life."

"I came into your life—my everything."

I smile.

"There's that smile I love—my last gift to you."

"What?" I brittle.

The sound of movement muffles and pads out from her side. She flicks the switch. Viviana's camera shakes to her falling back upon her bed. She holds up her phone's camera extending her arms as I see her face. I gasp; her skin is pale, sickly, red and dark circles consume her eyelids underneath. A bright red facial rash resembles the wings of a butterfly unfolding across both her cheeks.

"To live," she says.

"Your last gift is—"

"To live because life is so sweet!"

Her words are vibrant; her smile shines, and her eyes glow as bright as a burning flame. Her eyes speak more beyond the physical decay of her flesh.

"Death is coming for me, but you see these butterfly wings?" She points with her index finger at her rash. "This is proof that I can go through a great deal of darkness and still become something beautiful. Even though this veil doesn't allow me to see how truly beautiful I am—everyone else can. You're like that as well. Let go of your past Alice; trust the future, embrace change; come out of your cocoon! Unfurl your wings, dare to get off the ground to ride the breezes and savor the flowers. Put on your brightest colors and let your sublime nature shine."

Numbness grips beneath my pale cold skin. I've been out here for too long, but my heart embers to her words. She flips her phone's camera lens, and the screen reverts to her altar. "Look what is left there. The figure you picked out from my box—the Anne Stokes Dance with Death figurine."

"The grim reaper statue with wings."

"Yes, it's still there; it has never left! Life and death teach us how to live and that's my last gift to you."

Tears line my cheeks. "I love you."

Her camera switches back and she smiles. "Dance with me then— Dance me to the end of love."

I chuckle. "Isn't that a song?"

She laughs. "Yep, The Civil Wars cover it."

"Yes, I know! They're one of my favorites."

"Mine too!"

Viviana gasps. "Oh, the time! I have to take my medication. I'll call you soon—I promise!"

I glare and give her the evil eye playfully. "You better…"

"I will; till ashes fade away." She winks. I chuckle under my breath knowing she will love me till the end. We wave and our call ends.

The breeze plays a cool melody upon my cheeks. Snowflakes meander across the sky. My head is hazy from my conversation with Viviana and my body stiffens from sitting upon the stone. In front of me is the tunnel. Water roars and streams out of it. My eyes catch a black bird in the sky as it soars over the tunnel bridge; it's similar to the bird from my dreams. I rise from leaning my body against the wall. I scuttle onward and stare into the abyss of the tunnel.

Never once did I ever go through this tunnel. The darkness seems to devour the insides of its gloom. I shut my eyes, breathe a deep breath into my lungs, and stride forward. I think about my life: my mother, father, Viktor, Camila, and Viviana. The events of my life flash before me as I reflect upon them while I flounder through the darkness of the tunnel. Each step echoes and triggers a sequence of all the memories. Every stone is firm, slippery, wet, and broken. I slip upon the stones but press on through. Viviana's face flashes, our memories, and time spent thus far. The natural light at the end of the tunnel shines and breaks the darkness. I'm at the tunnel's end. The stream soaks my feet; it's cool, and flows. The truth of its gentleness shivers from the sky's delicate light. I transcend a past once lived…

A snowflake, when it melts, transforms into water, making it a transformation for new beginnings.

David Edgar Grinnell is a poet, author, and literary scholar from Cleveland, Ohio. He was born 1992 in Norfolk, Virginia, but grew up in the suburb of Bedford. In 2014 he attended Cleveland State University and graduated with his bachelors in English. Grinnell specializes in Romanticism, the Gothic, and draws inspiration from vulnerability. He reflects and portrays love alongside hope, melancholy, and even occasional despair. Currently, he is a funeral director apprentice at St. John Funeral Home.

Also by David Edgar Grinnell:

Moonglade

"My heart aches with every tender sweet kiss,
The touch of your embrace tugs my heart's strings
As the blue in your eyes is heaven's bliss,
My soul now, forever, and ever sings…"

Love, longing, heartache, and loneliness are illuminated in this heartfelt collection from David Edgar Grinnell. Building on themes of budding relationships, misunderstood feelings, and innocent first loves, *Moonglade* creates a narrative that is relatable to everyone looking for love and companionship. Immerse yourself in a world of gothic romantic poetry that shines a soft light on finding and losing love in the twenty-first century.

The Antiquarian

The pages of this diary belonged to a young British archeologist, Nicholas Ainsworth, known for his odd curiosity for the morbid and macabre. His expedition for deviant burials and historical artifacts in the Transylvanian Alps abruptly ruined with the approaching Nazi occupation, he seeks refuge in a mysterious old castle. As he settles into the abandoned gothic ruins, strange phenomena cause him to question his sanity...and if he is truly alone.

The Antiquarian

20 August 1936 Entry One

I've never recorded anything in my life. I shall write in this diary for academic, research, and personal use only. It is only fitting to start now since receiving my admission's letter to attend the University of London. As a British gentleman, I am eager to begin my scholarly ambitions as an inspirational archaeologist. Since I was a young boy growing up in Yorkshire, I've always had a curious mind and I would go exploring the countryside. While growing up I became fascinated by Yorkshire's rich Roman and Viking heritage and explored the many Norman castles, medieval abbeys, and even the national parks.

After my primary education, my father passed away from tuberculosis and my mother sent me to live with my wealthy Uncle Henry. Uncle Henry is my mother's oldest brother, but he and my father never got along due to their social class differences. My father was always offended by my uncle's appearance as he always dressed in fine fancy coats and ties and when he came to visit us in Yorkshire during the holidays, he would arrive in his fine Crossley 19.6 modelled car. Living with Uncle Henry in London is enjoyable, however, during my time here, thoughts of my father and mother remain in my mind.

My mother is a grieving widow… She met my father at what is now my uncle's residence. My mother and uncle hosted a party at the residence to support our military. My father was a soldier. He was drafted in the royal army during the outbreak of the Great War. According to my mother, father was never the same after returning home. He was fighting in the trenches and was returned home after being wounded in action. I imagine the horrid conditions of the trenches triggered his later illness. Father never talked about the war; his hands were always shaking as if he was always tormented by a looming spirit. I am fifteen and just like any young man away from his parents for the first time, I feel homesick. I am an only child. Solitude kept me company while growing up in Yorkshire. Though I was not completely alone, I had a friend named Irene. She was pretty with black hair, soft-hued skin, and brown eyes. She wore a dark bluish grey dress with lace designs upon her chest. Not only was she my friend, but we became much closer than that. We'd go explore ruins such as Whitby Abbey.

Whitby Abbey with its gaunt, imposing remains, is what I believe to be the most romantic ruin. It is set high on a cliff above the Yorkshire seaside town of Whitby. It was founded in 657 by Saint Hilda. Whitby Abbey over the years was a bustling settlement, a kings 'burial place, the setting for a historic meeting between Celtic and Roman clerics, the home of saints including the poet Caedmon, and inspiration for Bram Stoker, author of Dracula. I've never been too keen on superstitions, poets, or Victorian authors such as Stoker. That bit of information was given to me by Irene. She loved all the Romantic poets and, in her solitude, would spend time reading Stoker's novel, while I, was more fascinated by the over two-thousand years of history of the site.

I miss her… We spent so much time together around the Whitby Abbey grounds. Any enthusiasm or discovery I shared with her; she'd giggle at me with her hand pressed against her lips. She would be sitting, leaning against one of the fallen pillars with her book, and say, "Oh, Nicksie… You're so cute!" She bit her lip at me, "What did you discover?" I'd sit next to her, she'd put her book down, and listen to me rant and rave about everything. She cared; and when those deep brown eyes met mine, it was difficult for me to finish speaking. It was like I was in a trance; mesmerised by her gentleness. She gave me a kiss upon my cheek. I didn't see it coming because I was too focused on her eyes. The next day, I broke Irene's heart. I met her at the abbey and told her my mother was sending me to live with my Uncle Henry. The clouds were dark and grey, and a roll of thunder echoed as she stood there comprehending what I told her. We felt raindrops dancing upon our heads. Irene's breath shallowed; every breath drained her. My eyes strained against the sight of her. It tore my heart; watching her. Irene's soft skin turned sallow. She was like a ghost or a corpse and darted away. The rain picked up as sheets of water soaked me to the bone. From the distance, my sight lost her amongst the downpour. I haven't seen her again since…

Irene is always on my mind. Ugh, he's bloody at it again! Though Uncle Henry can never have any children, he loves me, his only nephew, as his own. Sometimes, Uncle Henry has many birds come to his residence. He is sort of a pig when it comes to women, but yet at the same time, he is a gentleman to them. I don't know how though… I mean, my uncle can never stay with one bird. I shall write at another time when my brain is not bothered by the rambunctiousness from these thin walls.

Yours Truly, Nicholas Ainsworth

21 August 1936 Entry Two

Finally, some time in silence and solitude this evening. I love my uncle dearly but he's such a ponce. It was early in the morning when I heard the woman he was with last night; scream at the top of her lungs at him. It wasn't the "velvet climax" either, but an indignant quarrel. My uncle mumbled something under his breath as I was getting dressed in my room. His room is next door to mine and that's when I heard his bird yell: "You're a daft bimbo! I'm Anna, not Pauline!" Then, a loud smack ruptured. "Cor, blimey that hurt!" Anna's feet thundered and shook my dresser, "We're done!" she roared and slammed my uncle's bedroom door shut. In a few moments, I heard his door creak open. The door from downstairs slammed and I tiptoed to check on my uncle. Wooden debris scattered from the door and a fissure had spread upon it. My uncle and I stared at each other as he chuckled, "Well, wasn't she just like a banshee?"

My uncle has brown hair swept up to the side with a brown moustache. He smudged his lips together while studying my appearance, "You need new clothes," he said rising from his bed.

His room had sombre red wallpaper with black eloquent designs. The wallpaper only covered half of the walls as the rest of it was met by a dark wood finish. His floor was hardwood and a giant rug covered the centre of his room. It matched the wallpaper. My uncle ravaged through his closet while in his white muscle shirt and underpants. He spoke to me as his hangers clicked inside his closet, "Nicky, it's time to get you a suit. Now, I know you're not used to nice things, but every gentleman needs a suit." I pressed my lips into a thin line, "Uncle, are you sure that is necessary?" He stopped and turned his head in my direction. His eyes squinted at me in disgust, "Don't be daft boy! Of course, it is necessary! My boy needs to become a gentleman especially when he's been accepted into the University of London." I scratched the back of my neck with my head down, "Yes, but it's not like I've been accepted into Oxford or something…" My uncle snagged a light-grey dress shirt. He pushed his arms through the sleeves, "It doesn't matter Nicky. A suit makes a man. In this world, people will judge you on how you present yourself. This is especially true when dealing with people like me who are higher in class. Believe me, there will be professors at the university who will judge you on your appearance." As my uncle had said this, he buttoned up his shirt. "Nicky, can you grab my tie rack hanger?" He pointed to its direction upon the wall. I mooched over, grabbed it, and brought it to him. He studied the rack, "I want what's best for you.

Don't do what your mother did." I bit my lip and clenched my teeth, "What do you mean, uncle?" Uncle Henry wrapped a black, silver, and white tie around his collar, "I am in no way speaking ill of your father, he served our country, and I respect him for it, but your mother traded her wealth for love." My knuckles popped from balling my hand into a fist, "Now, Nicky… Calm down. I'm trying to teach you a valuable lesson. Be careful who you fall in love with." My uncle tied a full Windsor knot, "What do you know about love?" I laughed under my breath. Uncle Henry pulled up the tie, adjusted it, and tucked the tail of his tie as he rose an eyebrow at me. "It may come at you as a surprise, but I wasn't always like the way I am. People are never the way they were before to shape who they are today." Those words struck me.

As I reflected upon my uncle's insight, he said, "Nicky, have you ever been with a woman before?" Irene flashed within my head. Those eyes and her standing before me. I mumbled under my breath, "Not officially, but there was a girl who had cared for me deeply…" My uncle nodded his head at me, "Well, there you go… Whomever this girl was, she will never be the way she was before." After my uncle's words, the last memory of seeing Irene creeped into my mind.

It pains me that I hurt her. I wonder if Irene will be as carefree as she was to me with other men. I would imagine not because of how she reacted to my rejection. It's like every breath she took from my words, they drained her of life and moulded her into a corpse. White as a pale ghost… Geez, here I am writing about superstitious rubbish. I've been listening to Irene's romantic intuition for far too long. I will be an archaeologist in the next four years. I cannot believe in ghostly rubbish. I do appreciate the suit my uncle bought. It's a blazer suit jacket with dark grey trousers, a red dress shirt, and a darker shaded red tie. I shall wear it on my first day at university. The first day of classes will start soon!

Yours Truly, Nicholas Ainsworth

26 August 1936 Entry Three

The University of London is fascinating! I didn't know that the university was the first in the UK to award degrees to women, which it did in 1878.

I like some of my professors and some not so much, but there is one who I believe will stand out from the rest. His name is Dr Ralph Gilders. He's roughly a middle-aged man with a short white beard. He lectured in one of the bigger lecture halls. He's one of the many associate professors in archaeology and wore a fine fancy suit. In fact, many students wore suits too. I'm glad I followed my uncle's advice on getting a suit of my own. The entire week before classes, my uncle lectured me on how to be a gentleman. He gave me a bloody etiquette guide recently published called Modern Manners by Frederic J. Haskin. The cover features a cartoon drawing of a gentleman and a lady sitting across from each other at a dinner table. There are so many things to memorise such as invitations, introductions, cards, calls, engagements, weddings, christenings, funerals, at the table, on the street, at the theatre, at the movies, restaurant or hotel, travel, telephone, and even how to dress. For example, "Is it regarded as effeminate for men to wear wrist watches?" The guide's answer: "If such an idea ever existed, the World War dissipated it. The wristwatch was found convenient and practical. Since the War, its popularity has increased rather than diminished." What an explanatory answer to a simple yes or no question… My uncle is paying for my education though and so I must abide by his rules.

Besides the headache on the etiquette of a gentleman, Dr Gilders talked much about himself. He said he is part of The Prehistoric Society. A learned society which is devoted to the study of the human past from the earliest times until the emergence of written history. He ranted on about his group of colleagues V. Gordon Childe, Stuart Piggott, and Grahame Clark. It sounds fascinating! The society organises regular conferences, lectures, and other events that make grants for archaeological research. Dr Gilders spent some time with Childe in traveling to conferences. For instance, last year, he visited the Soviet Union, spending twelve days in Leningrad and Moscow. Childe was impressed with the socialist state, and he was particularly interested in the social role of Soviet archaeology. Dr Gilders on the other hand, is unsure. He denounces European fascism, and he is outraged by the Nazi co-option of prehistoric archaeology to glorify their own conceptions of an Aryan racial heritage. Of course, why wouldn't he? I decided to visit him at his office to individually introduce myself to him.

Dr Gilders' office smelled like old books mixed with herbal tea. He was sipping on a cup of tea and munching on some crumpets. He swiped his hands to rid of the crumbs and reached for one of the many books upon his shelf. I caught a glimpse of the book but didn't get to observe what it was as I knocked. "Ah, yes come- in!"

"Greetings professor. I am delighted to meet you."

"How do you do? I am very glad to meet you."

"I am well, thank you. I'm Nicholas Ainsworth." Dr Gilders nodded his head and pointed out a chair across from his desk.

"I am much obliged." I sat down as the cushion squealed and sunk me in. I readjusted my posture in the chair, "Mr Ainsworth, do you care for a cup of tea?"

"No, thank you. That is quite a book you have there."

Dr Gilders' eyes gravitated to the book that was in his hand, "This, why yes… The Hebrew Bible. What can I do for you, Mr Ainsworth?"

"I wish to express my interest in working with you as I was intrigued with your involvement with The Prehistoric Society."

Dr Gilders smirked and his eyes gleamed, "Ah, an ambitious goal for a potential archaeologist." He sipped his tea again while extending his pinkie, "Very well." He placed his cup upon his saucer, "I'll give you the opportunity if you prove yourself in your studies. I'll keep a close eye on you, your performance, and how well you master the material. If you prove yourself worthy; we'll fund a field expedition abroad at a location of your choosing." I bolted from the chair as it squealed from sticking to my trousers. I shot my hand out, "I won't let you down sir!" He shook my hand, "Very good Mr Ainsworth. I look forward to it!"

What a goal and opportunity to work towards. I shall completely devote myself to my work and studies! I just wish I knew where it was, I would like to go, and what subject to explore in archaeology. An expedition to Egypt sounds too cliché. Maybe my studies will direct me in the right direction. Something to stand out amongst other archaeologists.

Yours Truly, Nicholas Ainsworth

28 August 1936 Entry Four

College life and academics are challenging to adapt, but all is going well. Yesterday before Dr Gilders began his lecture; a new student wandered into the hall. She had fair auburn hair, fine blue eyes, and dark eyebrows that nearly met. She handed Dr Gilders a card, he grasped it, and read its context. His lips sunk in his mouth, he nodded his head, and glanced up at her with his arm extended. Voices muttered and mumbled under their breaths about this mysterious girl. She was short and inclined, but as she ambled toward my direction, her features were regular and finely cut. She sat in the row below me where there weren't that many students seated. Dr Gilders resumed his lecture.

I've been studying ahead in my academics for Dr Gilders' class, but this girl's beauty distracted me from the actual lecture. I squirmed in my seat, my eyeballs shifted between her and Dr Gilders. Some moments, my ears tuned out the lectured words. This never happened to me before. It reminded me of how I was mesmerised by Irene's brown eyes. I frolicked the pen in my hands playing with it. It did not help. As I glanced back at her, she caught me staring, but I turned my gaze away from her. I tapped my pen silently against the long table to rid myself of the senses of her staring back at me. I couldn't resist; I gazed back down at her, but she fixed her attention to her notebook and scribbled upon it.

When the lecture finally ended and class was dismissed, I was relieved because I wouldn't see the mysterious girl. I feel guilty just writing about it. How can a heart be tormented by two women? One who is a complete stranger and the other a childhood friend who probably loathes me? I still believe I won't ever see Irene again, but yet she haunts me. Her figure when I told her I was leaving. That sadness and sorrow. Lately, I've been pushing more into my academics to distract my mind from her. It helps, but in my passion for study, it is sometimes not enough. I remember Irene and I used to gaze upon the stars. The Yorkshire Dales and North York Moors are home to some of the darkest skies in the country, with large areas of unpolluted night sky where it's possible to see thousands of stars, the Milky Way, meteors and even the Northern Lights. Here in London, I don't get to see that anymore. I miss it and I miss her. Irene is my first love and I was hers. When we gazed upon the stars, she rested her head gracefully upon my chest. She had an exquisite loveliness, a rich heady fragrance that combines the green freshness of lilies, the valley with a spicy bite of gingerbread, and the voluptuousness of a white rose. Her natural scent was like a wild bluebell with hints of sharp floral notes. My heart aches as the scent still looms over me in a delicate twirl. Sometimes, my chest still feels the weight of her gentle head upon me. It hurts, that I cannot find the emotions or words to describe it. I feel guilty for destroying what was once good and pure. The memory of places, feeling the shadowy impressions of a person who stood in the exact place I hope to visit once more, but Irene's experience leaves only vaguely discernible echoes that I will strain to hear.

Nicholas Ainsworth

31 August 1936 Entry Five

I am utterly disturbed… It is a reason for my brief absence from writing anything but writing about it may help me comprehend everything. I have developed the routine of spending many hours at the university's library devouring books of study. One day though, the library was quite crowded and there weren't many spots available to study in solitude. On the fourth floor, there was one table available to sit, but it was also occupied by the mysterious girl. She had books and papers scattered all around her, she scribbled restlessly in her notebook as if possessed by a vivacious desire. I mooched over, pulled a chair from across from her, and uneasily sat in it. She didn't seem to notice me at first until I placed my books upon the table. As I opened one of my books, I felt her gaze upon me. The tension was uncomfortable, I glanced at her open notebook, and saw what she drew upon a loose-leaf paper inside. It was a human skull with a giant stone lodged inside its mouth. There were illegible writings scattered all around the drawing. It was written in a language I did not recognise or understand because of her messy handwriting.

She slammed her journal shut, stared at me, and gripped her notebook tightly.

"My apologies... I did not mean to intrude. Curiosity gets the best of me. I've seen you at Dr Gilders' lectures; do you have inspirations to become an archaeologist too?" My voice croaked because of her gaze, but she bit her lip as if she wanted to say something. She unloosened her grip on her notebook and placed it back on the table in front of her. "That was a peculiar skull I saw you draw, it is quite good, and I imagine you hope to study human remains of the past?"

"Yes... Yes, I do."

Her accent struck me. She is not from any English- speaking country.

"Where... I mean, how do you do? I am very glad to meet you."

She chuckled under her breath as she batted her eyes,

"I am okay. I imagine it's your first time following a gentleman's code?" I smudged my lips, the words she spoke were slow, but good.

"Yes. Yes, it is..."

She laughed, "Well, do not worry so much. I appreciate your kind attempt. No ideal gentleman has spoken to me and so, I am flattered. I am Sasha."

"Nicholas Ainsworth... I have never heard of your name before." I fiddled with my pen.

"I imagine not... It's not a very common name in this country." I tapped the end of my pen against the table, "What country are you from if I may ask?" She broke her gaze and glared down at her notebook, "I..."

Silence.

"You're afraid?" I asked her.

She nodded her head, "If I say... You'll walk away and won't talk to me."

"As a gentleman's word of honour; I shall not."

Sasha stared into my eyes. Her blue eyes radiated with a tender glow. Those eyes gleamed in mystery, pain, gloom, and sorrow.

Finally, she spoke and whispered, "Россия."

I dropped my pen as her voice rang in my skull. The pen rolled off the table and fell onto the floor. My chair squeaked as I reached down and heard her gathering all her books and papers together. She was about to leave until I uttered, "No, please stay..."

"You think I'm monstrous because I am Russian."

"No..."

"That face of yours speaks more..."

"Sasha, I assure you those are not my thoughts."

She sank back into her chair, bit her lips, and shut her eyes. She clasped her hands against her face and wallowed into a short but silent sob. She rubbed her fingers underneath her eyelids, "You don't know what it was like over there…"

I pulled my chair to the side of the table and was closer to her, "Мy родители…"

"Your what?"

Her lips sank into her mouth, her eyes glared up to the ceiling and back at me, "Parents… My parents…"

"What happened?"

After I said those words, her eyes conveyed a tender gaze at me, she inhaled a sharp breath and told me her story:

"I was five years-old when the Russian Revolution was still going on… It was near the end of the civil war between the Red and White armies. My father fought against the Bolsheviks. While my father battled during our civil war, he entrusted my uncle to keep my mother, sisters, and I safe under his protection. Violence and harrowing screams rang throughout the night. Gunfire echoed and death always stayed close. We were in hiding from the Cheka. One night my uncle had awakened us and ordered us to put on our clothes. As much as we could wear because we were under the assumption that my family would be moved to a safer location. The impending chaos reigned outside our hiding place. My uncle told us to go into the basement and wait for a truck to come escort us. A few minutes later, a squad of the Cheka barged in and my uncle read aloud the order given to him by the Ural Executive Committee:

'Tikhonova Maria Vasilievna, in knowing that your husband is continuing his attack on Soviet Russia, the Ural Executive Committee has decided to execute you and your children.'

My mother, facing us, turned and said, 'What, Dmitriy?' My uncle quickly repeated the order and the squad raised their weapons. My mother tried to bless herself but failed amid the terror. Uncle Dmitriy raised his colt gun at my mother's torso and fired, she fell, and was pierced with at least three bullets in her upper chest and died. As this was happening, I fled to the back of the basement. There were some stored crates against the wall that was tall enough for me to climb. My eyes caught glimpses of my uncle shooting at my sister Varya with a bullet wound to the head. He then shot at Anya, who ran for the double doors. By this time, I climbed through the broken basement window. The remaining squad fired chaotically and over each other's shoulders until the room was so filled with smoke and dust that no one could see anything at all in the darkness. I heard my uncle shout commands but I cannot recall them because of the noise.

There were dogs barking from our hiding quarters and the sound of gunshots roared despite the caterwaul sounds from the trucks 'engines. I heard my uncle shriek at the men to stop firing and kill me. I heard wallows of pain and suffering from within those basement walls, 'Bayonets! 'commanded my uncle. I imagined my sisters being stabbed knowing it was their moans and whimpers inside. Tears streamed my cheeks as I ran faster. My heart pounded, my breathing wild, and I had no recollection of where I was running. I was possessed by a frenzy…"

Sasha stopped. She shrouded her mouth to control and muffle her crying. "I'm sorry… I must go…" She darted with her books and papers as a few of them fluttered upon the floor. I stood as she slammed a door. Her feet echoed down upon the stairs. They became faint as I grabbed a few sheets of her papers. In my hand was the drawing of the skull I saw earlier. I studied the writing and realised it was all written in Russian.

I am utterly disturbed… Her story. I believe my father would know of Sasha's suffering because of the fighting he did in the trenches. The claustrophobia. This drawing though, it intrigues me. I must ask her about it. If I see her again; I will return this drawing.

Yours Truly, Nicholas Ainsworth

1 September 1936 Entry Six

Sasha wasn't in class, but I did find her outside on the College Green field. She leaned against one of the trees and was reading. As I approached, I observed she was reading a book called, The

Vampyre. The title was engraved with gold letterings with a black hardcover, "John Polidori?" I said seeing the author name glitter from the sun. She glared at me, "Yes... How are you Nicholas?"

"I am well. I've been looking for you." There was a pause.

"Oh, may I sit down?"

"Of course."

I licked my dried lips, the breezed swayed my hair, and my eyes wandered over, "I deeply appreciate you sharing your past with me. Even though, I am a stranger; you confided in me."

"You gave me your word and you honoured it..."

"These are yours..." I presented the papers she left behind.

Sasha placed her book down, her face moulded into disbelief: "You saved them?"

"Yes, they looked important. I thought they were research notes."

She snatched the papers, "Yes, they are... My future dreams lie in these papers."

"What does it mean? What's the skull with the stone lodged in its mouth?" She picked up the book she once held, "See this book?" I rolled my eyes, "Yes, bloody vampires... So, what? What does this have to do about your academics?" Sasha pointed her index finger upward and she read from the book, "This is from the introduction of this volume: 'For many years vampirism was a serious subject of research. Medical authorities in the 1670s wrote Latin treatises about 'grave eating 'where the undead were dug up to find they had been eating their own shrouds and even feasting on their own limbs and bowels, according to research...'"

"Ok, rubbish!"

"It is but wait!"

I groaned; Sasha continued, "Sightings of vampires were reported in journals and gazettes in Poland and Russia in the 1690s. In Eastern Europe, for instance, where Bram Stoker drew inspiration for Dracula there have been numerous discoveries of corpses that have been 'staked.' Bulgaria has had multiple cases of seven- hundred-year-old skeletons with ploughshares, the hefty blade of a plough thrusted through them into the ground. Polish excavations unearthed skeletons with sickles placed around their waists or necks. Other techniques such as 'stoning 'have been found all over the world, from four-thousand-year-old Bronze Age burials pinned down with huge rocks, to graves from Ancient Greece weighted down with amphora fragments, to medieval English skeletons buried under grinding stones."

As Sasha read this to me, laughter built up inside me. I tried so hard to contain it, but after she finished reading, a wave of hot air exploded out from my mouth and cheeks, "I'm sorry for laughing Sasha, but I still call it rubbish. For instance, these claims of vampires are lacked by adequate scientific evidence. It cannot be excluded that a brick slid accidentally into the mouth." I laughed even more until my eyes caught her crossing her arms at me. Her eyebrows crinkled into a loathing gaze,

"I'm not trying to prove if vampires exist or not because they are just folkloric tales. My mother told me such tales to pass the time while in hiding because they were entertaining, but what I am interested in is to actually get to the bottom of these strange practices and resist misdirection."

I shook my head and sighed, "I worry that such literature biases could be influencing archaeology itself..." Sasha's eyes gleamed and glittered like a spark of inspiration, "Exactly, which is why as inspired archaeologists we must develop new systematic approaches by collating deviant burials into datasets."

Flights of fancy consumed my brain. Her words triggered a desire for knowledge and discovery. It all rushed like a fluttering dream, "Are you proposing we establish a comprehensive analysis to disprove these public fascinations?"

"Yes! Historically, archaeology hasn't paid much attention to deviant burials. I want to prove that these deviant burials weren't just some fringe practice, but to declare they are widespread across cultures. These so called 'discoveries 'of vampires are fuelled by abundant fictional coverage, but often I find it frustrating as an archaeologist, because many of the stories are based on unpublished findings that have yet to be thoroughly scrutinised."

I grinned, "Then let's start scrutinising and gather evidence!"

Sasha clenched both of her hands into fists and squeezed them vibrantly. She bolted towards me and hugged me, "Yes, a partner in crime!" I jolted from her embrace and thought about Irene, her drenched ghastly appearance flashed before me. It was like her sallow corpse stalked me and watched Sasha's arms wrap around me. The dark grim skies at Whitby Abbey ravaged inside my head; she's there with her soaked hair dangling upon her face.

"I'm sorry... Too much?"

Sasha's voice disrupted my trance. "What?"

"I didn't mean it as an advance towards you…"

"It's not you Sasha, I promise." My hands quivered, Sasha's touch lingered upon my shoulders. They were warm, but my body tingled against the imagination of Irene's embracement.

"Okay, but your eyes…," She said.

"Yes?"

The sun's rays glisten Sasha's blue eyes, "They're haunted," she said.

"As are yours…" My heart palpitated a burning ember throughout the chambers of my heart.

"Yes, but I am here… Away from danger and in the safest place to be." She smiled at me as her smile made me smile.

Ugh, I am a daft sod! My heart wretched by two women! No wonder Uncle Henry can't stick with one bird, but I'm not like him; he's a prat! I shouldn't write ill of my uncle, but I don't believe it gentlemanly of him poncing about with different women. One thing is certain though… I can't engage toward any advancement with Sasha because my heart grieves for Irene. It's not fair to Sasha. I still feel Sasha's touch as it revives my soul and reanimates my being with life. The blood in my veins flows warmly and vivaciously from her tender affection. I wonder what she thinks of me as… a friend, colleague, or… No… No, I can't fill my head with such nonsense.

Yours Truly, Nicholas Ainsworth

2 September 1936 Entry Seven

My teeth; I am gnashing them in an uncontrollable manner. My wristwatch reads: 05:00… The sun shall rise soon. I saw Irene.

She was here at least in a dream perhaps… I am unsure. The ticking from my watch is driving me mad. It's like it's keeping in time with me dancing with her. Yes – I was dancing with her at the abbey. At least that's what the shadowy place felt like. Whitby Abbey; my watch ticking in time with our waltz. A hypnotic lullaby with the beatings of my heart. As we waltzed and twirled, she rested her chin upon my shoulder. Her warm breath tickled the side of my neck, her lips barely touched my bare skin, and chilled me ever so tenderly I gripped the back of her dress. Overwhelming passion possessed me. I held her safe and warm as our figures touched gracefully together. My lips rested against her neck; they felt the delicate radiance of her beating pulse. It was once something my heart knew as it yearned for what I once remembered; her kiss.

Even after this dream, my neck tingles where Irene's breath tickled it. It makes me mourn with the idea I may never see her again. Why would she want to see me? I broke her heart. Nothing is almost as powerful as a first love. Someone you love so much and learning how to live without them is one of the hardest things in life.

Yours Truly, Nicholas Ainsworth

9 September 1936 Entry Eight

So many exciting things are going on! Sasha and I are becoming closer. We've begun researching a most comprehensive analysis of deviant burials.

She and I have tracked down obscure references from the musty basements of university libraries, eventually compiling practically a well range of burials from Anglo- Saxon Britain: a growing one-thousand burials so far. Sasha has been recording the data into a vast spreadsheet, which allows us to organise the information into categories. One of the categories I recommended was, "position of decapitated heads" which I wager these heads are commonly missing.

While on our research endeavours, I learned Sasha has a fear of basements as it was difficult to get her to stay focused. Her hands trembled just like father's. She was deciphering the old wrinkled and dried papers stored in the University of London's archives. Papers fluttered away from the pile she was observing in her hands because of the shaking. I picked up a few of the papers, placed them back in the pile, and as I was taking the pile of papers from her, my hands touched hers. An innocent touch which both of our eyes jolted from. "My apologies… I'm only trying to help," my voice quivered. She smiled at me, her blue eyes sparkled from the overhead light, and her auburn hair fell between her eyes. She breathlessly giggled, "I know… I appreciate it. You're helping me get through this…"

"Oh?"

My hands grasped the papers for her to study and read. "Yes, I don't think I could be down here without your support." Her eyes shifted between me and the papers.

She spoke, "Sorry, I don't mean to stare at you… it's just…"

"Just?"

"Looking at you while multitasking between deciphering these papers helps me. It distracts me from knowing I am in a…" She stopped as she trembled again as if abandoned in a storm.

"It's quite alright… You don't have to say it. Just keep your eyes on me while transcribing these sheets." Sasha bent down to pick up her notebook and scribbled upon it, "We'll be here for a while…" She bit her lips while copying the written text in her notebook.

"I am at your service my lady."

She laughed, "Alright, Mr Peng… We'll put that hypothesis to the test, won't we?"

"Indeed."

Sasha smiled at me again, "Confidence, I like that."

The time passed… My knees ached and my feet tingled numb. I stamped my feet against the concrete. The air in the basement was hot and thick as sweat trickled my forehead, "Ugh, this infernal copying is driving me barking mad!" I chuckled out loud at Sasha's words. She pursed her lips forward and groaned hot air out of her mouth. Her breath flipped her hair from her face. "I would have never thought I'd hear an expression like that from you, 'barking mad.'" Sasha held her pen and notebook in one hand while she stretched out her arms. The bones in her elbows popped and she twisted her wrists as they crackled. "I guess I've been in London too long…" she halted from speaking as her eyes squinted.

"What?" I asked.

She brushed the top of her fingers against the side of my left temple, "You're sweaty…"

"Ugh, it's so stuffy in here I could drink dog's soup…" "What?" She laughed and snorted under her breath. "Dog's soup means water."

Sasha shrouded her mouth from snorting, "You Brits are hilarious… I'm sorry to laugh that way."

I clicked my tongue against the roof of my mouth, "It's all hunky-dory."

She smiled again. Sasha tried to hide it by shaking her head, "There you go again…"

"What?" "Being cute…"

"I'm just being my natural-self."

Sasha sighed heavily, "What is it?" I asked.

"I just."

"Yes, speak up."

She suspired her breath, "I just hope as I spend my time here, I will never lose my Russian accent. The British accent is contagious."

"You sound good to me. Keep your Russian accent and don't Briticise it. Your Russian accent is beautiful." Her chest deflated from my words, "That's so sweet of you to say. My mother pushed me to learn English because my father believed it would become a universal language. You remind me of him a bit."

My eyebrows drifted apart, "In what way or manner?"

"Mother said he had a drive for education. He'd always tell her, 'knowledge is power.'"

I blinked my eyes in thought, "Is that why you're here for your education? To seek power?"

Sasha resumed copying more notes from the dwindling pile from my hands.

"Yes," she finally said, "The power to find him."

"To find him… But you study archaeology… Wait, did he…"

"Die?"

I sunk my lips into my mouth and pressed them. I waited for her answer.

She glared back at me briefly, "I don't know quite honestly… He joined the White Army before my birth and I've never met him. If he is dead, then the tools and education I will receive shall find him. My childhood was always surrounded by death. My family and I didn't have much, but father remained loyal to the Russian Empire. He briefly fought in the Great War and when father learned about what happened to the Romanov family, mother said he wept. 'They're just young girls…' he repeated over and over again according to my mother. Mother told me, he gripped her hand and saw a burden of tormented sorrow in his eyes, they were like my eyes… Blue. That's when he told mother, 'The Bolsheviks will die. I must fight for my girls.'"

Sasha took her pen and gritted her teeth to hold it. She placed her notebook down on the floor. She reached down between her chest and showed a necklace. It was a golden bronze locket. It was a perfect heart locket that was adorned with stacked layers of filigree and a delicate blue crystal heart nestled inside a bronze floral heart. She opened the locket, mechanics twisted, clicked, and turned. A beautiful melody played and raptured me. Inside the locket was a worn picture of a man in a uniform.

"That's your father?" She nodded her head.

"That melody… It's beautiful."

Sasha snapped the locket shut, the melody ceased, and she grasped the locket into her hand.

She released the locket, and it fell against her chest. She took the pen from her mouth, and spoke, "Yes, that is my father's picture during the Great War. Mother kept this locket with her and said it brought her luck and then she passed it on to me. The melody is Debussy's Clair de Lune. Mother used to lull my sisters and I to sleep with the melody. My oldest sister Varya told me before the revolution, her, Anya, mother, and Uncle Dmitriy would attend the Imperial Mariinsky Theatre. The Mariinsky Orchestra once performed Clair de Lune. My sisters fell in love with the piece that my mother eventually received this locket as a gift from my father. Father was discharged from the service and returned to us in 1917 before the February Revolution. He made it for her, put his picture inside it, and every night she played this for me and my sisters."

The more I learn about Sasha, the more my attraction grows for her. I am a hopeless romantic sod for sure. My uncle has been inquiring about where I've been spending my long hours. Every time I tell him, "Long hours at the university library," he notices my stutter. He rolls his eyes and says, "It's a girl." My face turns bloody red of course. I can't help it and my uncle even asked me to invite her over. I have to make a visiting card… The card for a woman is usually from 2¾ to 3½ inches wide, by 2 to 2¾ inches deep, but there is no fixed rule. The invitation will be set for Friday on the 18th of September… Bugger, I just realised that I don't even know Sasha's surname… How am I supposed to write one when I don't even know her full name?

Your third-rate gentleman, Nicholas Ainsworth

10 September 1936 Entry Nine

My tolerance level with Uncle Henry is going to burst! I know he means well when instructing me on the qualities of a gentleman, but he knocks me off my trolly… We've added more to my closet with suits and even a proper tuxedo. Uncle Henry made it clear with me and his voice was firm, "You will wear this tuxedo upon informal occasions after 18:00. It is appropriate to wear one at the theatre, at most dinners; at informal parties; when dining at home; and when dining in a restaurant…" I interrupted him, "Blimey Uncle, I know and such attire is worn at the opera; at an evening wedding; at a dinner to which the invitations are worded in the third person; at a ball or formal evening entertainment; and at certain state functions on the continent of Europe in broad daylight." My uncle's eyebrows rose, "Very good. So, you have been reading the etiquette guide. The hostess has written across her visiting card and you will give this invitation personally to Miss Sasha."

I jumbled my head to the sound of my uncle's words, "Wait, what? Hostess? Since when did we get a hostess? I thought you were just going to invite Sasha over for tea or something." Uncle Henry laughed, "No, my boy. This is an invitation to an informal dance. I've been seeing a lovely lady and she will act as hostess." Uncle Henry flashed the invitation as its contents were inside a black luscious envelope. A wax seal was embedded upon it with an elaborate letter Y and a black feather. I took the envelope as Uncle Henry cleared his throat, "By the way, you have more invitations to send out personally. Make sure you are dressed appropriately when handing out the invitations. You are representing me after all."

"More?"

"Yes, invite your professors and even your esteemed Dr Gilders. Them knowing you as my nephew, will give you respect." I stared at the addressed envelope and back at my uncle, "Why are you doing this?" My uncle warmly smiled at me, "Because I love you my dear boy. You are the only thing I have left, and I want you to be successful." I was speechless. I have never heard of my uncle establishing an informal event just for me. For me to rise and grow my reputation. I smiled knowing this growing reputation will help reach me closer to my dream of traveling across the world in search of deviant burials. I will have the respect, wealth, and power to do so. I have to play the gentleman's role. My uncle spoke again, "Come back home at 18:00, dress up in your tuxedo, and the hostess and I will instruct you on the waltz." I nodded my head and prepared to set off.

When I arrived at university later that day, I carried a packet of invitations tied with a fancy gold string. I traversed the university departments and halls. I left invitations by the faculty doors if no one was there, slipped them under the door, and handed a few in person. I bowed my head gracefully, arms extended, and said, "Greetings, my Uncle Henry Yates invites you to attend." At other times, I placed the cards on a table in the halls where appropriate or in drawing rooms throughout.

I knocked upon Dr Gilders' office, "It's open… Please come-in." The professor's eyes peered over his reading glasses with the Hebrew Bible in his hands.

"Mr Ainsworth, it is a pleasure."

"Dr Gilders, I wish to personally invite you to attend my Uncle Henry Yates 'informal dance." He received my invitation and studied the seal. "Henry Yates… The Henry Yates who donated funds to support our soldiers during the Great War?"

"Yes, sir."

"I respect the man. He raised up British morale with his exquisite parties for the soldiers and spent time at our hospitals to visit the wounded."

"How do you know of my uncle?"

He grabbed a letter opener and sliced the wax seal, "I don't know the gentleman personally, but my brother wrote to me about him. He said your uncle was a kind gentleman and visited him during his hospital admission. I couldn't visit my own brother because my life's work with traveling detained me, but your uncle kept many of the soldiers 'company. He listened to them, spoke to them, or just sat with them in silence. When the hospital was low on supplies, he gave some of his money so the hospital could afford the supplies. In some ways, he saved my brother because the hospital was able to administer the medications he needed."

I smiled about my uncle's actions. I had no idea of his kindness and here I thought of him as self-absorbed in his money. "I am sure my uncle will be pleased of your arrival." Dr Gilders grabbed a fountain pen from inside his desk, and scribbled. He handed me a card and I read aloud what he had written, "Dr Ralph Gilders accepts with pleasure for Friday, September 18."

"Keep up the good work in your studies, Mr Ainsworth."

After departing from Dr Gilders' office, I turned the corner and bumped into someone, "pardon me. I am so sorry…"

"Nicholas?"

It was Sasha. A smile creased from cheek to cheek seeing her, "Greetings," I bowed before her. She laughed, "Wow, is that a new suit? You look dashing!"

"Thank you, this is for you." I handed her the invitation. Her eyes grew wide, "Oh wow, so fancy and proper… You're full of surprises." She tore open the envelope and read the invitation to me:

There was confusion on her face, her eyes squinted at the words on the invitation, "Ms Helena Yates?"

"That would be the hostess of the event. It will be at my uncle's estate where I live."

Sasha's breath was sharp and tremulous, "I don't have the proper attire… So, I don't think I can make it."

"No worries, I can help you. We can get you a dress for the occasion."

Sasha dropped the invitation, bending down quickly to grab it, "Uh, um… You'd do that for me?"

"Yes, I would be honoured if you attended."

"Would you mind waiting for me? I was going to meet with Dr Gilders." I nodded my head to agree and waited for her about an hour.

Eventually, we arrived at a clothing store in London, but closing time dawned soon. Sasha was overwhelmed. She panicked by playing restlessly with her hands. She asked so many questions like, "Is it necessary to be in the latest fashion to be properly dressed? What is the difference between a ball dress and a dinner dress? When should jewellery or ornaments be worn in the hair?" All good questions, which I happily answered. From what I remembered I said things such as: "The well-poised woman makes fashion her servant. Others foolishly make themselves the slaves of fashion. Out of date fads should be shunned but new ones adopted only if found suitable.

Also, the formal dinner dress differs little from the ball dress, except that the skirt of the latter must be appropriate for dancing, while for the dinner dress, it may be closer fitting. As for jewellery, they should be worn at balls and dinners, but the size is merely of taste." I paced back and forth as I waited outside the dressing room. A store-clerk woman was assisting Sasha with her dress.

"Will my locket suffice?"

"Yes, that will be good."

After I answered her question, she sauntered out of the dressing room. I was thrown into a loop, she had her casual clothes on, and smirked. "Where's the dress?" I asked.

She twirled around towards me, "The store-clerk is packing up the dress now, so you won't see it. I want it to be a surprise for you. You told me what was needed for the dress and I trust the store-clerk's opinion on it. She has helped a few women pick out such dresses for fancy events."

"I see…"

Sasha walked closer toward me, stroked my cheek, and said, "Besides, I hope it will trance you for I am in a sea of wonders." My heart jilted from her tender touch and the whisper of her words. All I could croak out was, "Sea of wonders?"

She laughed at me, "Yes, a quote from Stoker's Dracula: 'I am all in a sea of wonders. I doubt; I fear; I think strange things, which I dare not confess to my own soul.'"

I groaned rolling my eyes, "Not bloody vampires again…"

"I couldn't resist. Vampires are beings of seduction and are mesmerising."

Her words were flirty by how she conveyed them so playfully, "what are you getting at?"

"Ok, time for one of the confessions of 'my own soul, 'I like you and I want to impress you." She kissed me on the cheek. My face withered pale. I didn't know how to react. She kissed me on the opposite cheek from where Irene had kissed me.

My heart soars with delight. No more living in doubt on what Sasha's thoughts are about me. I shall be ever so slow and gentle with her. I deeply appreciate her openness with me. It's different and gives me time to heal. I paid a fair amount of money for her dress. I was even late for my dance lesson for the waltz… I practiced upon Uncle Henry's bird while trying to lead: step forward with the left foot, right foot step sideways to the right, bring back with the right foot, step back with the right foot, step back sideways with the left foot, and bring your right foot next to your left foot. Uncle Henry would yell: "No, wrong! Step back with the right foot," or, "wrong, footwork…" Uncle Henry's bird, Helena is a pretty thing. Short blond hair, green eyes, and smooth skin. She's an American which surprises me. She has a high squealing voice and calls me "honey." Eh, Uncle Henry joked with me by saying, "I'm doing a lot better than our lovely king of England, Edward VIII with his American birdy." It drives me insane, but it will be worth it once I dance with Sasha at the party. I eagerly wait to see her.

Yours Truly, Nicholas Ainsworth

17 September 1936 Entry Ten

Absent from writing again. I find writing in this diary is helpful because of the annoying preparations for the dance. After long hours of study, a few random exams, and assisting Sasha with our project; I come home and help out with preparations. Helena and I have been going over the guest list by creating a list of our own to confirm who is coming and not. Impressive enough, two-hundred guests so far. My uncle chuckled, "That's pretty normal with my reputation. The last one I held here was when your mother first met your father. The guest attendance was about that size." My eyes grew wide at my uncle's confidence and easiness about all these guests arriving. Helena whispered to me that my uncle is like a British version of Jay Gatsby.

"Who?" I asked sitting next to her.

"Jay Gatsby, honey… You know the character from Scott Fitzgerald's novel, The Great Gatsby. Your uncle is so handsome and romantic… Like Jay!"

"Sure."

I didn't know what else to say, but bloody hell, is she really just into my uncle's money or is it the fact that she's into the British gentleman? Probably just for the money like many of the past ones who stayed here. Then again, if my uncle wasn't the way he was, he could have himself a nice lady. Some of those ladies wanted to be with him, but if only he could learn to control his attraction toward other women. Of course, I am one to write about such things. My attraction towards Irene and Sasha. However, I cannot keep beating a dead horse because horses are for courses. I am better suited for better things like Sasha. I am in a different situation and growing into a striving gentleman. Pretty soon, I will be sixteen come January. I wonder how old Sasha is. She is older based on what she's told me about her past. I just hope she's not too old... I don't know how my uncle will feel about me courting with an older woman.

Besides all this pish-posh, I have been working in solitude on a similar systematic study for deviant burials. I haven't told Sasha yet because there is nothing concrete, but my approach attempts to cover the whole of Western Europe from the first to fifth centuries. I want to confirm that deviant burials can be discovered well beyond Britain. Dr Gilders has been noticing the connection between Sasha and me. We've been sitting next to each other during his lectures and talk before the start of his class. I asked Dr Gilders if I could meet him to ask him about deviant burials.

"Deviant burials by what means are you seeking?" Asked Dr Gilders intrigued.

"I want to discover if deviant burials are beyond Britain." I handed him some of the notes that Sasha and I put together. He studied them over, gave them back, and said, "I must warn you. Applying concepts derived from later times and completely different cultural contexts is a risky exercise."

I bit my lips in confusion, "What do you mean professor?"

He exhaled and laughed, "Vampires… They're creatures of the night in folkloric sources as diverse as Babylonian literature. For instance, the shroud-eating Nachzehrer of Germanic tradition, and the Chiang-Shih, 'hopping vampires 'of Chinese legend, notions of corpses rising from the grave have long been documented.

However, what archaeological datasets reveal is that these ancient accounts are just stories that our ancestors told each other on dark and stormy nights. Many of them were genuinely scared, taking time and trouble to ensure that the dead stayed where they belonged."

I cleared my throat while shaking my notes in hand, "Indeed, but what Sasha and I are interested in is to actually get to the bottom of these strange practices and resist misdirection because as archaeologists, we have to develop new systematic approaches. The best way to do this is by collating deviant burials into datasets. We're not trying to prove if such blood sucking creatures exist, but to probe for historical influences on mortuary practices instead of flights of fancy."

"I see… The threat of vampires still captivates us today and that makes it more difficult to pin down your discoveries. After all, the science to debunk these myths is quite a bit stronger than it was centuries ago. Perhaps the undead stir up our deepest fears about our own mortality? Maybe they simply make for great cinema? For instance, I had the pleasure years ago to watch Nosferatu when it came out June of twenty-nine… Who the hell knows?" My eyes shifted to the floor with an utter groan of disappointment.

I am disappointed in Dr Gilders' lack of enthusiasm for the proposed investigation and project. Sasha and I have worked so hard for this… I must get Dr Gilder's approval for this project. The three of us could fund a project to go on an excursion to one of the many deviant burial sites to collect data. It's for the protection of archaeology! To debunk public fascinations with the undead such as Irene's romantic intuition about vampires. Well, here you go Irene… Real proof to show you the real truth about mortuary practices. To say to her: "Thanks to the process of decomposition, the corpse would be found transformed from its previous cold, pale, and stiff state. Fresh-looking blood would be seeping from the lips; the face would be ruddy; the body would be engorged, and have a 'fresh, new skin 'that made the nails and hair to appear to have grown. The corpse might even 'gasp 'if a stake was driven through its lungs, releasing foul and noxious gases!"

Your Humble, Nicholas Ainsworth

Moonglade

Heart to Heart

You rest your head and snuggle on my chest.

Amongst the blades of grass and gentle care

The scent of your long hair puts me at rest,

For what matters is this moment we share

Time wains; nothing ever lasts forever.

Do not worry, the future that awaits,

Enjoy what we have right now together

Listen, your heart will always have a place.

The warmth of the sun's rays fades a distance

The courtyard's water plays a softened tune;

Your body gives warmth to my existence.

As our souls intertwine between love blooms,

My eyes grow heavy and begin to close

You, my love, are the blanket of my woes.

Forbidden

The image of her beauty stains my eyes

As her short dark hair meanders in flight,

Oh thine, deep brown eyes, listen to my cries,

Thy soft warm lips beckon my soul with might

The echoes of thy voice set me alight,

But my mind and hands are forced in wastage,

The red in thy cheek and scarf tempts my sight

My heart's blood seeps to know thine own bondage,

Helpless am I, the woman who holds me hostage.

Red Wine

Shall love itself be compared to red wine?

The bottle shape glass conceals its beauty

Lovers twist the corkscrew, ready to dine?

Let it breathe or pour for the gomuti [1]

Its scent alludes to my affectedness,

We have swirled this relationship before

Its taste savors of my addictiveness,

The year of our vintage urges me more

Why call for the open bottle we had?

I left us to sour, haunted am I

Pick me up, take a swig, how is this bad?

Our taste rotten ruins us high and dry

As this hangover is knowingly wrong,

I cannot help but sing us the same song.

---

[1] Gomuti – A sweet Malaysian sap used in wine.

Dear Grace,

Drown thy sorrow

For thou hatest me and I hate thee.

Thine eyes displease the sun's morrow

Thou sobs for fun and its music please't me.

Thou art shrewest Grace;

Shag from man to man

Even Satan shuns thy face,

Get thee hence, find another plan.

If thou ever thinketh of me,

Know thou art the greatest burden

As thou art meant to be;

Crawl thy grave, receive thine guerdon. [1]

The angels and demons shall not care

Even the Lord will not heed thy prayer.

---

[1] Guerdon – Reward or payment.